The Longitude of Grief

a novel

Matthew Daddona

Wandering Aengus Press
Eastsound, WA

Copyright © 2024 Matthew Daddona

All rights reserved

This book may not be reproduced or transmitted in any form by any means, electronic or mechanical, including photocopying and recording, or by any information storage and retrieval system. Excerpts may not be reproduced, except when expressly permitted in writing by the author. Permission requests should be addressed to the author at matthewdaddona14@gmail.com.

First Edition. Published by Wandering Aengus Press

Fiction
ISBN: 979-8-218-24643-3
Cover Design: Jacob Kemp
Author Photo: Randee Post Daddona

Wandering Aengus Press
PO Box 334 Eastsound, WA 98245, USA
wanderingaenguspress.com

Wandering Aengus Press is dedicated to publishing works to enrich lives and make the world a better place.

For J.T.
(One day, all of this will make sense)

"One starts at mystery and ends at denial."—Unknown

Part One
The Ravenous Boys

Chapter One

High School; sophomore year

Henry Manero was born with one of those small hands that was hard to get used to unless you knew him. He liked to smoke cigarettes, a lot of them, and always insisted on holding them with his small right hand. He lit most of them without trouble, but the ones that escaped his grip got crushed in the process, and he would have to sit there with this stupid, confused look, or else grab another from his pack and start again. And again. There was no telling how long this process would take to correct itself because once he got in the habit of dropping a smoke, he felt that all eyes were watching him; and to prove he still had the God-aiding will, he'd overcompensate and find himself shit out of luck, the cigarettes lying there like confetti.

What he could've done is ask for help. What he could've done is not smoke.

But that was exactly the problem—people like his friends and family telling him to quit, which induced his generalized anxiety. And this, coupled with the general skepticism with which he saw his place in the future, made him morose.

He pitied himself but also his mom, who was singlehandedly raising him. When he saw how hard she had to work, how the days folded into nights that folded into weekends where the chores were never done, the money never bought anything new, he slumped into positions on the couch that mirrored the ennui he experienced in the world. He felt it in his toes, how they fell asleep first and gave the rest of his body permission to stay there. On humid days where the sun hung high and bright—

a shining nuisance to him—he drew the shades and slept long into the afternoon, waking only to eat or to flip the channels on the television before tilting his eyes back to dreams. Television hosts rhapsodized about presidential decisions to invade foreign countries; that's all they ever did. And sometimes Henry Manero heard them and listened, but mostly he did not.

It all seemed unreasonable: the idleness, the moroseness, the smoking. And it was, if not for his deformity. In school, do-well teachers with salt-streaked foreheads, with dimples burning holes through their cheeks, confused Henry's lack of participation in group activities with their presupposition that he couldn't keep up with other kids. In gym class, especially, where physical prowess masked signs of other personality deficiencies, where, for forty minutes, one might prevail simply by showing up, Henry opted for reading a book on the sidelines. Teachers figured it was a teenage boy's prerogative to be feeble if he couldn't help it. Except that no one had bothered to ask him if he wanted to be included, for if they had they would have been surprised by the answer: Henry Manero's lack of participation had nothing to do with his hand. He simply wanted to be left alone.

His identity as a loner, as someone for whom an element like wind could better direct his passions than he could, sprung from an early age. His was muddied by his mother's insistence that he was as special as anyone else, if not more so. "Show them who you are," his mother had told him as early as he could understand, "but never overplay your hand, never." The irony of this being possible was not lost on him, even then.

His mother Alma's worry for her son's lack of inclusion, first in school and then outside of it, eventually reached the recesses of her family and picked up speed once her nephews got wind of it. Alma called upon them—his cousins, three boys—to fill this void, and they, in turn, thought that bringing Henry around was doing a chore that your mother repeatedly asked you to do and that you couldn't get out of, though in this case the request came from their aunt, who had a penchant for crying for her son more than he cried for himself. The cousins' mother, Kristi, felt bad for her sister and had offered her own children as tokens, though the reasons for doing so were lost on her sons. The sisters weren't that close, and the cousins couldn't begin to understand the reasons for Alma's grief and their mother's charity when, from the surface, Henry was a healthy child.

Before the cousins got wise enough to ditch Henry for girls, they would drive over to his house, park, kiss Alma hello, politely deny an invitation to stay over for dinner, and drive away with Henry while Alma waved from the doorway. Sometimes she'd meet them on the lawn in just her slippers, no matter the temperature, and hold Henry and whisper that she loved him, even though the cousins were within earshot and would later mock him. But he never tried to defend himself against the cousins' insults, never, having heard from Alma throughout his childhood that they were the closest blood relation he had between her and his father, who lived four miles across town, where the woods climbed along the ridge and the bay shone yellow at night. On occasion, the bay proved to be a dumping ground for bottles from high school boys who had had too much to drink and encountered the cousins when they were in fighting spirits during their frequent car rides—the drunkest being Peter, the eldest, who always insisted on driving with a Bud Lite can while the other cousins harmonized their plans for the evening (they also happened to be decent singers). Henry never accompanied the cousins on their escapades across town—they wouldn't allow it—if only because they paid visits to his father, bringing him an assortment of pot and liquor while he supplied them with a safe space to indulge.

In the years since Holdam had been co-opted by developers who turned many of the farmlands into craftsman developments and its crumbling docks into seaside motels, the peninsula on which the town sat bustled with outsiders from the city who dreamt of turning their seasonal rendezvous into full-time arrangements. This meant that questions were frequently asked about the culture of the town, and about its safety. But if these tourists had stayed long into the off-season or had sacrificed their need for entertainment for the unpopular choice of feeling bored, they might've seen the cousins, Peter, Andre, and Sal, drive across the roads, stoned in their wandering, until they eventually made their way to the home of Benjamin Manero, Henry's father.

Benjamin Manero's house proved a convenient alternative to dealing with the police, with whom the cousins were already friendly. And though the cops would never admit as such to the newcomers who asked about the town's safety—they detested the sight of them and their money-turning tricks as much as the next local—they conjured the cousins' visage whenever they told newcomers, collectively, *This town is safe.* They imagined Benjamin, the patriarch of this arrangement, and remembered the complaints that were made to the office about him and his parties nearly on a monthly basis. *As safe as it gets.*

The cousins' peers, being other kids and thus more honest, would report seeing a line of high school girls entering Benjamin Manero's house, like virgins wading into the river, and flanked on all sides by the cousins, who would pinch their asses on the way in before greeting their uncle at the front door. Their greeting to Benjamin was always the same: a stern handshake, a forceful look into his eyes. Sometimes they let his name fly out of their loose mouths like a chant.

Unlike the high school girls, the women Benjamin invited over were his age, and they had harsh skin and eyes caked in bronzing makeup. Sometimes two or three of them showed up on the same night and would vie for Benjamin's attention, all the while judging the high school girls who eddied in and out, escaped to the bathrooms, and whispered among themselves. Peter would catch the girls whispering and try to lead them to more comfortable habitats—meaning away from the older women—until, eventually, they got drunk enough and found themselves ambling back to the living room on their own accord to snag a place on the overcrowded couch. The high school girls were haphazard at first—you could see it in their posture, the way they would sit on the armrests of the couch or hover in the doorway while the cousins and Benjamin fraternized.

After one or two in the morning, everyone would fall asleep except for Benjamin who, it was said, would walk in place in the kitchen collecting empties and organizing them on the countertops. Finally, at around three or four, after Benjamin dozed off, the cousins would wander out of the house and pile into the car and speed off through the woods back to their mother's home. Their home. And there they would sleep long into the next day.

All of this goes without saying: If you give people something to stare at, they'll make a mountain of troubles for you.

At some point during Henry's sophomore year of high school, word had gotten back to him that his cousins were spending a good deal of time with his father and that the parties had awarded them popularity. It was not that Henry wanted to be invited—he hated his father, hated that he was made to feel this way—but that gatherings for which he wasn't a part could somehow drive a stake between him and his cousins, cutting off an already tempestuous blood flow. And moroseness rose again like a frog in Henry's throat and only exited when Alma coaxed it out of him.

One night, just short of his sixteenth birthday, Alma found him crying on the back porch. Smoke hung in the doorway and circled around the single light that barely lit his face, highlighting his fringed stubble. He cried, turning away from her like the cat with the saucer, milking embarrassment.

Alma didn't feel the need to give him space; it wasn't her way. She leaned into his discomfort. Her breath rose, then fell to a gasp, and when he didn't turn around to address her, she sat down where the porch met the lengthy grass. She said his name, and he spat in a cup where his cigarette corroded the plastic.

"Mom, it's not fair," he began, before stopping himself.

"What's not?" She had somehow gotten him to face her, but it was short-lived. In turning back around, he imagined her face suspended there, illuminous and softly worn. He banged his hand on the table, knocking over the cup that held the cigarette. He looked away at the bare trees that creaked between hard efforts of the wind, and then broke down completely. That's when Alma knew it was safe to embrace him and hold him tight and feel that he hadn't grown that much since birth, that he was still small in so many ways.

Benjamin left Henry and Alma when the boy was six. Henry had never seen his father stuff suitcases into his car the way the movies show. He had not seen his mother cry on the front steps while he surreptitiously watched from the kitchen. His father had not planted a kiss upon his head in the middle of the night and say, *I wish it didn't have to be like this.*

Benjamin had prolonged his move over years and years. He had chosen a house four miles across town as if to make a point that he was always reachable. He moved away slowly but with little tact, purposely leaving some of his prized items at Alma's house. His leather jacket for one. Henry observed how that jacket sat in the back of their closet for years. Whenever Benjamin came over—to pay his boy a visit, and, on occasion, drop off an envelope for Alma—he'd open Alma's closet and feel for it. In turn, every time she opened the closet and dug in for her winter items, she brushed against the leather and smelled Benjamin's scent, a coldness that had descended upon it and never left. Did she secretly miss this scent? No, she was much too concerned about what throwing out the jacket said about her inability to get over her own pride than it did her sanity. And it was true that over the years she had succumbed to Benjamin's frequent drop-ins, like he was a stranger she had chatted up on a bus stop once and had now felt obliged to entertain. If he brought presents for Henry, she thought he had purchased something temporary like goodwill. If he came empty-handed and promised to bring something the next time, *I swear to god* he'd say, she convinced herself that his showing up was more important than anything money could buy.

And so, for the first few years after Benjamin had moved, Alma's home still bore his mark, and it wasn't long before Alma herself had expected gifts as recompense. When Henry was eight, Benjamin arrived at their house with presents for them both. Christmas was three weeks away and Benjamin was inspired to make good after months of inactivity. Henry was gifted a wooden baseball bat and glove but no baseball. Alma received a scarf and a shade of dark lipstick she would never wear. Henry thought it weird that his father would go through the trouble of buying a baseball bat and glove but no ball. When he asked his father when he could get one, Benjamin told him, "Learn to swing the bat first, son. Get strong enough to lift it."

He could be pleased, even without a baseball. Alma was a wreck, though. Thinking her gift a ploy by Benjamin to get her into bed, she stormed upstairs with Henry in tow, leaving the contents in their paper wrapping on the floor.

A half hour later, Henry came down on behalf of his mother to see if his father had gone. He heard a whirring from the garage and went to investigate and found Benjamin, stripped down to nothing but his boxers, pouring detergent into the washing machine. He looked overly comfortable performing this role.

"Don't worry, I'll be gone before your mother even comes downstairs," he said, and winked at his only son.

This memory lingered until it swelled, and Henry, at nearly sixteen, remembered this as he cried on his back porch over the news of his father's parties. He recalled that this was the first time he had seen a man stripped almost to the nude, how his father's body hair was matted to his body, despite the cold; how sweat glistened on his forehead and made his skin glow brilliantly; and the bulge, the bulge of manhood with its dark trail of hair leading down toward it and the hair from his legs growing up around it, and how it all began there.

Benjamin's parties had begun the winter of Henry's freshman year of high school and continued well into the next, when the ground, once thawed and a composite of colors, also revealed evidence of his transgressions. By spring, his neighbors' homes had begun to transform their lawns and gardens while his idled out of fashion like a sweater out of season. The roof tiles fell away like loose teeth, victims of an unkind winter. And his door—the yellow door, with its signature eggshell texture—paled next to the newly planted azaleas of his neighbor's yard, where the cedars almost leapt into his own. Every spring, he considered throwing a fresh coat of paint on the door, and maybe even changing the color, but he didn't want to draw any attention to his house and, evidently, to himself.

He had almost been caught once before and could not risk that type of discovery again. That fall prior, when the cousins were not as judicious as to whom they invited to their uncle's house, Benjamin woke up in the middle of the night to find a teenager in his bed. He had expected Sal, the youngest cousin, to be there when he tried to shake awake the slumbering lump of blankets, but when he grabbed too strongly at hips that he thought were shoulders (she was lying in reverse), he felt the curve of her figure and then heard her scream, shrill and puerile. She cursed at him and sprung to the other side of the bed until they were both standing face to face with one another, only the bed between them.

She was dressed, thank goodness for that, but the toss and turn of sleep had caused her shirt to slink low across her breasts, and Benjamin watched as the shirt collar came to life with each exhale. He watched the collar but also the movement of her breasts underneath and the absence of a bra, such as it was.

He waited for her to say something.

She nodded; it was all she could force herself to do in her shock.

When the awkwardness between them was too much to bear, he turned to leave but not without offering half a smile, a recognition of guilt (his own, but maybe hers?). She looked the other way, how Alma would whenever they were in a fight.

The situation seemed serious enough that by the time Benjamin made it to the living room, the cousins were already gathered there. While Benjamin bit his lip and paced back and forth the length of the couch, the boys asked questions of his discovery.

The boys ascertained that it was Dana who had, at some point during the night, drunkenly made her way to the bedroom and fallen asleep there. Yet none of their queries were answered before Dana opened the door, fully clothed, and proceeded down the hall without looking at her classmates or at Benjamin, who was standing in the kitchen, his head dipped in shame. She slammed the door behind her.

Dana's leaving upset was worse than her even falling asleep in Benjamin's bed, Peter explained to his brothers. It wasn't the original discomfort. It was that it had the power and potential to outlast the initial moment. And Benjamin had soon enough realized a flaw: the cousins had invited someone over who was too respectable. Dana was a good girl; such was the unfair, lazy distinction among high school circles. Even if she could party with the boys. From that point on, Benjamin and the cousins decided anyone who came over would have to be as disgraced as the cousins were.

News of Benjamin's parties had gotten to Manero—which is the name Henry was called by family and friends—by the following Monday. Whispers of Dana's name floated from mouth to ear until surrendering itself in the locks of girls' hair and the impressions of numbers on boys' sweatshirts. Those who previously didn't know Dana or could barely identify her now felt personally attached to her story and could recite atmospheric details to their friends without recognizing those fallacies or the potential harm they'd cause.

They were mixed up in the sheets, her hand was touching his.
Tangled.
She pretended to be sleeping.
She wasn't sleeping at all.
She snuck into his bed in the middle of the night.
She only ran off because she thought the boys had caught her.
She'd do it again, you know.
She enjoyed it.

Of course, these rumors neglected Benjamin's role in all of it. Manero could have noticed the condemnation of Dana as opposed to his father and kept quiet, but this lack of censure only made him more paranoid. He figured evidence of his father's wrongdoing would bubble out like a geyser, and his own reputation with it.

He was walking Holdam High School's hallways between classes, listless but wary toward his fellow students, when he saw his best friend Janine amid a circle of other girls. His anxiety must've been apparent, because she soon left her friends to join him.

"Hiding something?" he asked her.

"Huh?"

"You know."

"What are you asking, Henry?"

She was an odd girl, even by Manero's standards, with one of those mouths that always hung open and that one finds discourteous as first until realizing that the words produced by it are mostly well-meaning. She was average-looking, confident in her averageness.

"Were you at my father's last weekend?" he asked.

"God no," she said.

He knew she hadn't been, or he pretended to know. He had to make sure.

"But then you must have heard about Dana?" he asked.

"About what your father did?" she returned.

He nodded, felt bonded to her.

"I can promise you that I would never do such a thing," she said. "Go there. Although the prospect of sleeping with your father is tempting, trust me." There was that cynicism, Manero noted, the kind that attempted to blunt the truth before them.

Later that evening, Janine called him. "Let's get drunk," she said, as if pushing forth a lecture on "how and why to forget." Told him, just like that.

They met in a patch of stray woods a mile from his house and consumed an iridescent liquor. Janine strayed from the conversation of Dana, which was the point—to get blissfully, mindlessly drunk. To not mention her or Benjamin at all.

He got drunk and she didn't. That's how it happened with hurt, with the emotionally feeble living as if on borrowed time. An hour later, after the bottle was finished, he tried to place his hand around her waist as she was walking him back home. Which hand? He was shorter than her and had to lean into her weight to steady himself. When she didn't lean back into it, he said, "I'm sorry, I didn't mean to," and she said, "Yes, you did," and laughed. Her forwardness caught him off guard, but what had he expected? He released her hand and brushed one of his nails against her belt, which excited him somewhat. But then there was silence, which was just as bad, or worse, than denial, and he wished he had never tried.

They had only met a year earlier, though most of their friendship had occurred inside the classroom, and it was only since the fall that they had spent time on some nights and weekends, learning each other's likes by what they disliked. Manero might say *I like the Ramones*, and Janine might respond, *I don't like them at all*, and that's how it went, the two of them disagreeing with each other until they met somewhere in the middle. In all that time, Janine had never suspected Manero of having feelings for her.

They crossed a small road bridge that connected both sides of the bay and paused in front of a house, the sound of water lapping behind them. The house was long and serrated like a cargo train, but on its perimeter was a sleek black metal gate that reached toward the branches of the trees in the yard. Manero considered who would ever need a gate that tall, like who would ever be trying that badly to get inside? A year earlier, the cops broke up a high school party at this very house, and the kids there had thrown their beer over the gate into the bushes to retrieve later. Manero hadn't been there—of course he hadn't—but his cousins had, and Janine told him after the fact that the cousins were the last to leave the party, even when the cops had shone the lights upon the house and forced everyone out of their holes and called the parents of the kid whose party it was; it was the cousins who retreated to the basement and played Spades and shot tequila while the cacophony of feet fled in every direction. Later, when the boy who lived there went down to clean up the mess that had seeped downstairs, he saw the cousins painted in dark shadows, Peter's eyes the first to emerge before he said, "Hey, fucker." Manero imagined what it would have been like to ask the cousins to leave, and he thought it must be something like the black gates reaching to the branches, something between a closing off and an opening up.

He and Janine walked a half mile longer until they reached his own house, and judging by the lack of lights on inside, the way the wind carried the sound of more wind, Manero thought it was later than he originally imagined.

"This is me," he said, as if she didn't know. "Will you be okay getting home?" he asked, stumbling on a divot in his grass.

"I was okay getting here," she said.

"But I was there with you."

"Don't flatter yourself," she joked. She scanned him up and down. "Are you even tired? I mean, do you want to keep walking? Now that you've made it awkward between us?"

"You don't want to go home, do you?" he asked.

They walked down the unlit street, and she watched Manero's hands try to find extra room in his coat pocket, watched his body shake like a child's. His teeth chattered, incisor against incisor. "You're freezing," she said, "let me feel your hands." She took his hand, forcefully at first, before recoiling. "Oh, sorry," she said.

Manero let out a laugh, louder than she had ever heard from him. "You were so freaked out!" he said.

Janine giggled mouse-like; he was right about her being taken off guard. She had never touched his hand, nor had she ever been curious about doing so. Now that she had, she felt an uncomfortable rush that could only be explained by her needing to release it just as quickly. She didn't watch as he slipped his hand back into his pocket. The knowledge of rejection didn't require sight at all.

They reached the main road into town where a few cars proceeded into a slow and steady line of follow-the-leader, then disappeared where it curved behind several shops. There were a couple smokers outside Sophie's Tavern, illuminated by a Budweiser sign and the embers they cradled in their hands. One of them shouted epithets at a passing car, causing Janine and Manero to stop on the road opposite them. "Maybe we shouldn't walk that way," Janine warned.

They turned the opposite direction, into the wind that pushed needles of cold into their cheeks. Janine thought about how this walk had pushed the limits of their stamina and of conversation, how it was the longest time they had spent together.

Soon, the road straightened and extinguished the light previously awarded by the bar. The trees, though bare, tunneled over the road like a cradle for the moon. Idling on the side of the road across the street from them was a car with its headlights turned on. Janine picked up speed and avoided looking at the car, whose driver-side window was rolled down. Manero, by contrast, set his eyes directly on the car's driver.

"What do I do?" the man in the driver's seat yelled to them. Janine pushed Manero onward by his coattail. "No seriously," the man said now with some desperation, "What do I do with it? Look, ahead of you."

Janine saw it first: a buck bleeding from its head, its dead eyes penetrating the darkness. The man's car had taken a hard blow by its left headlight. A lot of blood was left over on the smashed light. The deer's head, if it were capable of moving, seemed to inch toward the road's median.

"I'm fine, I'm fine, but that guy's not," the man said unprompted, pointing to the buck.

Manero turned his head away from the buck and back to the man. "Are you okay?" he slurred, having not heard the man say that he was.

The man opened the door and got out of the car, careless to check if other vehicles were coming. "I just hit it," he said, "I couldn't help it. I broke hard, but it was too late."

"At least you're okay," Manero said. "Jesus." Manero crossed the street, and Janine reluctantly complied.

The man was in his late forties, with wind-swept black hair and a lip that pouted in a way that connoted repose rather than sadness. Underneath stucco-like stubble was a boyish face. He kept sucking in his lip, which made an awful sound. His voice reminded Manero of his father's—booming and layered, like a doctor's. But he didn't see his father's face at all.

"I was going about 50," the man said, "and you know how dark these roads are. I saw this buck at the last minute, and he just glared at me with this I-have-nothing-to-live-for look, so I slammed on my brakes to slow down and jerked the car sideways, and the buck ran at me. It fucking ran at me, right into the car." The man bent down to look at and apologize to the buck. "I'm sorry, too," he said to it. "I've been up twenty-two hours straight. Don't even know if I'm seeing straight anymore."

"Have you called anyone?" Janine asked. "The police can come, maybe call animal services or something."

"Police. God no. I've been -- never mind." He sucked on his lip again. "I don't know what to do," he said.

"Well let's get this thing off the road, put it on the sidewalk or something," Manero said, But Janine knew the man meant he didn't know what to do about getting home, about having to drive home with blood on his car, one headlight working, and the fear of cops on his tail. His breath reeking like theirs did, but of something more expensive.

"I guess I should shut the engine off for now," the man said, but he let it idle instead and stepped out into the frigid night. "So, what should we do? What do I do with it?" he said.

Janine had a feeling that the night was closing in around her—an impossible feeling, maybe—but soon she imagined the sun coming up and the cars beginning to drive by, and she saw herself on the road, and it was not herself, really, but a version of her lying where that buck now was. And Manero, where would he be? Here he was entertaining the stranger's question. Here he was now, but where would he be come morning? She kept circling the man's phrase in her mind: *What do I do with it?* She didn't say anything to Manero, but what she thought was: this man's going to pull out his cock. He's going to flap it like a sorry-ass tailpipe.

"What are your names?" the man spoke. And after a beat, in which Janine warned Manero with her eyes, he repeated forcefully, "Your names, huh?"

In the distance, maybe a half mile away, a car roared with velocity toward them. The man whispered a curse and stood flush with his car door. He adjusted his coat, tightened his posture, and took a deep breath that pushed air toward Manero and Janine.

Once the car passed, the man eased his posture. "You need a ride home?"

"We're good," Janine said. She looked at Manero, crossed him without saying a word.

"We're okay," Manero said.

"I wasn't asking you," the man said. "Was asking this bitch here."

Manero opened his mouth but couldn't get the words out.

"What do you think, huh?" the man whispered, turning his body away and shielding Janine from her friend. "No one has to know."

Manero caught his reflection in the man's car. His hair had the blade-edge smoothness of black that the man's had, but his lips were taut like a hand puppet's. In the reflection his nose looked exaggerated and his eyeballs small, like capers. "Have you ever been laid?" the man said.

Manero had unconsciously walked away from Janine and was now arms-length from the back bumper, illuminated by the faint brake lights and the moon. A sticker haphazardly placed there read: Class of 1983 Football Champions. Its bottom right corner was peeled off. Manero read the phrase—less a phrase than a fact; maybe less a fact than a personality trait—and tried to find the man for whom this fact was gospel. And then he thought, *Do I know him? And didn't my father graduate in 1983? Or was it 1984? And will I—*

"Shhhh," the man said to Janine, which brought Manero back to his senses. "It's okay."

"Janine?"

They were huddled by the front of the car, nearly crouched. Manero stood senseless and stupid on the other side, his hand tracing the bumper sticker. He waited for the figures to move, for Janine to signal that she was all right, but they only seemed to come closer together, folding into each other until they were like the dividing lines of a road.

"Janine?" Manero asked when he no longer saw her.

Then she screamed. Screamed until the words *help* and *help me* weren't words but noises that skyrocketed across the vastness. A porchlight flickered on in the distance.

"Fuck," the man said. "Fuck this." He hastened to the car and peeled off, its engine hiccupping before turning to a steady hum as it got farther away. When Manero rose from the ground—sent there out of shock upon the sound of blowback from the exhaust, his knuckles bloodied from the concrete—he saw the dead buck, its eyes agape as if having watched the scene and chosen to stay silent. Janine had stopped screaming, but that's all Manero could force himself to hear. In the aftermath of the plume of exhaust, she too was gone.

Chapter Two

The cars that drove through Holdam in the summer disappeared by winter. Left behind were the local utility vans of jacked-up men and cars driven by mothers who towed their children in backseats. Manero had been one of these children craning their necks, watching winter in a pattern of muted hues: large oaks that bent their bodies back or the few lone, spiritless offices that squatted just outside town limits. From the winding woods and their tall, spindly trees from which the town was cut, children watched bulldozers move through plots of land to make room for houses, which real estate barons squeezed into what they called "developments;" and when the houses in the developments were completed, the deer roamed wild and free.

There were weekly meetings at the town board in which mothers presented fresh complaints about road dangers set off by deer, describing how they would pop out and, dim-witted as bats, veer into their cars. Standing in the town hall, the mothers, pink in complexion, would hand their babies to their husbands so they could preside over the room and one by one launch into their myriad grievances to which their children were speechless witnesses.

The men got behind the women's complaints. These amateur sharpshooters would cite some historical ordinance permitting deer culling by citizens and ask that the town double down on these efforts. The men were mostly keen to argue anything, such as the mayor's unconscious calling the deer packs instead of herds or his petty decision to put up more deer caution signs on the road ("Deer cannot read!" the men cried, though everyone, even the board, seemed to agree on this point). But whenever the fighting outlasted the cause of the argument, it was the women who wrestled the aggression from the men's throats, who were able to successfully shout over them.

No one dared argue the deer's beauty. At dusk, when the light looked like the entire town was praying, they shot between the rows, hopped over property boundaries, and crossed roads at the rate of cars. Were they going home like the cars were? It was hard to say. What the men, especially the men, would never admit is that they enjoyed these luminous connections between man and animal, or that they sometimes gave the deer names while watching them from their kitchen windows.

Inside the town hall, however, men reverted to emotional reasoning and their guns, though they swore they wouldn't shoot unless the town permitted this culling or if a deer happened to cause a car accident to someone they knew or loved. Namely their wives and children. This is all to say that the debate over what to do with the deer existed for a long time, increasing in fervor whenever an accident occurred. Without such debate, the topics of interest grew rote and mostly superfluous.

For instance, people in town recall how Deb Anatola petitioned for three weeks to have a handmade sign counting the dead in the War of Afghanistan, or as it was generally labeled then "the war in the Middle East," placed on the main road leading into town so that drivers would have a constant reminder of it. When the mayor ordered that the sign be taken down, Deb Anatola started leaving traces of her protest everywhere: sticking signs on private roads that listed the number of casualties in blood red, as well as posting flyers on electricity poles throughout town that read "Together We Can Create Peace," below which was the name of an arcane protest organization like Citizens With Consciences. (This particular organization angered a lot of folks, since it supposed that to be unaffected by the war was to lack a conscience, and just as quickly as Deb Anatola tried to gain supporters, she attracted just as many enemies). She was treated like a person-of-interest, talked about with a skepticism that would have merited larger crimes than just her littering. Critics of her exploits followed her whenever she performed her errands, just waiting for that "batshit, crazy old woman" to pull a stack of signs from her bag. Mothers would send their kids into the supermarket and tell them to trail Deb Anatola down the aisles, and the kids acquiesced if only because it gave them freedom from their parents. After Deb got cancer-sick, she told her husband that she kept hearing children's voices every time she tried to sleep, that the sound of their little laughs made her feel comforted.

It was a curious symptom that as time went on and problems amplified, people seemed to forget their original outrage, not to mention the war itself. When Deb Anatola died in the latter months of 2004, just as another war was under way, her family placed signs in her honor that read: "We're at peace. Rest, dear angel." The town ordered these signs be taken down hours after she was laid into the dirt.

Henry Manero was six when Alma took him to a town meeting for the first time. Alma had worn a black floral dress, and years later, and for no essential reason, Manero remembered this tiny detail. He remembered how the men, some of them with their wives and kids by their side, had ogled his mother as she navigated between the cars, tracking her as she squeezed her hips between the rear-view mirrors to make the quickest dash to the town hall door. Though Manero could not have understood then that his mother was attractive, he recognized the attention she received as something for which to aspire.

Alma had just come from work at the bank, in which her boss' boss, the regional manager Mr. Edgerton, came in to observe for the day. Mr. Edgerton had been swept away by Alma the first time he came in to observe two years prior, spending most of his day behind her teller station, not observing but watching her. Alma noticed that the difference between observing and watching was like the difference between sighing and breathing; and that Mr. Edgerton was taking her in. For the entire afternoon, Alma felt him behind her, how his breath hung heavy in the air and he muttered "Mhmmmm," loud enough for her to detect. At other times, his throat-clearing sounded like discerning grunts, and if Alma thought it was about her, she turned around to face him, only to find him smiling with pinched lips.

If she felt uncomfortable it was because Mr. Edgerton hadn't said a word about her job performance but only asked personal questions: Where did she work before Lewingston Regional? Was she college-educated? Did she have a family? Did she live close by? Would she recommend anything fun to do in this town?

For Alma, the question of what to do in Holdam was usually extinguished come happy hour at Sophie's, where she and her friends met on Thursday nights. Sophie's was the namesake of the 80-year-old woman who owned the bar but who, in her later years, wouldn't be caught dead there. By the time Sophie had reached retirement age, she relinquished bar management duties to her only son and spent her afternoons sipping gin and tonics under the stylish portico of the neighboring Townsend Inn, where she caught the reflections of gentlemen much too young for her.

Sophie's son did little to reverse the charmless affectation of his mother's bar, and in fact might've stepped back any half-ass effort Sophie herself had made in the past: during the Christmas season he often forgot to turn on the lights that were strung around the banister leading to the entrance, and in the spring he neglected planting anything new (one thing which you could've depended on old Sophie for), so while the bar was known for its aesthetic indifference, those who were long-term customers secretly wished it would try, if only a little.

Sophie's always had the effect of feeling like waking up from a short but productive nap. The sun sneaking in under the blinds captured dust colonies forming in mid-air, like a grainy photo. This was unfortunate for the newcomer to the place, who would judge the bar by its filth and its patrons clinging to their smudged glasses and tonguing them until the last drop. Lucky for Sophie's son, his loyal patrons were not interested in bringing the bar's faults into the light. This was of particular importance when it came to his refusing to acknowledge the non-smoking rule that had gone into law in 1998. Since he didn't enforce the law, his patrons were keen on tipping him more, if only because their ability to smoke kept them firmly planted in their seats, trading cigarette breaks for more drinks. Whenever patrons from out of town complained about the smoking, he would order a false warning to his favorite patrons and send them to the back door, which they'd crack and position themselves in the middle of, their eyes still glued to the sports game and to him in anxious acknowledgment that his order was adhered to out of necessity rather than respect.

Alma and her friends were regulars in 2004, but it was always she who was the first among them itching to leave, who nervously checked her wristwatch while her friends (who were also mothers, though still happily married and, arguably, less wracked by guilt than she was) commanded the jukebox in an attempt to find Harry Nilsson's "Coconut" for the umpteenth time, which always made Alma a little woozy having to listen. But it was their song—the four of them, all friends since high school—and every time they sensed Alma was gearing up to go, one of them would put on "Coconut" and watch Alma grimace through it. Then they'd all clink their neon martinis and wink at the bartender, who would say, "Shots, ladies?"

They were younger then, and Alma, fresh off Benjamin leaving her, enjoyed this weekly outing even if it meant complaining about him. But if the topic of divorce was suggested by anyone but her, she'd become defensive and accuse her friends of not entirely understanding her situation. And what situation is that? they'd ask. Alma would explain how Benjamin's moving away was well intentioned given his proximity. As if sculpting a primer on how-not-to-love, she invented the fibs that kept her relationship with him alive, beginning with the biggest one of all: that he still cared, a lot.

She didn't say it like that, not exactly. What she told her friends was, "He still cares for Henry," but the words came awkwardly, as if someone had scripted them. In her imagination, there was Benjamin—shirtless, tan, his figure thin but not Vitruvian—and he was cradling a younger Henry in her home. Their home. In her mind, he still lived there. Whenever Benjamin would drop by her house, she'd rush to the bathroom mirror to check on her appearance. It wasn't the type of self-check that required time and elaborate effort, but it was enough to keep her aware of the vanity it comprised. That kind of preponderance didn't just go away because her friends decided it was a bad idea.

He still touched her, too; not in a way that would have turned sexual (in fact, the year before Benjamin moved away was entirely devoid of sex, something for which he eventually blamed her), but in a way that made the space between them feel extra vulnerable. She should have understood that the knuckles he placed upon her neck whenever she turned her back to him in the kitchen weren't so much a comfort as they were a threat, like a storm that never blew away. If she had shared this detail with her friends, they would have scorned her. They had kids, too, though younger than Manero was. And as aimless as Alma would have appeared to them, she also possessed the virtue of being a more experienced mother, or, as they told her, "the first to be there to watch their kid fuck up." They meant this sarcastically, but there was a part of them, Alma detected, that also believed it. Manero was only a child then, still small enough to be held in her arms if needed, and his talent for crying for attention was a trait the friends noticed whenever they were over Alma's house, and was also the reason, perhaps, that Alma didn't take him anywhere—certainly not with her to Sophie's on Thursday nights.

No, on Thursdays Manero was watched over by his Aunt Kristi, and the two of them would play a never-ending game of hide-and-seek, in which she would stow away his favorite book—a chapter book with a shiny gold spine—and he'd have to upturn the house for it. This would keep him occupied for twenty minutes, until he'd start his endless questioning and she'd answer by supplying clues that weren't very helpful but that kept him distracted while she scanned the television. The game was unfair to begin with, since she would hide the book in a place much too high up for a child his size to look; after a few times he'd catch on to her strategy, and she'd reverse the logic, sometimes never hiding the book at all but sticking it under her misshapen ass on the cushion. Whenever the spine proved uncomfortable, she'd remove it and start reading aloud, drawing Manero from his search and back into the living room. Very rarely would she feel bad for leading him on. Sometimes, she finished a chapter.

If Aunt Kristi brought along her sons, Manero's cousins, the mood drastically turned. Peter, playing the leader, would devise a plan to sneak outside the house, ring the doorbell so that his mother would be forced to get up, and then run back around the other side of the house to his partners in crime, who would all replace her on the couch and change her TV drama to a show they preferred. After the second or third time, Kristi would catch on and yell from the couch, "Hey, idiots, you're going to wake Sal!" though her yelling was usually louder than the doorbell itself. Even at a young age, Manero wished everyone would just keep quiet and leave his home. And if it were true, if Sal was asleep and not just idling upstairs, he wished he could've spent more time in the supposed quietude of his youngest cousin.

One evening, someone else rang the doorbell, and Kristi, mistakenly thinking her oldest son was up to his games again, yelled to him, "Peter, I'm going to kill you if you ring that doorbell one more goddamn time."

"Mom," he called, "it's not me," but by then Kristi had turned the TV louder. *Buffy the Vampire Slayer.* The doorbell rang again.

"You think this is funny, right? Henry, answer that goddamn door please. I'm sick of chasing my idiot son around."

Henry Manero did what he was told and walked in his aunt's direct line of the TV while Peter and Andre froze in the other room. The doorbell rang once more; as if connected to Kristi's vocal cords, it made her wail, "The fuck?"

Manero recognized the voice at the door before he saw who it belonged to, and by the time he fully realized it he had been scooped up in the man's arms.

"My son," Benjamin said.

It hadn't then occurred to Manero that the nights his father came over were also the ones Alma had gone to the bar, but it hadn't escaped Alma's suspicion apparently.

Upon returning later that evening, Alma picked up a scent of cologne, more sour than sweet, and had a terrible feeling that someone had been there, though Kristi nor the cousins nor her son would confirm that this was true.

The next morning, while stepping outside to lead Manero to the bus stop, Alma saw boot tracks in the mud in front of her porch. The previous night's darkness had prevented her from noticing this, but there were Benjamin Manero's boot-prints: voluminous and familiar.

After that, her Thursday nights with friends were less frequent, and when they did occur Alma appeared beleaguered, a disposition that her friends immediately recognized as distrust. Of her sister, of her godforsaken husband, of the town, and of herself. Thinking back to Mr. Edgerton's question—*Would she recommend anything fun to do in this town?*—she could now answer, No, she definitely could not. She never could.

The topic of debate at the town hall meeting was about a planned development that many locals despised, Alma included. For most of the hour-long session, the six-year-old Manero had stayed still in his seat next to his mother, but it was summer, and nearing the end of the meeting the heat weighed on him and sent him to sleep. Alma hadn't noticed at first—she was busy trying to detect how much bullshit the town was seeding about residents' taxes not going up—but when she reached for her son's hand, she found it mysteriously gone. She looked over to find that his body had fallen over, that his head was resting on the arm of the gentleman beside him. She was startled, but not wanting to wake her son she shot an apologetic glance to the gentleman, and the arm that had been borrowed. Alma noticed how quick the man was to return her eye contact, like he had been waiting for it and needed only her approval. He was older than she was and stocky, and if he had been any less handsome, she would've called him fat. The man, maintaining a cautious distance by keeping his elbows from touching hers, whispered to Alma, "That's okay, don't worry, I'm sure he'll wake up soon."

When Manero awoke, he was in the fat man's arms. Years later and approaching adolescence, Manero would try to convince himself that he could recall details from this moment—the foothills within the man's cheeks as he talked to his mother; the enormous forearms wrapped around his bottom, the man's bright green eyes—but he most likely invented these. In reality, what Manero had done was this: when he noticed that only a smattering of people was left in the hall, he called out to his mother, which made the fat man grip him tighter.

"Oh, I'm sorry, little guy," he said. "Your mother got tired of holding you, so I took over a bit."

"It's okay, Jonathan, you can give him back to me," Alma said.

The fat man called Jonathan was slow to release the boy, and in the transfer from his mitts to Alma's delicate fingers, Manero slumped to the floor and sat there in petulant protest.

"I think he's a little cranky," Alma whispered.

"I don't blame him," Jonathan said, peering at Manero, who refused to face either his mom or Jonathan. "I still can't believe some of the clowns they let into this place."

"Sometimes, I think we show up here to talk over each other," Alma said. "The development's gonna happen and that's that."

She held Jonathan's gaze while feeling for her son on the floor, this time finding the smooth curve of his head. Manero felt a preternatural pull to follow the length of her arm to her torso, and he stood to lean his head against it. That's when he really concentrated on Jonathan, studied his rubbery, amiable lips, and saw that his mother was doing the same, that she saw something sweet in all the extra skin.

It wasn't three weeks later when Jonathan showed up for dinner at Alma's. Manero watched from the window as Jonathan pulled his black Chevrolet pickup to the curb and took plodding steps to the front door, as if trying to fit inside footprints somebody had left there. He was deliberate, and his weight did little to offset this lack of grace. At the dinner table, he filled the occasional silence by clearing his throat before speaking, and then smiling even when something wasn't funny.

Manero was interested to learn that Jonathan Bartlett was a farmer, one of the few remaining in Holdam, and asked him about animals.

Do you have sheep?
No.
Chickens?
No.
Horses?
No.
Cows?
No.
Antelope?

Manero was also disappointed to learn he didn't have anything he asked about.

"I'm not that kind of farmer," Jonathan said to Manero. "Things without legs and arms. Potatoes. Corn. Carrots. Herbs. I know, it's not glamorous, but, hey, I have a dog. I'll let you meet him if your mother allows it." Manero and Jonathan looked at Alma and got neither approval nor push-back, which seemed enough.

After dinner, Jonathan cleared the dishes and performed an awkward dance around the table in order to pick up the plates of pasta and salad. He took the plates to the sink and washed them, turning on the faucet loud enough to drown out Alma's demands not to do so. When she was on one side of the kitchen and he was on the other, his shadow felt gravitational. Soon, he and Alma were face to face.

"I lied when I said I didn't have an animal," he said. "I had a cow, but we had to put her down last September, and I had her for so long that sometimes I forget that I had to do it."

Alma laughed, if only because his admission seemed so desperate yet inconsequential, strung upon him like a medal of guilt.

"That's okay," she said. "Don't worry about Henry. He won't even remember."

"I just had to tell you outright," he said.

"Thank you. You're a good one," she said, craning her neck to kiss him. He lowered his and met her halfway. It had been some time since they felt something close to this kind of comfort. "I've known about you. That sounds crazy, I know," he said, smirking. "I mean, people talk."

"People talk? Around here? No way."

"Oh no, never. You're right," he said, laughing.

"What do people say?" she said after a few beats.

He wasn't sure if she was being coy or if she really wanted to know. "People? All sorts of things," he said. Her eyes, which had shown warmth, turned serious, and they leveled him. "They say you must be strong."

"Is that all?"

"I'll be honest. They say you're doing it all alone, raising your son. That must be hard. Can I ask you? Is his father still in the picture?" He already knew but, out of courtesy, needed to ask.

"No," she said. "I mean, not really. He lives over there." She pointed her hand past the kitchen window into some vague direction toward the darkness. She stared out the window and couldn't tell whether the darkness felt close or distant.

"He lives over there," she said again.

Jonathan nodded.

"And you know that he's still my husband?"

"People told me that, too," he said.

"You must've lived here a long time, Jonathan," she said.

"My whole life."

"Long enough to know that people know the truth about everyone here," she said. "Even when that truth is, well, not what it seems. I want to divorce him, you know."

"I know," he said, but here was no way he could've.

Alma lay awake that night and marveled at the speed at which all of this had happened: the town board meeting, Jonathan, that conversation in the kitchen, ideas concerning the future. But all things being relative, she also realized that nothing had transpired that was out of her control. They had eaten and then she had kissed him and before he left, he embraced all of her and whispered, "Your son will be safe, I promise."

In the room beside these thoughts, Henry Manero slept soundly. Alma finally closed her eyes as the sun was coming up.

Chapter Three

On the nights Jonathan Bartlett slept over, his shoes lived in a neat row outside the front door. He had an overly polite habit of taking them off before entering her house, ever so conscious as not to dirty the dusty hardwoods that Alma tried hard to keep clean. With great effort, he bent over to remove each one, taking extra time to undo the laces and avoid future tug-and-pull, as he called it. Then he tapped each heal to clear any remaining dirt, before, as Alma was keen on pointing out, leaving them outside. They were ugly, cumbersome loafers—a style Jonathan adopted for no other reason than to placate the weight that his feet bore—and perhaps not much else needs to be said about someone's shoe choice except to illustrate that these shoes were what Alma focused on whenever the distasteful memory of Benjamin surfaced. The reason being simple: She was the one who had to worry about Benjamin Manero pulling up the driveway on a random Saturday morning and seeing another man's shoes on the porch.

But did Jonathan have to fear Benjamin, really, given his size? Alma considered size synonymous with strength, the same way kindness might be confused with sincerity. Drawing scenarios in her head, she imagined Jonathan prevailing over Benjamin when the time came—striking him with the same force that his shovel made to excavate dirt. A tiny hole caving into larger superfluous damage. Growing weary of these potential consequences, and the ways in which violence would have belied her need for calmness and serenity, Alma simply instructed Jonathan to keep his shoes inside.

Jonathan did have something to fear, it turns out, but wasn't intent on admitting his preoccupation with Benjamin. Instead, this fear manifested as a defense mechanism, whereby during he and Alma's early nights together he repeatedly asked her if it was okay if he slept over.

Okay? He snuck this question in during the worst times, too. Pre-build-up. Mid-kiss. Post-orgasm. During these moments, if Alma had been forced to describe Jonathan in archetypal terms, she would've offered the words 'meek' or 'uncommitted,' but, seeing the earnestness with which he always asked, she would have also called him 'respectful.'

They had been dating two years by the time Jonathan decided he was running for town board. It was early May and they were seated at the kitchen table when he announced his candidacy. After chasing the last of his food with his coffee and closing the government section of the newspaper, he said, "Well that's that then. I'm running."

"You're running?"

"That's the idea."

"For what?"

"Dale comes from a finance background, you know that right? Before he purchased that fat land of his, he was an international fund trader. I'm not really sure what that means, but if someone that smart sees the problems around here, we should listen, right? And so, me and Dale were at the café one morning and he says, why not you, Johnny? You were born here, you know what's what." Jonathan sipped his coffee and swallowed pensively. "Of course, if I do run, I mean if it gets serious enough that I have a chance of winning…"

"Wait, you're talking about what? Running for office? Running for town board?"

"Haven't you been listening?"

Alma shrugged. He had mentioned the prospect of his running before, but not with this amount of focus. In the past, his rambling had been akin to a force you complain about but are too busy to get your mind and spirit to alter.

"Alma, you're my girl," he said, taking a beat, meeting her eyes with a confusing mix of professionalism and devotion. "But I'd also like you to be my running mate."

The announcement might have caused a tiny ripple in Jonathan's universe, a change in which days became brighter and optimism shown as a sliver of light on the horizon. But for Jonathan, who was already an early riser, revelation didn't come in the form of a cathartic image, his farm silhouetted against a comic-book sunset perhaps; it came in altering his fashion.

He changed his outfit of light blue jeans and scuffed boots to an oversized blue suit with ostentatious white pinstripes that he had bought from a thrift store—a move that, in his mind, made him look readier for his political undertaking. Alma, finding the change jarring and altogether unnecessary, couldn't help but smile, thwarting her disaffectedness by reminding herself that, if nothing else, her boyfriend was trying as best he could. It was true she called him boyfriend by then, the name sounding like a French overstuffed version of what Jonathan might serve for dinner: *Chicken a la Orange with a side of Boyfriend.* Whereas Benjamin was her "ex," a word that sounded pencil-thin, scarecrow-like, "boyfriend" was brimming, full of potential. Jonathan was *boyfriend.*

The election was to take place in the fall, by the time Manero was to turn eight, and without fail Jonathan started to immerse himself in local discussions and editorials. His habit of reading the paper every day was supplanted by now commenting on the caustic tone of the reporters; or by suggesting that he could write more vigilant news reports, ones that didn't favor big business over the little guys who were "struggling to get by." He took stances on issues like tax credits for business owners and zoning boards, topics he liked to casually throw around in conversations with friends at dinner, but also on issues that possessed no import to anyone, least of all Alma. "I'm in favor of a better transit system," he'd say. When she'd tell him that there was no transit system to repair, he'd respond flatly, "Well, now, that's the problem isn't it?"

The Algonquin formerly announced his candidacy on the last page preceding the Classifieds. What was otherwise a toss-away burb by anyone's standards—with two-and-a-half paragraphs devoted to the other candidates and only a sentence to him—Jonathan nonetheless bought thirty copies of the paper. Showing the blurb to Alma, he proclaimed, "I'm hoping that the next article about me will also feature you. As my running mate."

While the formal announcement of his candidacy, if you can call it that, elicited in him a great deal of pride, he chose not to gloat. Rather, he turned serious: he favored going to the library after work more than he did having a glass of wine on Alma's couch. He'd return home with his plastic bag full of three or four books—ranging in topic from government to environmental science to the occasional 19th century novel—and read on the back porch, listening to the faint drone of the tractor operated by one of his employees.

He was drawn to a biography of Ulysses S. Grant, particularly for its black-and-white photos of Grant that comprised the middle insert of the book. He ingested the 352-page biography in just over a week, staying up until two in the morning for three nights in a row to finish a chapter or consult the sources in the back, which he had worked into a supplemental reading list. This compulsion stirred him awake at night and were he to flip on the lamp to find his water glass, it was Ulysses' mug on the front cover that greeted him.

He found himself trying to replicate this stare on the front cover—that famous one, with Ulysses wearing his Union blues, that big chin anchored above his upper chest, his silver eyes directing us to an action somewhere distant. He'd crinkle his eyes, as if he could automatically add age to them, and suck in his top lip to make it appear smaller. Alma would punch him in the arm if she saw him attempting this face in public, though no one else was keen to his gross affect. The only thing they noticed is that he became more reticent, preferring to listen rather than speak.

"Listening is easy when you realize how much people like to talk," Jonathan told Alma one evening as the two of them were walking through his fields with the sun setting behind them. In the months after Jonathan announced his candidacy, they took meandering walks through these fields, and Alma felt as if she could become lost in them if Jonathan were not beside her. She never calculated which way they were turning and for what reasons, but Jonathan seemed to be driven by the change of smells along the grasses and would always lead them back to his house.

As Jonathan explained the importance of listening, accomplished by doing nothing else but talking, Alma was startled by a loud crash. She squeezed his hand. "What was that?"

Then he heard it. A second crash, followed by drawn-out creak, like floorboards being slowly yanked from their roots. A few barks followed. "Shhhh, hold on a second, I'll go and see," Jonathan said and ran toward the shed.

The fields at night, with Jonathan's small yellow house pitched under the sky, reminded her of violence. Maybe it was how the stillness never seemed interrupted here, how a loud machine plowing a row would eventually be forgotten, swallowed by another sound, and that, no matter the interplay of loud or soft or far or near, all would be lost to the landscape. It was like imagining violence: if a woman screams in the middle of a farm field, does anybody hear her?

Jonathan thrust the shed door open. "Oh no. Shit. Alma, come here," he cried. In front of him lay a rabbit, punctured in the torso by Jonathan's golden retriever that had dragged it across the wood planks and scattered tools in the process. The rabbit, ensnarled in the jaws of the dog, bled a figure eight across the floor.

Alma squeezed her body through the door that Jonathan hadn't managed to get out of the way of. "Guess Freddy finally got the thing," he said. "He's been chasing something all week." He crossed himself, whether in solemnity for Freddy or the rabbit, Alma couldn't tell, and muttered a word of praise to Freddy before looking up. "Aw, it'll be okay," he said to Alma. "You're okay, you're good. You'll be good. I'll clean this up."

Alma could reason that farm-living implied farm-dying too, and that sometimes those that got dragged through the jaws of that conundrum were the most helpless among us. But the death of such a small thing compounded with the largeness of her partner signaled a futility.

She followed Jonathan through the fields and back to his house. She watched his slouched gait, his shoulders like mounds against the dark sky. When they reached the back porch, Jonathan said, "It was good you heard it, Alma. That thing could've stunk up the entire shed if you hadn't."

"All that blood," she said. "I know you're not bothered by it, what I mean is you're used to it. That didn't sound right either."

He kissed her and said, "I never told you the Ford's Theatre story of Ulysses S. Grant, did I?"

She had heard so much about Ulysses by then that the mention of his name recalled the image from the biography's cover. She scorned this image, saw it even when she was trying not to.

"I read that Grant was supposed to be at Ford's Theatre the same night Lincoln was assassinated. Isn't that something?"

"What do you mean?" Alma said.

"I mean, say if Ulysses was there. Maybe it was him who would've been shot," Jonathan said. But, not believing this revisionist history, he added with a drawn-out breath, "Ulysses would've stopped the bullet and saved Mr. Lincoln. He owed him that much."

"But hon, what would Ulysses do about a dead rabbit in a shed?" she asked him.

"I think he'd kill it again, he said. "And then recite a prayer. He was that kind of soldier."

Jonathan Bartlett's campaign was like a comet in an already busy sky, an elusive but earnest attempt, and then gone too soon, nearly forgotten. Through his good humor and naïve curiosity, he had tried to unite Holdam residents in believing that change was possible, by which he meant a return to the earth, to mother nature, to the intractable ways in which its people and their children were tied to each other and their communities, but by the time he had become organized enough to promote his front, a candidate with financial means and a million-dollar smile had swooped in and elicited a comet of his own, which burned bigger and brighter and to which everyone, including Jonathan, followed to its logical conclusion. The other candidate had won a position on the town board, and Jonathan had very sorely lost.

Three years had passed, and Manero was now eleven years old. As Alma's relationship with Jonathan was burnished by their years together, Manero's initiation into Jonathan's life happened more slowly. Alma was cautious not to allow Manero's life to be influenced—no, altered—by another man, lest the boy's confidence was not fully formed. She worried that Manero lacked the means to interpret what another man in his life meant, but seeing as though he still didn't know what he wanted out of life in general, had no discernible hobbies as far as she could tell, she also realized she was likely being overprotective and that she would, at some point, have to let down her guard.

This moment came in November when Jonathan decided it was time to clean out his shed, and he solicited the young Henry Manero for help. Alma allowed this, if only because it gave her time alone on a Saturday, her only day off work, and because, for the entire week prior, Jonathan had argued his case. "A boy's gotta work," he told her. "Otherwise, he'll only ever stay a boy." She granted Jonathan permission, but not without first issuing a warning, considering his hand: "Henry is eager. He will want to lift everything. Please don't let him."

Saturday came, and Alma dropped off her son and watched as he walked from the car to Jonathan's front steps with timidity, each body part weighted down by layers of extra clothing. Jonathan, greeting him at the front door and sensing Manero's nervousness, the peculiar way with which he moved through the world, said to him, "You ready for work?"

"Yes," Manero said quietly.

"No, no, no. You're not ready yet."

Jonathan waved goodbye to Alma on behalf of both of them and rushed the boy into his kitchen, where the oven had been turned on to keep him warm while he sorted through his mail. The room smelled of hot metal.

"Here, sit down," Jonathan said, pulling out a kitchen stool. "Take off those shoes, your jacket. You won't be able to move in those. Take this." He opened a box and took out a fresh pair of black work boots. "Try these on. Let's just say they don't fit me anymore." Manero was unable to see how they would have ever. They were a size meant for a young man. "That's a joke, Henry," Jonathan said, laughing.

Manero slipped into the boots, falling into them. Jonathan had had to guess his size after all.

"They look good," Jonathan said. "Feel good?" Manero nodded and uttered a thank you. "Here, take this too," Jonathan said, sliding a steaming mug to him. On it was a printed forest with the words, "Find Your Place." Its handle was chipped where a hawk dove from the sky. "Coffee. Wakes you up," he said gutturally.

Manero brought it up to his face. "Ow," he said taking a sip.

Jonathan smiled. "Get out of that tight coat. You look –" He stifled a laugh. "Fucking A."

And so began Manero's first memory of work: standing around and listening to mice whimper in the lower cavities of the shed. While Jonathan moved materials and swept under tools and re-oiled the finer machines that were housed there, Manero watched and listened, unsure of what to do.

"I'm sorry about the mess," Jonathan said, attempting humor again. "Kidding! That's why we're here, right? To clean? Hey, do me a favor. See all that stuff next to you? Get it into this bag." He handed Manero a black contractor bag. The stuff Jonathan referred to consisted of a pile of clothes, some dirty plates and silverware, an ashtray, a couple magazines, an oversized gym bag that was filled to the brim.

"What is this?" Manero asked.

"The result of me being nice," Jonathan said. "I let one of my workers stay here for a week when he got thrown out of his house, but he turned it into a month. And then he told one of his hombres, and they both bunked up here. Never cleaned up either."

"Where'd he go?"

"Niceness is not an open invitation. Remember that."

"Their stuff is still here," Manero observed.

"Don't worry, it's all trash," he said to Manero, referring to the pile in front of the boy. "Get rid of it."

A half-hour into their efforts, they both hit a rhythm, with Jonathan developing a quiet apathy for his surroundings. Everything in his path was thrown away, and between them three additional trash bags had collected. After Manero swept the last of the dirt, Jonathan put his arm on the boy's shoulders. Manero observed the dark hairs that protruded through the opening of his sleeves. "Good boy," Jonathan said. "Good job."

"What's next?" Manero asked.

Jonathan laughed. "Oh, eager, huh? Do me a favor and wait here."

Jonathan crept toward the shed door, went out, and closed it behind. The lock clicked, and suddenly the prospect of being stuck inside a small shed—the fear of which made the dimensions seem even smaller than they were—was heightened. But Manero, checking the door and assuring that it was indeed unlocked, chalked this fear to his imagination. He peeked through the crack of the door, though, and found the source of the constant clicking sound: perched on a dolly that was being steadied by Jonathan Bartlett was an oversized white desk. Jonathan busied himself with a gold keyhole in the desk's center and made sure that it locked and unlocked correctly.

Manero closed the crease of the door and scampered to the center of the room, reminding himself of one of the mice that scampered beneath the floor. Listening intently now, he heard the awkward roll of the desk as it landed in uneven grass patches, heard Jonathan harrumphing to the wheels' squealing, and finally—as if ruining his own surprise—Jonathan saying to him, "Okay, okay, now give me some help with this. Open the door!"

Before Manero could get to the door, Jonathan pushed it open with a gratuitously loud thrust. "This is...for you!" he said, his body blocking the sight of the desk. "Here, come look." Jonathan squeezed around Manero until he stood behind him. "Touch it," he said. "It's got a lock and everything. Just one of many things you're getting—"

"For what?"

"I'm going to make this your very own room!"

Jonathan marveled at the space as if for the first time, unaware of how large he looked within it. His head came up a few inches under the palleted roof, and standing next to the desk, only a foot or two smaller than the length of one of the walls, Manero regarded Jonathan's gesture as well-meaning but grandiose. But because he was still only a young boy, estranged to the customs of well-meaning but grandiose men, he said sheepishly, "Thank you?" And then catching himself, remembering his manners (or was it the voice of Alma that reminded him?), exclaimed, "Thank you so much!"

It wasn't long before the cousins were dropped into this new world. When the work to the shed was completed the following spring, just as the traffic in Holdam increased and construction to nearby developments resumed, Alma invited the cousins to Jonathan's farm to celebrate Peter's and Andre's birthdays. Though three years apart—Peter about to turn fifteen and Andre twelve—the boys' birthdays had always been celebrated together, to the extent that, given Andre's height and outsized strength, many in school thought that the brothers were the same age. While this difference was of no consequence to Kristi, who enjoyed celebrating the boys' birthdays together (it spared her from having to buy two cakes), it inversely affected Peter, who felt that he had been dragged to Jonathan's house and forced to spend the day with Manero. As was natural by this point in the boys' ages, the celebration became less about the boys themselves than it did about the adults, who had taken their conversation to the kitchen where white wine and Ritz and grocery store-bought Gouda awaited, and from which the cousins were barred from entering until later, much later on, when the single cake would be served. So, while the adults got half-drunk and staved off mid-afternoon headaches, the cousins followed Manero into his newly completed shed and shut out the world behind them.

"You're lucky," Peter said to Manero upon looking around. "You're a bitch, but you're lucky."

Sal, still two years younger than Manero, nodded. If he was too young to understand his brother's cruelty, it didn't seem to matter.

"I've moved in. Look." Manero pointed to a mattress on the floor, atop which blankets were piled in a lazy state.

"You sleep here? For real?" Andre said.

"Sometimes."

"No way," Peter said.

"Those are my blankets right there," Manero said, pointing at them.

The cousins approached the blankets as if inspecting a disturbance underneath, and Peter swiped the sheet off the bed, a whipping sound that startled the rest of the boys. A spider the size of an ear lobe crawled out and all four boys jumped back. *Shit*, they said in unison.

Peter laughed. "You sleep with…spiders?"

It was true that Manero had only slept there once, and then only accidentally and only half a night. A month earlier, the second night after Jonathan's project was completed, Manero had fallen asleep on the mattress, and when he awoke, he saw Alma beside him. Jonathan was still awake but dipping into sleep on a metal chair he had set by the desk, which also held his jacket. The jacket was sloped so that it appeared to have life in it, like it could fall away or rise at any point. Manero saw this and shivered.

Now, Manero eyed the spider that made its way into a crevice along the baseboard, soon to be swept into some hidden spider-history. "They don't bother me," he lied to his cousins. "They're always here."

Hours later, after cake, night came over the farm and Peter cut the light from the single bulb affixed to the ceiling while the cousins told stories. They seemed to be all versions of the same one, in which Peter had scared his younger siblings into numerous situations and the younger boys submitted to his will. Manero listened to them, and as they turned more elaborate, more sinister, he tried inching closer to Andre as form of comfort. Though Andre noticed, he wouldn't dare risking exposing his cousin. Rather, he turned the attention to Sal, who was still a child then. They all were children, but Sal's face hadn't lost the baby fat his brothers had. He was only starting to grow into his teeth. A couple of his top ones looked like they stood guards to the younger adult ones, and his mouth's bottom row was growing in crooked, though he hadn't yet developed the self-consciousness that would soon cause him not to smile.

"Henry, I don't believe you. That you slept here alone," Peter said. "I heard your mom talking to mine one day, about how you would come down to your mom's bed in the middle of the night. When was that? Like three months ago! And that you'd sleep on the other side of the bed until it was morning and then she'd take you up to your room, holding your hand until you got there. And your mom told mine that she was worried, that you were too old to be doing that. She asked my mom for advice, and I heard her say, 'My kids never had that problem.'"

"Man, why are you telling him that?" Andre asked.

"I just don't think that he had the balls to sleep here by himself," Peter said.

Manero felt a stinging in his eyes like there was sweat where none appeared. He felt his shoulders get hot and wondered if his cousins felt that heat too, that pulsing discomfort. In that moment, a challenge had been issued, and Henry Manero knew it. But even if he could sleep through the whole night, what would that prove? More importantly, what would it disprove?

"Who cares anyway?" Andre said. He was one to always shift the conversation, like Manero's emotions were a weathervane that only he controlled. "I don't care. Do you care, Sal?"

Sal looked at Peter, who rolled his eyes.

"Yeah, I don't care at all," Andre said.

A little after one in the morning, everyone fell asleep except Andre. Each boy's slumber had given the night extra length felt by the next boy, so that when Andre was the last one awake, he heard every outdoor sound as a flat-lined harbinger. The nighthawks called out to no one from the other side of the field, and from somewhere near an animal rustled in the trees. And when there was no discernible object upon which to frame a sound, there was the wind penetrating the shed.

Andre shivered, and in wrestling the blankets back from his brothers ended up thinking it silly that they had all resigned themselves to a cold, earthen spot for the night when there was a house waiting for them. No, not Jonathan's house, but his own, in which he and Manero often spent nights. His room had a lock—an old hook and eye—that his mother hadn't yet suggested he take down and which he used to keep his brothers out. Sometimes he saw Peter's eyes peeking through the door while he and Manero played, and other times, when he was far from the door, he imagined him there, like a manifestation of Peter's spirit. But when he and Manero slept, they did so soundly, without fear that the brothers could enter.

Looking at Manero sleeping in the shed, Andre thought it a shame that his cousin couldn't stand up for himself. He shook Manero awake.

"Come on," he mouthed, and then waved a hand in the dark that Manero couldn't see.

"What the hell? What time is it?"

"Shhh, let's go," he said deliberately.

Andre stood and took three long strides toward the door. Manero followed but was careful not to make any movements that would alert Peter. Sal was no bother to either of them; he was curled in a senseless ball and hugging the wall.

Manero followed Andre to the door. "Does this lock?" Andre whispered, pulling Manero close. "From the outside I mean?"

Manero understood what Andre was planning. He smiled and took a big step until he was flush with the desk closest to the door. Steadying his hands on the surface, he opened the top drawer and withdrew a pad lock. "Here," Manero said in a voice just above a whisper. "Let's do it."

If Manero wanted to prove to himself that he could—that he would—use his small hand even in times of haste, he had misjudged his anxiousness. The lock slipped from his fingers and dropped into the dirt where it momentarily disappeared. "Shit, shit," Manero said.

The boys craned their necks down toward the earth and felt around. But finding nothing they moved a foot back where fresh grass met the extant dirt. And there it was, the lock, an imprint within the imprint their shoes had made.

"Sorry, here," Manero said, reclaiming it and handing it to his cousin.

Andre found the latch and secured the lock. Then the wind took what space was left between the door and the frame and slammed it. Then slammed it another time. And again.

"Hey, hey," a voice shouted from behind the door. But Andre and Manero were now a few yards away, disappearing into darkness, and couldn't hear what Peter had followed with. "Hey, what the fuck? Are you fucking kidding me? Manero, what the fuck? Manero? I'm going to kill you."

Chapter Four

Years later, and for no apparent reason except to claim his innocence during the incident that follows, Sal told Andre, who eventually told Manero, that the problem with locking one inside of a shed is that it's not a very successful method given its proximity to the ground. Not ten minutes had passed when Peter realized that the windows, which were perched just above their heads, offered escape.

"I'll throw you out first," Peter told Sal. "Just don't, don't kill yourself, okay?"

"Alright."

"Wait."

"Okay." Sal fumbled at the glass, his legs dangling within Peter's extended arms, waiting for his brother to speak again.

"Hold on," Peter repeated. He dropped Sal and closed the window. "If we go out, if we leave, it's going to be a problem getting back in. We can get out but not back in. You know?"

"Okay. So?"

"So we stay," Peter said, "we're in control now."

Sal assisted his brother in pushing the white desk against the door, the first step for securing a successful blockade. The next step was arming themselves.

Peter remembered the secret spot Jonathan had created in the floorboards, a compartment that Manero bragged to him about and had used to store candy among other items, and so he lifted the latch and extracted a switchblade. Unbeknownst to everyone, Peter had stuck it there before bed.

It was a rusted, off-brand Swiss Army knife that Peter's friend had stolen from his own father that Peter convinced him to borrow. Peter had told his friend that he would only play with it for a day or two, but weeks had gone by and, still, he hadn't returned it. When the friend asked if he could have it back, Peter baulked and said he had to look for it. How long does looking take? the friend wanted to know, to which Peter responded, "If you are so worried, you shouldn't have given it to me in the first place."

Peter taught himself the wayward personality of the knife. He'd switch it open and then close in his jacket pocket, invisible to everyone, and in conversations see how many switches he could do. When walking, he'd picture the knife tumbling inside his coat as if in some type of lonely struggle with itself. He'd imagine what he would do if a stranger approaching him tried to attack, and he'd rehearse the steps in his mind: grab and twist the person's wrist, reach into his inside pocket with his right hand, draw it, switch, and cut.

Or he'd wonder about the reverse effect, of what could happen if, when trying to retrieve the knife, it fell onto the ground and was scooped up by his opponent and used on him. This made him more eager to refine his skills, but on whom or what? He decided on the inanimate for it had no chance of fighting back. First at school on the white wood paneling that bore the bathroom radiator, in which he inscribed his first initial— how cliché, and yet how recognizable clichés can be—before moving on to three-and-four-letter words. *Dead. Sex. Hate. Love.* Clichés still, but this time with an iota of intent. He switched bathrooms to avoid being caught, and after several attempts of making his mark had gotten used to the knife's feel, the flexibility of its blade and how it never stayed too long in the wood. He could hold the knife and feel his hand grow warm, or not and simply imagine it as such.

Andre had caught on to Peter's antics relatively quickly, especially when all he saw at home was his brother flipping the damn knife, launching it into the air and catching it as its lowest point, and sometimes in front of their mother who said nothing. She'd notice it and tell him to put it away, her nonchalance worse than her never noticing it, or so Andre thought.

Peter kept it up at school. Added a couple more trenchant words in the bathroom. *Suck. Dick. Fuck.* One of these words, or likely all of them, got the attention of teachers as well as the principal, who called for an emergency assembly. Imagine the sight: a roomful of barely pubescent boys and indifferent girls listening to a well-manicured man in his late thirties talking about "inappropriate words being carved into the bathroom. Not only is it a disgrace, but it's a destruction of school property. There are major consequences for vandalizing school property. Do I need to explain what vandalizing is to everyone?"

Everyone, including Peter, whose legs shook and whose Pumas kicked each other with defiance, shook their heads no. Nobody needed any explanation; they just wanted to see their principal recite the words. Someone in the back of the room shouted at him to say them, and the principal responded defensively, "I'll say one thing. Whoever it is, he's not going to be writing anything for long, long time."

The teachers who sat among their students or hovered in the back of the auditorium couldn't help but feel that this sounded like a potential threat, even if they found themselves agreeing with it. A couple students who picked up on the subtext dropped their heads in shock. *Did he mean he's going to break someone's hand?* The ill-intended comment didn't elude the principal either, who scrambled to amend his verbiage. "What I mean," he said, "is there will be a suspension. Assembly dismissed."

The teachers led their students out row by row, each collapsing on the other like a set of china, until the room reached cacophony. Guesses were made by students as to whom the culprit was while their teachers tried as best they could to shut them up. The noise (and guesses) spilled out into the hallway, and it wasn't until the students filtered back into their respective classrooms that, for the first time in nearly an hour, the racket settled down. But it was only temporary. A minute later, Owen, the school's obsequious brat, rushed out of the second-floor bathroom and yelled to no one in particular, "Another one! The cutter did another one!" Owen didn't realize that he had given the perpetrator a moniker, but everyone just as soon referred to him by that accidental name. However, unbeknownst to everyone and to The Cutter himself was the fact that a secondary copycat cutter existed and who had made his mark while the rest of the school population left the auditorium. He had done one better, though: instead of writing three or four-letter words, The Second Cutter had composed a full sentence. "You Know Who I Am. I Love You," below which he inscribed the initials HM.

It is true that the emergence of two cutters made an otherwise straightforward case complicated, but it is also true that the appearance of a complete list of initials provided a breakthrough. The principal, upon inspecting the newest sentence in the bathroom, which had been carved into a stall door as opposed the radiator shelf, said, "Get me a list of all boys in the school with the initials HM."

Now, it is empirically viable that the discovery of words in the boys' bathrooms would have led one to believe the cutter was a boy, but the rush to judgement on behalf of the principal and several educators was also shortsighted. And it took a female languages teacher with the gift of eloquence to ask, "Are we sure it's a boy?" to which her male colleagues looked at her with cold suspicion. "The second clause," she said, "I mean, it's just not something I'm sure a boy would say." This might have been correct, but, still, what about the handwriting, the male colleagues asked? It's sloppy, crooked. Look how deliberate the 'Ys' are. It doesn't have any of that pretty touch. "What's that supposed to mean?" the languages teacher asked, and the men dropped their heads and mumbled, Oh come on, you know.

The list was assembled, and it was determined that four boys and one girl had the initials HM. Henry Manero was considered a suspect along with the other children, though his innocence was championed by the principal as soon as he was called into his office to answer questions. The principal, assessing Henry's hand with wandering eyes, skipped over asking Manero which hand he wrote with for fear of embarrassing the young boy. He said instead, "Look, I know you're a good kid, Henry, so I'll be straight with you. This is a formality, that is why we're calling up kids with the initials HM and, unfortunately, you're one of them. I appreciate you listening, Henry, and I'm sorry again you had to come in here. If there's anything I can do to," he considered Henry's hands again, and then leveled his sight to the boy's dark eyes, the black hair sweeping along his brow line and falling over his right ear, "to help you, you let me know. Oh, and if you happen to hear anything, you'll tell me, right?"

Henry Manero nodded, though he did have a suggestion. "Sometimes they say it's the person you expect the least," he said. "I don't know if that helps or not."

"No, no, that's helpful," the principal said. "If you had to guess, if you had to pick anyone in this school, who would it be?" The principal's eyes wandered to a larger roster sheet on the corner of his desk. "Don't be embarrassed now," he said. "This conversation remains between us."

Embarrassment was not Manero's issue, but loyalty was. He didn't doubt that his eldest cousin was behind this somehow, but his mother had always told him to protect his family at all costs. What was it she said again? That it was the only one he had? And though Manero would later learn that this was a truism to be flouted, at that moment, sitting in the office that smelled like Altoids and rubber erasers, he defended his cousin's name. The name he finally threw out was Martin Hladik.

Martin Hladik's initials were a reversal of HM, and the principal noticed this coincidence almost immediately. It wasn't until later, when Manero was telling Andre about what had gone down in the principal's office, that his cousin said, "Smart, man. Same initials, but backwards." It was also smart because Martin Hladik, besides possessing a name that sounded Olympian, also had a soiled reputation. He was tall and wiry and wore oversized clothing, and he had supplemented his default insecurity with a meanness that bordered on irascibility. He talked fast and laced his sentences with insults. He spoke to girls with the confidence and candor of a man with money and good looks, of which he had neither.

Once the principal had absorbed Martin Hladik's name, he had also conducted the rest of his investigation with limited scope or imagination. He ruled out all possibilities of the carver being anybody but Martin, and he pursued any likelihood of proving this true. He had told Martin's teachers to alert him by phone whenever Martin was to use the bathroom during class, and at one point, after receiving such a call, he rushed up to the second floor and followed the boy in.

"What are you doing, Martin?" the principal asked. The boy was already at the urinal, which was too small for him. He stopped peeing as soon as he felt a presence lurking there. Turning to face Martin, the principal asked, "Do you have anything in your hand" and then catching himself, quickly amended. "No, no, please don't answer that. But when you're ready—I mean when you're sick of these games—you can answer. You can fess up. I'll be waiting."

"What do you want me to fess up to?" Martin asked. "You watching at me at the urinal?"

Later that afternoon, the principal called yet another emergency meeting in the gym, this time for boys only. They piled onto the bleachers, some of them going as far as the upper row even though there were only about a hundred kids present. The principal started by articulating the understandable concerns that many parents had about a knife-wielding young kid, and that if the defamation of the school's character and façade didn't come to an end *right here, right now*, there would be consequences. Several of the boys, seated on the top bleacher, mocked his pronunciation of consequences, his Bostonian accent dragging out the 'con' of the word. Noticing this, the principal asked the ringleader of the gang, identified only as such because he happened to be laughing the hardest when spotted, to step forward.

The boy, Dillon, surveyed the scene, but seeing no clear path forward given the arrangement of bodies, stayed where he was. The principal demanded once again that he come forward, and this time Dillon did, first shrouding his smile and then navigating the path forward by putting up his hands as if blocking a spotlight. Some kids oohed and ahhed, which made Dillon' face redden, and when the kids below him started to lean their bodies in opposite directions, like flippers on a pinball machine, Dillon determined a fixed route and moved down the bleachers with speed. He underestimated his vision in seeing the gaps, however, and tripped and fell, spilling onto several jackets and backpacks. The first sound—Dillon's fall—incited a riot of laughter, but it was the second sound that silenced it.

From the jacket of Dillon's coat spilled came a knife, a brand-new Swiss Army model that slid across the hardwood and stopped right before the principal's shoes. Before Dillon had a chance to reclaim it or to explain its presence, the principal had swooped in. "Well, it looks like we can take this into my office," the principal said, leading Dillon out of the gymnasium by his shoulder. The rest of the kids—Peter and Andre and Manero included—remained seated but looked like they were suspended there. Comically transfixed, still disbelieving.

It turned out that Dillon confessed to some of the carvings, though it didn't matter to which ones. When asked why he did it, Dillon told the principal he had tried to the copy the original carver, but that he couldn't stop once he had made a habit of it. "I wanted to make each one better than the last," he said.

"And why HM? Why those initials?"

"Heavy metal," Dillon said. "Heavy fucking metal."

Peter imagined Henry Manero's face as he held his knife, turning it over in his palm as he approached the desk that he and Sal had pushed against the shed door. And perhaps the incident that follows is avowed by Manero's imagination and not by actual events, but one of the benefits of memory is that it shows deference to whom was there. In this sense, everything eventually reported back to Manero was observed firsthand by Sal, not an impartial onlooker either but an active participant.

The boys approached the desk imprudently, ripping the drawers from their tracks and spilling their contents. There were books, many of them, some with illustrated covers and others that were clothbound and hardback, with the titles either obscured or entirely missing from the cover. Sal opened one of these, smelled the golden pages, and winced. There were also miscellaneous toys of little import or interest to them, except for a baseball glove that had been stuffed in the bottom drawer below several old school reports, all high marks. They had seen this glove years before when Manero had shown it off to them, a gift from his father on his eighth birthday. Peter pulled the knife from his pocket with the opposite hand. Sal, watching him and admiring the glove, pursed his mouth as if he were about to ask a question, but whatever he had planned on was forgotten once Peter slashed the middle of the glove with the knife. Perhaps Sal expected something exciting to pour out of it, for he leaned in as if watching a dissection, but the cut was quiet and clean, and as soon as Peter completed it, he tossed the glove to Sal and switched the knife closed.

"Man, that's a good –"

"It's cheap," Peter said. "It's shit."

"What are we even doing?" Sal asked. Standing there—the contents strewn around the room, the glove slashed in half, the desk perched against the door—Sal, for the first time since he could recall, became wary of his eldest brother.

Then there were sounds. First, inhuman and shrill, but Sal soon recognized them as voices of a conversation in progress outside, carried out by the wind. He heard Manero ask, "Do you think they're still mad?" but did not hear Andre's response. Then, louder this time, he heard Manero say, "Should we go back?" The footsteps trailed off.

"Did you hear that?" Sal asked Peter.

"No, what –"

"Shhhh. Listen." They waited several seconds but heard nothing. Peter pinched something in his palm and turned it over, producing it to his brother, as if fake-punching him.

"What is it?" Sal asked. "What are you going to do?"

"Man, stop asking questions," Peter said.

They were marbles he had found in the desk, and one by one he began to launch them across the room in random directions. Two of them hit the walls and dully stopped their course, but the other three came dangerously close to the window and made a snaring rat-a-tat against its pane. Sal jumped back. "God, what's wrong with you?" Peter said nothing and walked across the shed to reclaim the marbles. Sal, tracking his brother's forceful steps began to realize he was acting like a sieve for Peter's antics, absorbing his freneticism out of pressure to fit in and letting the rest filter out. He began sweating. He thought about would happen if Andre and Manero were to come back and see them like this.

"Relax, man," Peter said. He returned to where Sal was standing and juggled the marbles in one hand. "They're not coming."

"How do you know?"

Peter didn't answer but seemed sure of this. His gait, which before was stalking and menacing, eased. "Come here," he said, though he didn't indicate a direction, just walked toward the desk. "Take this."

Before Sal realized it, he was holding Peter's knife. And beyond the shock of possession, he was disappointed to discover how ordinary it felt. If he weren't looking down upon it, he would've mistaken it for a pair of nail clippers. It was only when he switched the blade that he noticed its discoloration.

Peter guided his brother's arm, and by extension the blade, to the desk. Sal was only a foot taller than it, and Peter not much more, and peering over its surface they were amazed by its smooth contours and soft edges that conflicted with the rest of the shed, which splintered out in all directions.

"Write your name," Peter said.

"What? No."

He smacked his hand on the center of the desk and demanded, "Your name, here. Sal, write it." Sal's hand moved automatically, but it stopped as soon as he realized how difficult it was to pierce the wood. He looked up at Peter, who smiled encouragingly. "It gets easier. Write," Peter said.

By the time Sal had formed the floor of the letter L, a terrible regret came over him. He dropped the knife on the wood and walked behind Peter, shrouding himself from his own crime. But then he craned his neck around his brother to check again on his work. Had he really done that?

"You're a natural," Peter said.

"Will it come off?" Sal stuttered. "Can it be erased?"

"Come off? It's a masterpiece!" Peter laughed. "Ya know, maybe they won't notice," he said. "Come on." Peter signaled for Sal to pick up the other side of the desk in order to move it back against the wall, but several knocks compounded by anxious laugher interrupted them.

"Hahaha, did Sal shit his pants?" Andre asked from outside the door. "Or how 'bout you, Peter? We got you, huh?"

"Yeah, yeah," Peter mumbled, still holding the desk on a tilt.

"Sorry, we had to!" Manero yelled.

"You got us," Peter said lazily, like the words were stuck in his mouth.

"You ready for us to open?" Andre asked.

"Yeah," Peter said. "Yeah, go on."

"I don't hear Sal," Andre said. "Is he crying still?" He mumbled something to Manero that Peter and Sal couldn't hear.

Inside, Peter turned to his brother but saw only the outline of where his body used to be.

"I'm not crying!" Sal yelled back from underneath the bed, where he had retreated. Peter thought he heard the latch open and Sal drop the knife inside.

"Alright, we're opening up!" Manero said.

Opening a door is as apt a symbol for a beginning or ending as anything, and this door opened with the severity of a thousand streaming lights. Though it was black outside and poorly lit inside the shed, Peter felt frozen in the symbolic spotlight. And just before Andre gasped, before Manero shrieked with the tenacity of a caged animal, Peter—sensing his moment, basking in the attention—raised his brows, bared his teeth, and launched the rest of the marbles he had stored in his pocket as hard as he could across the shed before sprinting away.

The window Peter smashed made time feel like it was beyond time, and what followed was an apogeic silence. Then, when the silence discontinued, the shock rang out and the boys who remained were left gaping at the hole in the window. Forgetting for a moment the disaster of belongings that awaited them at their feet, they turned to each other with antipathy and then turned further to yell at the sprinting boy behind them. "Peter!" Their words fell flat, felt insignificant when compared to the sound of marble hitting glass; Peter was gone.

The break in the window was not bigger than the base of a water glass, but Peter had hit it almost directly in its center. After the marbles hit, Peter and Andre heard them roll and take their time rolling. They kept hearing their dull, top-heavy sound, but not seeing anything below the window they were left to wonder what exactly had been thrown.

Then Andre saw one, blue and red and yellow, in a shower of broken shards. He picked it up, careful not to stab himself, and held it delicately between his thumb and index fingers. Manero immediately understood and bent down to search for the other marbles, and since the floor was sloped a bit toward the center of the room, he followed the slope toward the center where his eyes met the bottom of the mattress and, coincidentally, Sal. His cousin was sprawled face down on the wood, sobbing, with two of the marbles pooled at his knees. When Sal finally had the courage to look at Manero, it was with the shame of a thousand bandaged knees.

"Where's Peter?" a voice said.

How long Jonathan had been standing there was unclear.

Sal knew that the absence of Peter solidified his guilt, but he didn't say anything more on the subject. Jonathan plodded forward and placed his hands on his hips, his body like an orbit he was trying to slow.

The boys had subconsciously lined themselves up in a row, awaiting Jonathan's judgement. Manero knew Jonathan not to be the violent kind, but he watched to see if his hands would leave his sides. He imagined what Benjamin would do if he were woken in the middle of the night by a loud sound, about how the violence would be reciprocated by additional violence. But Jonathan didn't stir, and he did not speak. He held his gaze at the window before bringing it back to the boys. Then he turned, walked to the desk, and lay his hands upon it. He stood frozen there, and if he were a learned man it would have appeared natural—a genius presiding over his work—but Jonathan Bartlett simply looked withdrawn.

It was Sal who came forward, who, still sobbing, uttered, "Jonathan, I'm sorry. Please, please don't tell my mom. I'll do anything I can to fix –"

"Please," Jonathan said harshly, his back still turned. "You shouldn't be apologizing to me. Henry, what do you think we should do?"

Manero hadn't expected the question to feel like an indictment. But seeing Jonathan's hands, how it traced something on the desk, he knew it concerned Jonathan's prized creation. "Sal, what did you do?" Jonathan asked.

Manero approached the desk and traced his hand along the engraving.

"What do you want to do?" Jonathan asked Manero again.

In the distance, Manero thought he heard a howl, or maybe it was the wind whistling through the new hole in the window. And then he heard Sal's sobs but could think only of Peter, whose absence was magnified by these cries. Peter, who had never shed a tear in his life as far as Manero could tell. Peter who had never been quiet and whose disappearance was now deafening.

Chapter Five

Jonathan Bartlett had made the mistake of thinking Peter would come back to the shed, like a thirsty dog that had erred in his ways and would eventually plead forgiveness. But he was also worried about Peter's safety, thinking him the kind who would drift farther and farther away as to avoid possible punishment, who would run from danger by running closer to it.

Everyone had heard stories about cars stopped in the middle of the night on roads in their town. About teenage girls picked up by men and their boyfriends beaten to pulp. Or about one man who sported a high school football team bumper sticker and would approach boys and girls and offer to drive them to the liquor store or to 7-11 in exchange for, well, no one knew. Either no one took the offer or those who did were too embarrassed to talk about what transpired. The irrationality of a scenario like that happening to Peter stirred in Jonathan a newfound paranoia. What if a car hit him and kept driving? What if the car had meant to?

Jonathan considered chasing after Peter, but chasing after someone would've required a direction, a sense of knowing however vague. "Too far," Jonathan said aloud, though to himself. "It's too late."

"Come on," Sal said, "you can take us. You know the way in the dark."

Jonathan could admire Sal's zeal, his nascent wish to see punishment served, but he also didn't believe its authenticity. "We'll all just wait here," Jonathan said. "I'll wait until you tell me you're tired of me being here."

It wasn't long before he and the boys had fallen asleep, knocked over like soldiers into half-fast slumber. When they awoke it was morning and Alma was beside them, her eyes glazed over, her breath heavy with panic. She had only needed a couple seconds to survey the shed, find it in disrepair, and notice that Peter was gone to sense that he was responsible. "I'm going to call his mother now," she said.

"Now, now, wait a second," said Jonathan Bartlett, snapping awake, embarrassed that he had spent the night inside the shed. He kept scanning Alma's face to see if she was mad at this fact. "I don't want to scare her. I mean, what are we going to say? We were watching your kid and, er, sorry, we don't know where he is now?"

Later that morning, Manero would overhear his mother giving Jonathan lip about his not returning to bed the night before. She'd question what kind of man—what kind of *boyfriend*—would let someone sleep alone after a disturbance. And he'd respond by questioning her independence—I thought you were such a strong woman, he'd say harshly. But here, within the shed, Alma's voice rose to a confident, unnerving pitch. "And Sal," she said, addressing the youngest one, "You're going to come with me on a drive. Don't think you're off the hook just yet."

"Yes ma'am," he said obligingly.

Manero almost felt bad for Sal when he heard it.

Peter later told Sal that he'd awoken that morning to the acrid smell of smoke and was perplexed to find the room perfectly still. For a second, he imagined himself in his own bedroom, with his mess of clothes and video games on the floor, but the first thing he saw when he fully opened his eyes was the TV on mute. It was an infomercial for a kitchen device that minced, sliced, and chopped vegetables—though not necessarily in that order—according to the words on the screen.

And the smoke. He smelled it worse than before and convinced himself that it was permeating the room. He dramatically wiped his eyes and then heard a large pop, like a firework, and ran to the living room window where he saw Benjamin Manero in the driveway trying to have his way with an old car engine, turning and turning the transmission as it continued to resist; it responded again with a bang so loud that both Benjamin and Peter covered their ears in the aftermath. A plume rose from the engine block and Benjamin rushed to the hood to relieve it of its pressure, and then walked away like a man turning his back to an insult. The screen door creaked and then snapped back to announce Peter.

"Morning, Uncle Ben," Peter said.

"You didn't hear me struggling out here? This fucking Pinto, bucks like a horse, piece of shit."

"I just woke up."

"You didn't hear me struggling? Couldn't help a guy out?"

Peter was looking elsewhere, beyond the Pinto and heap of junk on the front lawn, past the driveway that wound to the street. He was focused on a car idling on the edge of where the lawn met the pavement. Benjamin paused speaking momentarily and Peter heard the hum of its motor.

"Uncle Ben, who is that?"

"Been out here since six trying to get this thing going. Luckily the neighbors don't mind. But who gives a shit, right? Soon as I get it, I'm gonna replace the rotors, axels, splash it with some paint, sell this thing like new. Fucking Pinto."

"Uncle Ben—"

"What?"

"Who is that?" He now had his uncle's attention. Benjamin shot his neck around and squinted until he too saw the car, a blue SUV.

"Son of a bitch," he said. "I gotta get you home."

She was tall but soft around the edges, like the petals of some flowers. Looking at her, one sensed the confident stride of someone who had come into good fortune—be it money or providence—but had harnessed it as some window into her soul. She peered at them from the blue SUV without making direct eye contact, diverting her attention through them, and Peter thought he didn't recognize her features as he did the voice, a grating racket that belied her elegance.

"Hello, Peter," she said, exiting the car. "You've gotten so big."

He smiled with indifference.

"Peter, you remember Sylvia?" Benjamin asked. "Your cousin's godmother?"

That's who she was. Sylvia, about whom his mother and Alma spoke with declamatory hatred, who hissed her name from wine-stained lips from within their respective living rooms. Once she was in a photo in Alma's living room and then she was not. Once, Manero had said to his cousins, "My mom threw Sylvia in the trash today. She broke into a thousand pieces. Maybe it was an accident." Peter knew better when he heard Manero say it. An accident would have been throwing out the glass and sweeping off the photograph, sticking it on the refrigerator for safekeeping. Not wishing it would have just gone away. From the bits of conversation Peter overheard from his mother and aunt, Sylvia had pursued Benjamin with the passion of a fan. She had shown up at, back then, Benjamin and Alma's house—once when she was much too drunk to drive home from the dinner party she had been at, and another time, two weeks after, to ask Alma and Benjamin if they had any desire to go away with her on vacation one day.

That afternoon, deep in the recesses of a living room where Benjamin had drawn the shades, he made a pass at Sylvia while Alma was upstairs changing for dinner. In the kitchen adjacent to where Sylvia was seated on the couch, Benjamin removed his shirt to change into a new one and walked by her as he tried to fit it around his large shoulders, like it were a towel swinging on a drying rack. If not for her friend's footsteps upstairs, Sylvia would have held her gaze, but she looked just long enough to catch sight of his brown nipple and the black hair curling over it. She was both appalled and delighted but said neither of the sort. "I'm still here," she joked when he saw her noticing him.

"Oh, I know," he said, laughing. "I was hoping you were."

He jogged up the stairs to join his wife. Spotting her in front of the mirror as she put on her new face, he said, "You are beautiful, you know that right?"

Back downstairs, Sylvia imagined Benjamin's snake of a torso as it molded into its shirt. How she wanted to watch that image again and again before allowing him to come clean, to shed the layers and rip off her own.

Sylvia took full responsibility for the affair that soon ensued, and she told Alma—using whatever words one might try when absolving oneself of such an unfortunate situation—that she was sorry. Alma told her she understood. And before walking out, of her own house no less, Alma slapped her former friend in the mouth.

Peter hadn't received any of that story, not that it would've mattered if he had. He was transfixed by her in the morning light. It was the way she took his hand in hers, pulled it toward her chest, and then squatted so that their faces met and said, "My dear, you are an angel." She tussled his stringy hair and plotted a kiss above his eyelid. She rose like a ball of pressure and exploded into tallness. Then she fell sideways laughing into a much shorter Benjamin, who could barely contain her.

Their affair hadn't stopped—at what point do you stop referring it to as an affair and instead refer to it as a relationship—and he was still in the throes of a passionate and irrational fixation with this woman who shared none of his wife's qualities except for her being a woman. But Benjamin also had enough sense to know that Peter would report this sighting to Sal and Peter, and they to Manero, and Manero to Alma, thus promulgating the cycle of hatred that began with his ex-wife and siphoned down to Sylvia, who, sometimes when they were in bed, would lament the loss of her best friend like it were an item of jewelry that had slipped from her tiny wrist. *I don't know when we lost contact. I should've paid more attention.* And she, possessing all the emotional capriciousness that Alma didn't, would burst into sobs upon Benjamin's chest and bury her face in his hair. Then, lying on her back for hours, to him it seemed, she'd force her knees up in petulance and kick her feet to the base of the sheets. Benjamin, having no patience for this, stroked her hair and said nothing, and then got up and walked to the bathroom without her ever noticing. When she emerged from her grief, she'd sometimes find the bed and room empty, would hear the TV downstairs and assume Benjamin was there.

Benjamin wanted to make a deal with Peter. If you can keep this a secret, I'll defend you, he thought to himself. If you don't say shit about Sylvia, I'll ensure you're not in trouble.

Meanwhile, Peter's memory of last night came into focus. He imagined the search party that his running off must've produced—Alma and Jonathan Bartlett thumping through the grass, turning over grates and containers in the barn as if, somehow, he could be under them; he imagined Manero and Andre pretending they were looking for him but secretly celebrating his absence, retreating to the edge of the yard to drive golf balls instead; finally, he saw Sal coming loose as a screw, protecting him first and then, turn by turn, tattling on him, telling Jonathan the truth each time he pressed harder. In Benjamin's front yard, staring at Sylvia's legs shaped like a suspension bridge, he only thought that whatever bad he had done last night would look worse in this morning's light. He looked at his uncle and said, "Uncle Ben, can I ask you something?"

"Ask away, son."

Peter looked at his shoes and then back at Sylvia. "Alone, I mean."

Benjamin led his nephew to the side of the house where the sun couldn't reach them, and their eyes opened fully. Peter saw that his uncle's eyes were bloodshot; he rubbed his own as a reflex.

"I'm in trouble," he said.

"Mhmm. I'll tell you what —"

"Will you call Alma and Jonathan and tell them —"

"I'm calling your mama."

"But why?"

"To tell her you're safe. That you made a mistake."

"And then what? Uncle Ben? What are you gonna tell my mom?"

Kristi had always found her sister's relationship with Benjamin hasty and awkward, and she didn't fully blame Benjamin for its failure. Alma was too meager a personality to ever contain a man like Benjamin Manero, Kristi thought; she, being older and more prone to failure, decided as early as sisters form opinions about their respective loved ones that she was a better match for his temperament. Furthermore, if her kids' positive relationship with their uncle was any indication, they could well as be *his* kids, though she only suggested this once to Benjamin, and just as quickly rescinded it when she thought about how Alma would react if she'd heard. She'd still had some loyalty, though on her terms and hers alone.

"It's worth a shot," Benjamin said, leaving Peter outside to make small talk with Sylvia as he walked into his bedroom with the phone. When he stepped out minutes later, he said, "I wouldn't worry about anything, Peter."

And Sylvia said, "What's he got to worry about?"

And Benjamin said, "Nothing. Like I said. It's taken care of."

And Sylvia smiled and said, "He's such a sweet, sweet kid."

Benjamin Manero had told Kristi that Sylvia was over, which prompted one sister to call the other (there was that errant loyalty). But he also told Kristi that Peter could stand to learn some proper manners from his uncle, which she hastily agreed with. Kristi had yet to ponder the efficacy of this plan, but not being one to think about anything for too long, decided that her son, from which a wellspring of trouble came, didn't have anything to lose from this proposal. Driving her son home from Benjamin's house that morning, she convinced herself that the inevitable punishment he'd receive would be better delivered by a man than by her.

This plan of theirs was extinguished once they got home and found Alma and Manero on their front lawn. Peter had barely opened the car door by the time Alma started to accost him. "The reason I'm here," Alma said, pointing fingers at Peter.

"I know." Kristi considered Peter, expecting him to bow his head in reverence, but instead he ran into the house. The three of them followed, the silence between them hovering inside the dark living room.

"Peter!" Kristi screamed. "Peter, get your ass downstairs now." Peter flew down the stairs and stood behind his mother. "No," she said. "Not there. Come stand, in front of your aunt." She led by the shoulders and positioned him between herself and Alma. "I want you to say sorry," she said. "To Aunt Alma and to your cousin."

"Sorry," he said.

"Like you mean it," she said.

"Aunt Alma, I'm really sorry. And Henry, man, whatever it takes, I'll make it up to you. I'm so —"

"Save it," Alma said bitterly, which caused Peter to slink back and Manero to marvel at his mother's ability to make him slink back. "Do you know how selfish, how disgusting—" Alma caught herself. "Are you aware of what you've done?" Peter nodded. "Look at my son," she said. Peter looked at her son. "Look at his face. Do you know what it's like to wake up to your kid crying? It makes you feel so helpless, which is the worst thing a mother can feel. Feeling like she can't do anything to help her boy. Do you know what that desk meant to him? His father got it for him."

Manero was embarrassed by his mother's verbal accident. He felt his stomach well up.

"My Jonathan got it, I mean. It was a gift," Alma said.

"I know that," Peter said.

"So how do you explain what you did? Sal told us, how you made him write his name. And the marbles and the broken glass. The shed, it's a goddamn mess!"

"Enough!" Kristi screamed, her voice shrill.

"What do you want me to say?" Alma yelled back. "I'm angry."

Kristi sighed. "I know you are, you just—you just can't keep defending your boy, Alma. Let the child speak. Henry—"

"Don't tell my son what to do," Alma said.

"I'm just—"

"No, you're doing what you always—"

"Shut up!" This time it was Manero who yelled. If his voice were a ghost, it had traversed through Alma and left her there, used up.

"I don't want you to apologize," Manero said to Peter.

"But Henry," Alma started.

"I want you to make a promise," Manero said.

Everyone looked at Peter. Perhaps they expected an explosion, the kind that would have erupted into a screaming match with Alma and Manero divided on one side against him and Kristi. Lines would be drawn, a victor proclaimed. But Peter extended his arm and offered a hand; he had nothing else to give.

"Okay," he said.

"Wait," Alma said, "this isn't that simple, Henry. This isn't just one of those things where we just move on."

Manero shot his mother a disproving look. "Okay," she said. "Okay."

"I never want you in that shed again," Manero continued. "Ever. I don't want you near it. I don't want you at Jonathan's house or at my house. I don't want you touching my things. And I don't want you to make Sal do those things, either. I don't—" He paused, felt the tears form, and his breath get hot. "Okay?" he said. "Okay?"

He looked at Alma, as if asking her if he had said the right things. He had expected tears, but not like this, not in front of everyone. He felt his mother's cheek against his and then felt Kristi's chilly hand against the back of his neck, could tell that she wanted, as best she could, to comfort him. He moved farther until it was just him and his mother in their own cocoon. He allowed Alma to embrace him as he continued crying.

When he finished, the house was still. He could hear this from within the bathroom where he had retreated. The others had talked about him while he was in there—first about remorse and guilt and then about plans, how they intended to repair this fracture—but the voices were hushed, and he only heard a pot clinking in the sink, being washed. He turned off the faucet that he had run to mask his crying. He wanted to reenter the world of the living.

He found Kristi in the kitchen fiddling with the pot. As soon as he entered, she ran to him and threw her big arms around his chest, and said, "My baby, my baby. You have always been such a sweet boy. Peter is sorry. Peter is more than sorry, he just doesn't know how to show it.

Please know that I'm going to make this right for you, okay? Henry, tell me you're okay."

Henry Manero left her embrace and nodded. "Where's my mom?" he asked. "I'm ready to go home."

"Soon, baby. I'm making dinner, will you please stay?" She moved to the wicker basket on the counter's edge, which held baked goods like bounty.

"Where's my mom?" he asked again. But he just as soon heard them, his mother and Peter on the front porch, out of sight and their voices subdued. Manero walked to the infinite space their sounds had left.

"Wait, wait," Kristi said. "You don't have to go there. Stay with me for a second." He stayed, if only because her expression prevented his going forward. "This shed of yours," Kristi said. "It must be really nice."

He nodded.

"Jonathan, he must really love you. You must love him."

Manero didn't know how to answer. He yearned again for the voices, his mother's.

"Your mother, does she love him?" she asked intensely. "No, sorry. It's not my business." She took his hand and swung it up and down as if shaking a die. "I just want you to be okay," she said. "My son, he means well. You have to know how sorry he is."

Alma reemerged from outdoors with Peter stumbling behind, like the conversation had left him shaken. Conversely, she appeared tall and strong, and she marched toward her son standing in the hallway, forced his chin up effortlessly, and whispered, "You listen to me, Henry. I'm telling you this because you need to hear it, so you pay attention now. You see your cousin there? He thinks he can take advantage of you, and he can. Because you're weak now, Henry, and he's strong, and he's going to continue to beat on you until you can stand up for yourself. You need to make yourself strong, Henry, or else this is going to keep happening. Weak versus strong, weak versus strong, over and over. And you know who wins? It's never the weak, believe me. The weak have a license to lose, it gets renewed yearly. You have to stand up for yourself, Henry. Now look at Peter and tell me what you see. Right there, right there, look at him!" Her voice had gotten away from her; she was now yelling. "Come on, tell me what you see!"

Manero looked at his cousin, but it wasn't just his cousin there. It was his mother and his aunt, too, and they had gone pale waiting for him to answer. He formed the words and felt his lips tremble, saw the words hover there like fruit flies, itching to populate. But they didn't come out. He tried to force them but produced only air, and then the tremors of a good, long cry. He cried until he thought they stopped looking, but they never turned away.

Chapter Six

Like Henry, Benjamin Manero was afraid of the dark.

When Benjamin was eleven, he fell victim to a punishment instituted by his father—a man hardened by the Korean War, though, ironically, having never seen battle—and was forced to lie in the hallway outside his parents' bedroom for one night.

Benjamin slept in the hallway between two white walls scuffed by numerous hands having brushed their surface over the years, their sources unknown. Some of those prints had disappeared in the darkness when Benjamin lay there, but in the light closest to his parents' door the smudges were illuminated in ways that felt disgraceful for a boy having to spend the night beside them. When it got hot during the night, he reached out with both hands and feet for the walls in the hope they contained coolness, but, remembering the walls' grime, he didn't want to further smudge them, a crime for which he would have been found guilty. So, he kept both hands and feet in line, soldier-like, in a way that would've better served his punishment.

This attention to order made him more spiteful, and in the middle of the night he woke up angry. His back and hips hurt. His eyelids were heavy with resentment. He set his sight down the hallway toward the kitchen with the hope that it would be morning and that he could crawl away, though, in reality, no one was standing guard and he was free to leave if he could permit himself. But seeing as though it was still fitfully dark, he made himself imagine someone in the kitchen, that the materialization of someone—if it was a person—would be enough to distract him until his father woke and relieved him of his post.

He envisioned his mother, soft and bed-worn, saw her busy with pots and pans and her myriad spices on the countertop. She made eye contact with him and held it as if looking through him and back to her bedroom, before continuing her work. Was his father in the bedroom? And if so, did his weary countenance communicate something deeper about what lay behind the door? If Benjamin moved, would his father hear it?

He moved. He straightened out and walked to the kitchen where, as he expected, his mother wasn't. But below him on the counter was a bowl of cereal with a spoon dropped into it. At the surface, bubbles from the milk were still forming. He questioned whether his mother had been there all along, if that had really been her staring at him moments ago, but deciding against that absurdity, he stuck a finger in the cereal. A mirage, likely left there from earlier that day.

"Benjamin, what do you think you're doing?" His father's voice came from around the corner. "You're not in your spot." His father entered and stood before the counter. He didn't bother to turn on the light.

"Dad? Dad, where's Mom?"

"Your mother's sleeping. As you should be, yet here you are. Your finger in my, in my fucking cereal?" Benjamin's finger dripped guilt.

"I'm sorry," Benjamin said. "I thought I saw Mom in the kitchen, and she was making –"

"Your mother's sleeping."

Benjamin's father discarded the cereal in the sink and walked young Benjamin back to his spot on the floor. Benjamin felt the brush of his father's pajama leg and the short gust from the space left by the bottom of the door as it shut. For another few minutes, he saw shadows from behind the door swing from one side to another. When the shadows stopped, he thought he heard his father say, "Maybe I'm too hard on the kid," he heard his mother respond, "It's late. Go to sleep, hon."

Morning was bright and pronounced in a house from which no shades hung, and the light slunk around the corner to the hallway where Benjamin stretched from sleepiness. At some point, he had fallen asleep— was it hours or only minutes ago?—and he woke to a quiet house, his parents' bedroom door still shut. This was odd, he thought; he had never witnessed his father sleep past first light. Benjamin rose and walked to the kitchen where everything was as he had found it hours ago, the cereal bowl in the sink. Outside the kitchen door, with a view unto the backyard where the tops of oaks painted a line between the sky and the dirt, two rabbits chased each other and disappeared into the bushes that hugged the side of the house. In the distance, a family of dogs barked until their sounds were consumed by the hum of a lawnmower.

What time was it? It felt too early to tell time.

"Hello?" Benjamin called out. "Mom? Where are you?

"Here." His mother's voice was distant and somber.

He walked to the bedroom, crossing the spot that had absorbed him hours earlier, and leaned his head against the door. "Mom? Are you in there? Where's Dad?"

"Your dad is—I'm here. Come in, sweetie."

Benjamin entered and saw his mother huddling her knees on the bed. Her black hair, usually framed in a bob, stuck out in different directions. "You okay, Benjamin? Do you need anything? I can make you breakfast—what time is it? It must be late. Are you starving? Do you need to go back to bed? Your bed, I mean. Upstairs. Why don't you go upstairs and sleep some more? There's no way you could've. Slept. There's no way that was comfortable."

"Is that Benjamin?" It was his father who spoke, whose voice sounded miles away, on an ocean liner somewhere.

"Yes," his mother said to her husband. And then to Benjamin: "Hon, why don't you go in the kitchen and I'll make you something in a bit? Is it nice outside? It must be lovely."

Benjamin noticed how unusually dark it was in their bedroom. The shades were drawn; the unmade bed subtracted hours from the day.

"Benjamin, how are you son?" his father asked him. "How's my boy?" he asked his wife.

"He's good. You good, Benjamin? Benjamin's good," she said.

"Tell him to come here," his father whispered.

"Your father wants you," she said to Benjamin. "But you don't have to go if you don't want to." She looked in the direction of the bathroom. "Don't go over there," she whispered.

"Come here, Benjamin," his father said.

"You don't have to go anywhere," she said again, this time louder.

Crossing a minefield of clothes, Benjamin walked around the bed to the bathroom. The door was shut and the shower was running. Benjamin knocked, but it was barely loud enough over the stream of water.

"You can go in," his mother said before turning away resentfully.

"Is he in the shower?" Benjamin asked.

"No."

None of this made sense. The contradictions, the shallow answers.

He cracked the door and watched steam escaped like a bat-winged vision. He saw his father's legs, crossed at the ankles, the hair thick and matted. When he opened the door farther, he saw his father seated atop the toilet wrapped in a towel. He was crying but swiping at his tears with his wet hands, sending droplets of water onto the floor.

"Shut the door! Quick, shut the door," his father said with such persistence it scared both of them. "God, I hate you seeing me like this. Like this!" He laughed to himself before turning sullen again. "Your own father, crying."

Benjamin said nothing and turned half of his body toward escape.

"We cry, you know. Fathers. We do, even though we don't admit it. Even if we're caught crying, like this, we deny it. I'll deny this, watch me. You watching? You'll talk about this with your mother in a few years—'Remember that time I walked in on Dad in the bathroom?' —and I'll tell you that you don't know what you're talking about, you're crazy, you're seeing things, you were a boy with such wild fantasies even the weather couldn't contain you. What am I talking about? I know, I know, it makes no sense!"

Benjamin had never seen his father so animated, discomposed by his own mind. Up until now his father's disposition was rank with rule and order. Even time was a sort of list. *One night on the floor. You'll spend one night on the floor, Benjamin.*

"I saw you last night, on the floor. You were sleeping." His father spoke between sobs. He lifted the towel to wipe his eyes, which left his bottom exposed. "I didn't know how you could sleep like that on the hardwood, but you didn't shake or stir. And I watched you for a while, must've been minutes, and you didn't move. You could've been dreaming. And then I started thinking about what kind of person—no, what kind of father—makes his own son sleep on the floor, like you were a dog. Worse than that. A dog's abandoned litter. After I fell asleep, I woke up imagining you there, and when I couldn't sleep thinking about you there, I got up and went to check on you, but you were gone. And I was mad at first that you left because you had ignored my order, so I went searching for you. In the middle of the night, searching for my son. Nothing. I went upstairs to see if you had gone back to your bed, but the bedroom was empty. Nothing. I went to the bathroom, nothing. Went to your sister's room. Just her in there. I went back downstairs. I checked the basement.

I called out. Then I turned on the light and started scouring. I turned over a cushion for God sakes, thinking maybe you'd be under there. Turned over a blanket. Pulled a book from its shelf. And that's when I started panicking—Oh no, did he just run off? Am I going to have to call the cops?—but right when I started panicking, I heard a noise from outside, right by the basement doors. And it was loud, like the earth was being smashed. And I didn't want to open the basement doors in case it was, you know, a stranger or something, so I hurried back upstairs and went out into the backyard and yelled, Hello? Hello? And it was you who answered. And do you know what you said?"

Benjamin shook his head.

"'Fuck you, fuck you, fuck you, fuck you,' and you were stomping your shoes in the dirt. Right outside my bedroom window, too." His father took an elaborate breath and gawked at the memory. "Do you remember that son? You were sleeping, I know it, but do you remember that at all? Do you know you were cursing like that, right by my window?"

"I don't...what? I was cursing? Was I sleepwalking?"

"Yeah. I mean, I hope so. Because I tried to get your attention and your eyes looked fierce and lacked any understanding, and when I shook you, you didn't stop repeating how much you hated me, and I gotta say, son, it broke my heart. Fuck, it broke me."

They breathed together. Sweat had formed as an additional streak above Benjamin's head, but he couldn't distinguish between the salt of heat and the salt of disgrace.

"I'm sorry, sir," Benjamin said. "I'm sorry that I don't remember. I didn't know that I could sleepwalk. I mean I never have. And I'm sorry but I don't remember. I only remember the cereal you poured."

"The cereal?"

Benjamin's mother walked into the bathroom, and the three of them were like pieces of driftwood that came closer and then apart. "Benjamin, why don't you go outside? Let me talk to your dad for a second," she said. The boy didn't move. "Please."

His father grabbed his wrist forcefully. "No, stay, son. You're staying." His mother, reacting to this aggression, also pulled her son, though away from the bathroom, and closed the door behind them. Benjamin thought his father would follow them out, but he didn't. The water continued raining down.

"Benjamin, follow me," his mother said. She led him outside, like she was a tour guide through sleep and sleepwalking, one after the other, bedroom to hallway to outdoors. They paused under a holly in the backyard that looked new and extra bright, like they were seeing it for the first time.

"God, did he scare you? I'm so sorry." She embraced him. "Your father, he's been having these things." She said it with such delicacy, like a sentence she'd trip over if not careful. "He's not right. I don't know what it is, but his moods are all over the place. He's been crying a lot. He's been waking up in the middle of the night and just bawling. Crying but worse. And I've read a lot about soldiers coming home from wars—shell-shocked they call it—and having these strange moods. But your father, he—"

"What?" he asked, after she stopped talking. She ripped a leaf from a branch and poked herself but didn't cry out.

"He didn't see any action," she said. "He never saw any battle."

"What does that mean?" Benjamin asked.

"I'm not really sure," she said. "Maybe that he shouldn't feel so strongly."

"He needs help," Benjamin said.

"I know, honey. I know."

Over the next few months, his father's actions became more unusual. Reticence was not the only word for it, because just as diffident his father was, he could also become loud and wired. He'd animate his speech with pronounced hand gestures and allow his eyes to go crazy with performative glare. In showing his wife and son a large tree knot in the backyard, for instance, he couldn't stop talking about trees in specifics. He told him that he wanted to count all the trees in the yard to make a physical catalogue of their properties, and then move on to the shrubs and the flowers and the ivy.

"Not until you're well," Benjamin's mother had said to his father. "You need your energy."

"No, you're right. Not until then," he responded.

And though it unnerved the young Benjamin to think about it, he never asked his mother the kinds of questions that continued to keep him up at night: *Mom, was I really sleepwalking? Was I really outside like that in the middle of the night? Did I really see you in the kitchen?*

How many trees had come and gone since his father's death? Benjamin would stare out his house's windows as an adult all these years later and think of those lazy days at the end, in which his father trembled on the edge between life and death as if in a verdant dream; he could find solace in the rope swing that still hung from one of the trees, its knot a couple threads away from tearing; he could consider following the dirt trail until it reached the end of the property where a dry patch burned across the lawn. But whenever Benjamin looked outside, his thoughts flashed to the hallway, the one where he had slept a single night as a child; and in a bizarre juxtaposition of dark and light and interiors and exteriors, he felt both young and old: he hated his father for turning to such cruelty and yet, he yearned for his company again, however cruel.

After his father died, three years after the incident in the bathroom, Benjamin could once again occupy his room without fear of admonishment or danger, and it was his mother who sometimes made the trip up the steps in the middle of the night to check on him. And though she never tried to wake him, he listened to her footsteps shuffle in the hallway while wondering, partly, if her coming up there was out of concern for his well-being or something else, deeper down, that drove her to do it. A feeling that, despite their relative space to one another in the house, they had never been that close.

But it was she who outlasted the grief of losing her husband so early when nobody, least of all her son, thought she could, who, by the end of her life had banished her husband from her memory entirely. This could have been the unconscious result of old age, but it was more likely intentional on her part: that after he passed, she decided that her sanity was regularly informed by her ability to appreciate life independently and without instruction from him (though she could never unhear his imperiousness).

Neither could Benjamin, it seemed. So of course, after his mother passed years later, and Benjamin was an adult and in the midst of leaving Alma, he assumed responsibility of his parents' house. More accurately, their old bedroom, the window of which looked out into the backyard where the tedium of the oaks reminded him that nothing had really changed there. And it was here where he also heard his father's nagging voice, which, he convinced himself, was thanking him for returning. And though he needn't be thanked as much as silently acknowledged, he thought, isn't that what living is all about? Picking up the pieces of your family?

This choice—call it freedom or adulthood—inspired him to make a change in his life after Alma, and he started the only way he knew how: by recruiting his eldest nephews Peter and Andre to help him clean up the backyard.

Under Benjamin's supervision—this being a stretch, for he was gone for most of the time, lost in some mundane task within the house—Peter and Andre had gotten rid of the swing set that was Benjamin's as a young boy. Then, as best they could with only four hands between them, they cleaned up the shrubs and ivy that consumed the yard. And, within a couple days' work, the house transformed into one that resembled sanctity and livelihood, although, like many things in Benjamin Manero's life, that too was temporary. Only a month after recruiting the boys' help, Benjamin replaced the newfound cleanliness with a collection of his life's work: selling and trading people's used items. He rejected, smartly, the label of 'junk man,' such as what his type was naturally referred to as, but his backyard became a dumping ground for the idiosyncratic passions of other people.

There are assumptions that junk collectors are so taken by their collections that they become increasingly attached to them, and, worse, start to assume the same passions as their original owners. There are examples of this everywhere one looks. Show up at a summer yard sale in Holdam and peer at the vast collection of Gene Clark or Sarah Vaughn records that nobody buys and consider that they came from the same source; and then consider that this same source likely acquired those records from a myriad dustbins and dollar store sales, and so on down the line. To say nothing of those glass milk bottles of yore that people like gazing at but which hold no real function.

Benjamin, however, never adopted the passions of his customers, never collected voraciously and habitually. He paid attention to the demands of his clientele, as few and far between and motley as they appeared to him. And their main interest? Furniture. Thus, the yard, after being disposed of its brush and foliage, grew roots in the form of chairs and pedestals and bookshelves and coffee tables, all of which multiplied in volume and were only moved inside whenever the weather turned inclement.

The nephews' help was not limited to just cleanup: when winter came and snow was certain, they were once again recruited to help Benjamin move everything into the garage. During these times, the house transformed into a curious mix of items that bore no relations to each other. When they were children, the cousins found pleasure among the drawers and hollowed out spaces, and they designed set pieces that corresponded with their moods. A talk show one week. A stage another. Then an office in which Peter stalked the rows of cubicles (fashioned from cardboard) and played an executioner boss on the hunt for "disrespectful employees." Sometimes, Benjamin suggested his own machinations, culled from the rooms and spaces that his childhood house held, even electing to use the hallway—*that hallway*—for dramatic effect. Naturally, once the boys got older, the furniture became more a distraction than a game, an affront to their senses. All that dust and splintered wood. The lack of space. Andre was convinced the allergens kicked up all that moving were pernicious to his health, and, if he could avoid it, he tried not breathing in. His face took on a mix of consternation and befuddlement that Peter and Benjamin would mock. *Oh, look at him. Mr. Holier Than Thou cannot be bothered with a little asbestos.*

If the cousins had to take a guess, they would have said that at least half of the items Benjamin sold in his yard had been poached from innocent owners (read: stolen), and that the reason he hadn't yet been caught was that he had enough awareness to never steal from houses in neighboring towns. And he never had enough money with which to boast anyhow, thus avoiding suspicion. Benjamin's financial insolvency was most acutely observed inside the house, though, where not a single renovation had been completed since he had moved back in. The bathroom tile had been ripped up to be replaced, but that day never came, and now the floorboards flaunted the musty reminder of a past time. The sheetrock that was supposed to provide the template for a soon-to-be finished basement, hung on some walls but not others.

It was years before the suggestion of a visitor reached Benjamin's ears—and not just one visitor, but lots of them—who, just like the cousins who suggested it, wouldn't dare judge their uncle by his tactlessness but embrace the opportunity that his house offered. Who could disappear into it for a while. Who could find pleasure among the refuse.

"I think you should have a party," Peter had said. "And we can host it."

Andre thought that Peter's suggestion had crossed a line. Peter was seventeen then and Andre two years his junior, the same age as Manero. But in hearing it, Benjamin hadn't explicitly said no. He asked what kind of party his nephew had in mind.

"You know, a *party*," Peter responded. "Booze, girls. You live alone. You're a bachelor."

Andre thought he heard his brother say, *You're a bastard.*

"What do you know about parties?" Benjamin asked.

Peter looked uncomfortable for a moment but then told him everything he knew. "I know that if you're lucky you'll get laid. And if you're double lucky, you'll remember it."

At several of the parties they had crashed in the recent past, Andre watched his brother slingshot through crowds until he caught someone's attention, or more likely, somebody caught his eyes—those intense brown eyes, their stoned pupils. When he was in the presence of a girl he was interested in, he always did the same thing: removed his baseball cap and held it by his side. And then he tussled his hair, made the curls bounce on his forehead.

There was fear on some of the girls' faces, Andre noticed. He knew it the second he saw it. Even when these girls were smiling, he observed how tight their mouths were, how their eyes scanned the room for friends who could yank them from that conversation. Eventually, Andre would show up and tower over his brother and sidle between him and the girl, and the girl, sooner or later, would use this imposition as an excuse to retreat to her friends. Peter, disbelieving of his adverse effect on the girl and the conversation, would tell Andre that it was only a matter of time. "Until what?" Andre would ask.

"Until they learn better," Peter would say.

Now, in their uncle's living room, Peter and Andre could agree on the fact, albeit silently, that Benjamin had his share of female visitors. They could feel their feminine touches if they looked closely enough. The aqua blue soap holder. The hand towels in the bathroom. A magazine here or there that Benjamin had no business reading because, truth was, he didn't read. These sightings felt like clues their own mother would have left, or, better yet, Alma. Yes, sometimes their minds went to their aunt—could they be absolutely sure that she still didn't come by? They could not.

They set a temporary date for a Saturday three weeks later. It would be the last Saturday in April, and Peter would be turning eighteen the day before, which was cause enough for a celebration. "And don't worry," Benjamin had said before the boys left for home that evening, "I'll even buy you a fucking cake."

When the boys got home, they awakened Sal to tell him that they had negotiated a spot where they could celebrate Peter's birthday, but that under no circumstances could this location be divulged until that night, and then only to friends.

"And what about Manero?" Sal asked. "Our cousin?"

The boys hadn't planned that far. What about him?

"Manero can't know," Peter said. "No way Manero can know."

"Really?" Sal asked. "It's your birthday. You're not going to invite him to your birthday party?"

"He hasn't talked to Benjamin in, what, five months? Six?" Peter clarified. "Andre should know. Andre, how long has it been?"

"Six months, give or take," Andre said.

"That long? What happened?" Peter asked.

Andre tried to sift through the memories like flipping through playing cards, but each time he got closer to landing on one, he dropped the deck and the memories went limp. Andre thought that Manero must have understood by now that he and his brothers would visit Benjamin on the way to their own house. He must have known that when driving across the bridge and seeing Benjamin's light shine across the bay, they wouldn't just pass through like Manero did. They would stop, and they would continue stopping. And each time, the memory of the last time would linger.

"I'm not sure. I mean, I don't know. I can't remember what it was," Andre spoke to his brothers. Silently, he recalled that whenever Benjamin spoke to him and Peter, he hardly mentioned his son. No, he never mentioned him at all.

Chapter Seven

That Peter and Andre couldn't recall the last time their cousin saw his father isn't surprising. After all, they weren't there. It began the day prior to Manero's sixteenth birthday, when, on a Friday, as his classmates were pouring out of school and dashing to their cars or those of their friends and parents, he exited where the crowd finally thinned and the noise tuned to a tedious sigh. Somewhere amid that first crowd were Peter and Andre (Sal, at thirteen, was still in the lower school then), and following them out minutes later was Manero, who, being so much shorter than the other boys, directed his eyesight toward the ground as if counting the cracks and mentally piecing them together. He wore a camo jacket, the sleeves long and drooping toward irony, and his hair was parted messily. When he reached the steps, he looked back at the school a final time before meeting the paved concrete that led to the sidewalk and thus, to Benjamin's Toyota truck.

He hadn't expected to see his father. In the two years since entering high school, Benjamin never showed up to greet him after school nor did he tote him through town like a tiny human appendage the way other parents did. For one thing, Alma had forbidden Benjamin access there—as if she could control this reality, as if she could've been alerted to his trespasses—but it was Benjamin himself who restricted his own visitations, part out of neglect but mostly out of embarrassment of running into an old classmate or, worse, an old girlfriend and finding himself on the receiving end of a battery of questions. *What are you doing with yourself now? Where are you living? Are you picking up your kid? What's his name again? What is he like?* In potentially having to answer these questions, Benjamin would've had to pretend that the real memories he was making with his nephews also involved his son.

That's what he called it: *making memories*. A phrase he inherited from his own mother when she was alive and had tried to reconstruct their relationship after his father's passing. Making memories, as in trying to appreciate that the differences between he and his son were great and their similarities few.

Benjamin called Manero to his truck, lowering his voice when he realized he'd caught the attention of other kids. When Manero didn't budge, Benjamin was able to persuade him by leaning into the horn for two, three seconds.

"Dad, stop," Manero mouthed, and his father opened the passenger door from the inside and signaled with his eyes to get in.

Flashes of Manero's brief life played out before him in the kids he saw as his father drove. Their errant arms and legs, the backpacks that sunk them backwards. The mothers and fathers who walked beside some of the younger ones, carrying their kids' belongings. Such care.

They drove, but Manero hadn't a clue where they were going. He shifted uncomfortably, like he had dropped a quarter and couldn't decide whether to fetch it or let it roll into the graveyard between the seats. He scanned the street signs, squinted as they passed.

"Don't worry, son," Benjamin said, noticing him. "We're not going there. I know your mother's rules."

They drove over the bridge. The bay below them was tinted green and unpleasant in the sunlight. Two docked skiffs made parallel waves. Farther off, where the land cut into it to form a C-shape, a man fished off his land. Above, a few birds circled each other.

"Where are we going then?" Manero asked.

"We're building a memory," Benjamin said. To make a memory, first you had to build one.

Where the woods ended, a flatter road continued, bisecting farms on one side and a strip mall on the other. Benjamin indicated that the strip mall used to be a Ford dealership, and before that a potato farm. He told Manero that when the Ford dealership was pouring over concrete to create their parking lot, the laborers would come across potatoes that had been left behind by the farmers, and that every day, for two weeks straight, they'd bag them and take them home to their families.

"Can you tell me where we're going yet?" Manero asked.

A few miles later, Benjamin's truck turned right into a vacant property adjacent to Jonathan Bartlett's. Manero could see Jonathan's house across the field, but he'd never seen it from this perspective, and when he asked his father why there were here, his father said, "Oh come on, don't you know already?" They parked where the gravel met the overgrown grass. Between them and the swath of land that led to Jonathan's was a small house; bricks had been dropped as a makeshift walkway. Twenty yards behind them, a For Sale sign hung near the road.

They exited and slammed their doors at the same time, which shook the truck's body. Benjamin leaned on his side of the truck before walking to Manero's. He put his arm around the boy's shoulder, and Manero felt a slight chill. Above them, the trees whistled a song. "You know this house?" Benjamin asked.

"The house?"

"The man who lived here," Benjamin clarified. "He was an old man, lived here his whole life. Imagine spending your entire life in one place. Do you know how old he was? When he died I mean?" Manero shook his head. "Ninety-three," Benjamin said.

"Did you know him?" Manero asked.

"No. I've seen him around. Probably same as you. Do you know how he died?" He asked it like he was ready to pounce on the answer.

"Old age or something, that's what I heard," Manero said.

"Right, right, you heard," Benjamin said. "Did he tell you?" Benjamin indicated the field across from them. "Jonathan doesn't tell you the truth."

"What do you mean?" Manero said.

"Want to know how he really died?" Benjamin asked. "Bastard fell down the stairs. That's how he died. Cracked every rib, his leg was fractured in three different places. His face was all bloody, teeth through the lip. When they found him, his eye was so swollen it looked like his face was a giant black hole, just sucking in the rest of it." He covered his own eye for effect. "Do you know what this means, Henry?" Manero shook his head. "It means no one was there to watch over him. They didn't find him until three days later, and he had lost so much blood by then that it was too late. Three days until someone came, and you know who it was?" Manero turned away. "A mailman delivering a package, who found it weird that the old man didn't answer the door like he usually did. That it was so silent. And the mailman called the police and asked them if they could call someone in his family to check on him, and that's when they came down themselves. And they found him. Right on the bottom of the basement steps."

Manero focused on the image of the old man, the darkness of the stairs illuminated by—what?—the paleness of his leg when the cops found him, maybe. He saw the blood drip and then pool. He thought of the black hole that his father described, a bruise the size of a small island on a paper map. Something foreign and unpronounceable. Then he considered the stillness of the home before him, its weatherboard siding sloping down in sad rivulets. In the weeks since the old man's death, the landscapers stopped coming (Jonathan had told him this, too), and now the dogwood spired without purpose and reached past the porch banister. The door had a sign on it, though Manero couldn't see what it read from this distance.

"You live here your whole life, in the same freaking home, and you get a death sentence at the stairs," Benjamin continued. "People need to know they're being taken care of. That old man had no one, until it was too late. It was like his death provided a reason to care. We're all searching for that reason." The intensity with which it was said startled Manero. A motor from across the field started and then stopped. "I want to give that to you son," Benjamin finished.

Manero laughed, formed the roundness of the word *son* in his mind. He couldn't think *son* and not see *sun*, and he was blinded by the latter. He turned his cheek away and felt the heat atop his thick hair. "Thanks, but I'm not that dead guy who lived here."

"No, you're not," Benjamin said, "but I worry that one day you...you're not seeing the bigger picture. Does he take care of you?" This time, Benjamin pointed across the field. "The lump?"

"Jonathan is nice," Manero said.

"Jonathan is nice," Benjamin repeated coldly. His eyes twitched and the space between them furrowed and fell.

"What does that mean?" Manero asked.

"You're so stupid sometimes," Benjamin said. "How do you not see it? This thing, with your mom I mean. With her and Jonathan. It's just temporary, a drive-by. A distraction. He couldn't even tell you the truth about how this old man died. How can you trust a guy who can't even tell you the truth about that?" He scoffed. "Old age!"

Manero felt sweat pool at his lower back and a heat that enclosed his shirt and trapped it there. He clenched his fingers and exhaled. "What's your problem?" Manero asked. "You took me here to tell me about...Jonathan? You say that he lies, but what about you? You left mom. You left her and never said why."

"And I need what, to give you a reason?"

"Not me..."

"Then who?"

"Us!"

Benjamin could appreciate his son's tiny explosion. Having watched him emerge from school an hour before, he didn't think it possible that such a small person could navigate that building let alone the world. He had heard stories from Manero's cousins about his son's occasional fits of anger, his outbursts that popped up from time to time like a runny nose, but he never believed them. Now there was proof.

There was an incident at gym class months earlier in which Manero's anger flared after he was designated to right field during softball. Given that there were no lefty hitters, he never had an opportunity to catch a ball, not once. When a righty batter accidentally pulled the ball to the left and there was potential to make a play, he was shoved out of the way by his own teammate who made the catch. The teammate was a girl, captain of the softball team, and whose aggression could match anyone's. After she made the catch, he pilfered the ball from her glove and threw it as far as he could toward the opposing field where the geese congregated. The girl called him a bad name, and the rest of the players, his team included, booed him, and then he ran to the locker room where he sat in the unused shower stalls for the remainder of class. Benjamin, upon hearing this story from Andre, said, "I hope he punched her in the fucking jaw." But he had done nothing of the sort. When Andre came into the locker room to check on his cousin, he saw Manero cradling his right hand, bleeding from where his knuckles had squared the punch against the lockers. On the shower tiles were a few squirts of blood.

Benjamin watched as Manero raised his voice and righted his posture, absorbing his son's petulance. "And you took me here, why?" Manero asked.

"See that for-sale sign?"

"Yeah."

"I bought this house."

Manero's face narrowed. He slunk away from the truck and plodded to the grass where he dug holes grass with his heels. "You're a liar," he said, turning back.

"Alright now, hold on a second," Benjamin said. "Let me explain."

"Is this why you brought me here? To tell me this?"

"Henry, come here." Benjamin felt the urge to lunge for his son so that he didn't have to put up with the charade of shadowing him, but as Manero got away he followed him across the grass toward the right side of the house, which sat in clear view of Jonathan's farm a hundred yards off. Several bodies occupied the fields across from them, one of whom was Jonathan.

Manero tried zeroing in on him, scouring for Jonathan's hips that made his entire body move from side to side in a secretive dance, before he heard his father increase his speed. Manero picked up his pace, as a result, and the two were soon involved in a cat-and-mouse game around the house. Midway through the second lap, Benjamin, noticing how ridiculous this must've appeared, said, "Son, you're right. I'm sorry. I shouldn't have said anything. What do I know? What do I know about Jonathan? You hear me?"

Manero hesitated. Thinking his silence more effective, he turned, glowered at Benjamin, and continued walking around the house.

"You hear me, Henry?" Benjamin persisted. "I said what do I know?"

Manero lapped the house a third time—it was a small house, he noticed, upon rounding it and making himself dizzy—and then ran north to Jonathan's farm.

"Henry! Where are you going? I want to you to tell me. I want you to tell me, what do I know about Jonathan Bartlett, huh?" Then, sensing that Manero was slipping farther and farther away, he screamed, "What the fuck do I know about Jonathan Bartlett? Tell me, Henry!"

Manero ran toward the red door of Jonathan's house. It was a loud door, louder than the house was, and a feeling of security overtook him when he saw it. He looked back to see if his father was following him. He ran faster, thinking that at any point Benjamin just might.

"Fuck Jonathan Bartlett!" he heard his father scream again. "Fuck him to his fat core!"

The men who were working Jonathan's field stopped what they were doing. Their shovels, which they pierced into the dirt, stood beside them like third legs. They called to Manero—first to see if he was okay and then to mock his foolish way of running—but he kept running until he reached the door, invisible to their calls.

He was discouraged to find it locked. He knocked and one of the workers who wasn't snickering said, "Boss isn't here, hombre. He gone." The worker approached, his boots skittering across the hard dirt. It hadn't rained in a couple weeks, and every sound was amplified by this crunch. Manero turned. The worker seemed to be about the same height as him but was built in the chest and shoulders. He wore a brown t-shirt that was stained with new and past mud. "Didn't say where he go."

Manero nodded a thank you and turned back to the door, expecting it might open this time.

"I know you. Jonathan, he talk about you," the worker said. "Say you live here sometimes. Say you live over there?" He indicated the shed, fifty feet to the right of him, but Manero's eyes scanned the field where his father likely still was.

"I sleep there sometimes. Though not as much these days. I've outgrown it, you know?"

"Yeah, you sleep in the big house then?"

Manero laughed. "This house you mean? Yeah, well, sometimes too. It's a long story." He paused. "It's not that big inside, though. Really. Pequeño." He made a tent with his fingers.

The other workers stopped to gawk. In between slow digs, a couple of them lit cigarettes.

"Who you run from?" the worker asked.

"No one. I think he's gone anyway," Manero said.

"Gone? Who gone?" He turned back toward the field. "Gone? Eso?"

Manero didn't see the man at first. He only saw grass, a couple sparrows blast from a tree limb, the long exoskeleton of a farm sprinkler on the edge of the property, but then he did see it: the head bobbing and the body's urgent walk. He could've been yards or a mile away depending on how deep he chose to focus. "Shit." Manero said out of breath. "Shit, that's Jonathan."

The entirety of the scene took place in slow motion: his father's fists raining down on Jonathan—or were they raining up?—landing squarely on the fat man's jaw until there was a crack that echoed across the wide, emaciated field. Benjamin, after landing the punches, checked his knuckles to see if they had split, if the sound had come from his hand or from some distant entity, but Jonathan's descent to the ground proved that they were his own doing.

Manero had made himself scarce by hiding behind a burn barrel, while his father kicked at Jonathan's stomach. Kicked him hard until

Jonathan let out a gasp like a steam fitting, then kicked him in the shins, and when Jonathan tried to squirm away, Benjamin let him get a few yards before kicking him again.

Stop, Manero yelled, but nobody had heard. Not his father who continued to lay into Jonathan. Not Jonathan who continued to writhe in sluggish movements. He outweighed Benjamin by at least eighty pounds yet didn't bother to raise his fists.

"Piece of shit," Manero heard his father say. "Want to get up? Get up." Jonathan rose and Benjamin clocked him again. "A shame," Benjamin said. "A big shame."

This time, Jonathan landed the opposite direction and caught Manero's eyes peeking out from behind the burn barrel. Manero wasn't sure if their eyes had really locked, or if their directionality was mere coincidence, but the act was confirmed when Jonathan grinned, like he was setting down to a plate of breakfast foods. Manero thought that Jonathan enjoyed the pain, that he found comfort in it, and Manero could've screamed out, this time louder, this time from in front of the burn barrel, but he didn't. What did this say about him? he wondered. Did he like pain too?

Jonathan rose a final time and had barely centered his weight when Benjamin wound his fist back and squared it against Jonathan's face. He didn't flinch but fully absorbed its impact, stumbled, and fell back in the direction of Manero. His smile, previously manufactured there, had faded.

In the moments after, Manero couldn't understand why Jonathan hadn't reacted. Or if reacting was, in Jonathan's mind, the decision to not strike back, then why hadn't he made any noise? It was as if pacifism and silence were synonyms for appropriate behavior, and in Jonathan's world they were.

That's when Manero realized that he had to do Jonathan's yelling for him, and when he was convinced that Benjamin had left—not just exited the field but had driven away, had taken his cursed existence onto the road—he reappeared from the burn barrel and rushed toward Jonathan, the workers behind with their own brand of concern, though theirs didn't contain tears or screams of rage. Screams of panic, maybe, but not of rage.

"Jonathan!"
"Jonathan!"
"Jonathan!"

Who was screaming and who was crying? Were they one in the same? When it had appeared that the workers were closing in on him, Manero swiped at his tears, afraid that their seeing him cry would've made him appear weak. He only cried in private, and even then. Was this private or was it public? Did crying on private land full of public people make it okay or less so?

"Jonathan!" It was him. He heard his inside voice and his outside one too, like a chord. So many chords optional to a scream. "Jonathan, are you okay? Why didn't you...hit him?"

"Hit him?"

"My father." The word didn't sound right, but he was too dispossessed to alter it.

"Why would I?" Jonathan was helped up by the workers as Manero looked on, his hands perched on his hips in idle remonstrance. Jonathan's left eye was already swelling, soon to meet his upper cheek in a tug-of-war game of damage. His face produced in Manero the undesired effect of guilt—Manero felt bad that this had happened as a result, perhaps, of his running away from Benjamin, but it was hard to view Jonathan's fight-avoidance as noble; in turn, this made him feel even guiltier, like Jonathan, in his fragile state, needed further protecting. But Manero would not have been able to defend him. Even if he had been, he would not have wanted to. "Your father," Jonathan said, "will get his." Jonathan Barlett spit blood into the dirt, and Manero thought that he saw one of his teeth dislodge. It floated away in the wind, speck of plant dust that it actually was.

In the days that followed, as Jonathan's eye swelled and his lips broke into sores that the fat sun did nothing to help heal, he was taciturn whenever Manero asked of his motivations.

"Why didn't you fight?" Manero would press.

"Because I didn't want you to have to see that," Jonathan would say. "You don't forget that kind of thing."

"But what I saw was worse."

"Okay..."

"You have to do something."

"Let's just drop it, kid."

"If you don't, then I will."

And then Jonathan would laugh, and any potency the conversation had had would be extinguished. The difference between the two men, Manero thought, was that one man broke things and the other refused to pick up the pieces. But at least the one who did the breaking acted. At least he had a will. Picking up the pieces was reactionary, and even then, Jonathan didn't react.

Still, any bit of action versus inaction didn't solve the issue of Benjamin having bought the old man's house, of whether any of it was true. Alma made it her sworn duty to find out, and on the first Saturday following the fight, unbeknownst to Manero and Jonathan, she drove across town to Benjamin's house.

Objects were strewn across the lawn. A dresser with its drawers emptied leaned chaotically against a dumpster, and it was unclear to Alma whether it was supposed to be going in or was on its way out. A table was staged with chairs around it, and on top of them gaudy window curtains, shades of mustard yellow and dull orange. Farther along the driveway, where the gravel pitched up and resembled a speedbump, an engine block was shoved on the grass, its guts rusted.

Alma parked and noticed that Benjamin's truck wasn't there, and she relaxed a minute before stepping out. The air felt like rain, and she considered the engine block and the assorted objects on the lawn. Benjamin was not home now, but his absence couldn't be mistaken for entrepreneurship either. It was entirely possible that Benjamin was idling away at Sophie's or entertaining a new female friend or—could it be true, no, please God—arranging plans to move into the old man's house. Alma panicked, remembering her reason for coming in the first place, and considered again the dumpster. Perhaps those objects were all going in after all.

It could be minutes or hours before Benjamin returned, and the sun could go down and the night could become all-consuming. That potential darkness would do her in, she decided. She would only see Benjamin in the light. How long would that last? Minutes, hours. Then there was the sound of fresh gravel turning, spilling, and she watched Benjamin's wheels emerge. He was going unnecessarily fast, and it wasn't until she swung her arms in his direction that he slowed down. His windows were up, and he was listening to loud rock music that she didn't care to recognize. Their eyes met and the music got quieter. He mouthed her name.

Alma had become so comfortable saying no to Benjamin for so long that perhaps she needed to say yes to get what she wanted. But she declined when he invited her in for coffee, and again when he insisted. When he insisted a third time, this by touching the fringes of the bottom of her blouse, she slapped his hand away. "Don't be stubborn," he said. "You won't get what you want that way."

Resignedly, she followed him in through the door, the darkened hallway, and into the kitchen where she took a seat at the table, atop which papers were tacked unevenly like blown-out forts. At the counter adjacent to her, he poured water into the coffee machine. "Still coffee, right?" he said. "Don't tell me you're a tea person now, like those douche bags."

"Douche bags?"

"Tourists, you know. People not from here."

"Still coffee."

The coffee smelled sweet and leaked steadily into a pot that looked like it hadn't been cleaned in years. Alma didn't have to concentrate to notice there was barely a clean surface in sight. It was a fact as clear as the disarray in his yard.

"You didn't come with him," Benjamin said. "I'm surprised."

"Surprised? You'd think I'd ever let you near him again."

"Funny that he needs protecting." They locked eyes and Benjamin scratched his beard. "How is his face?" He smiled, and he was still so handsome. She hated this fact.

"What you did was…fucked up," she said. "Why would you do something like that?" Alma didn't tell him that Jonathan was laid up for hours, that he cried in the bathroom, that he cursed himself for losing a fight to her ex. For not fighting back. What she said instead was, "You will not go near him again." And then added, "And, no, he doesn't need my protection."

Benjamin poured the cups, stirring in sugar for Alma and keeping his black. She took it from him soundlessly. "Then why are you here?" he asked. "To press charges?"

"Tell me honestly," she said. "Did you buy that house? Is that why you took Henry there? You know, he's petrified. He doesn't want you there," she said.

Benjamin laughed. "Really? I'm sorry for laughing, but really? You think I bought that house?"

"No? Why else then?"

"To make a point. You're still so much like a child," he said.

"A point." She crossed her arms and bit her lip. "It's a joke to you then?"

"No, it's a point. A point is like a story. Do you know what it says?" Alma shifted her weight. Outside, the rain had started. "That he can get as close to Henry as he wants, but I'll always be next door. What do they call that—a symbol? A metaphor? A warning?"

"It's one thing to think it," Alma said, "another thing to fight someone to prove it." Benjamin laughed. "Stop that," she said. "Don't laugh at me."

"It's not you," he said. "It's his size. Have you seen how big he is?" He let out a howl.

"I told you not to laugh," she warned. They were only a few feet away from each other, so close their hands could have met if they extended them. Benjamin had swung his legs so that they pointed in her direction. In her silent rage, she pictured her son.

"Take a joke, babe," he said. The lines across his face ran vertically, and in the middle was a coin slot. In all their years together, she had warned him that this would come, and he had always refused to wear sunglasses. You end up looking like one of those winos who drinks in the sun, he told her.

"Don't fucking call me that," Alma said. "*Babe.* Where the fuck do you get off?"

"See? You really can't take a joke. Who made you like this? So serious, so tired."

And she was tired. She wanted to stand up but couldn't gather the momentum. He moved his hand toward hers. She traced with her eyes his fingers back further until she reached the base of his hand. The places his hand had been.

"You still are —pretty," he said. "Even if you are tired. Those other women, Alma, they were never real. Have you ever wanted something for the sake of it? It was like that with them. But you're real. You're still real."

Alma rose and moved into the kitchen where the rain shone through the window over the sink. It was so quick that she was at the table and then she was not.

"I'm late," she said. "Shit. I need to get back."

"Come on, a few more minutes. We just started." He made it sound clinical, and the way he clasped his hands reaffirmed this.

"What do you want?" she asked.

"You're the one who came here," he said. "You tell me."

"You think your actions don't have repercussions," she said, "but they do. Even now. Your telling me that I'm real, that I'm pretty—you lie through your teeth. And I don't care, Benjamin, I really don't. But Henry does. And more than remembering his father as violent, he'll remember you as a liar. That's infinitely worse."

Benjamin felt an impulse to unload on her, but what she said transported him to another place, to those fields where Henry had said the same thing. *You're a liar.* His words became hers, or hers became his, and soon he was staring at Alma and seeing his son. They had the same dark eyes and habit of brooding, and Alma, despite her confident choice of words, could not help but look down at her feet.

"His cousins," he said after a while. "Your nephews. They seem to be fine with it."

She looked around. She wasn't sure when he had gotten up, but he now stood under the entryway into the living room, portal to the undivulged. If he moved another foot, he'd have vanished.

"What are you saying?" she said hopelessly.

"What am I saying?" he mocked. "What am I saying?"

"Yes? It's late, Benjamin, I have to—"

"They're here all the time. Your nephews. Right where you're standing, they are."

"When did this start?" she asked.

"I can't remember. It's been a while."

"Does my son ever come?"

"Our son."

She shook her head.

"I think it's time," he continued. He indicated the front door. "You're late you said."

The living room was less cluttered than the kitchen, but it lacked the aesthetic of a woman's touch. A real woman's touch. Mismatched furniture was arranged around a postage stamp TV, and the rug under which everything had remained from when Benjamin's mother lived here. In the dim lighting, the stains looked indistinguishable from the floral patterns, and both spread outward from the edges and reached the center where Benjamin and Alma found themselves, and each other.

"You know when people say, 'You look pretty even when you're angry?' I think you look prettier than that. Come on, why don't we do it right here?"

Alma smiled. "You never were smart."

"Come on," he said. "Come on, right now. It'll be fast."

Benjamin anchored his hands on the wall above her, and when she tried to squeeze away, he slid his hands in any direction that prevented her doing so. The veins in his arms were the color of sky, and they were tightening.

She pictured something peaceful—that spot along the bay that the locals called The Bog—where she'd go after long days to sit and watch the rain. Watch the little boats become unmoored. Watch the tide rise, the seagulls perch and then dive and scour.

He sent a punch that landed high over her head and caused the sheetrock to split. She ran.

Part Two
The Wake of Bodies

Chapter One

High school; sophomore year

...They must be miles away by now

Manero rose from the pavement, crossed the street, dusted off his shirt, and picked out small rocks from his hair.

...And if she's with him, then she could be dead.

He was uncomfortably warm, so warm that he took off his jacket and threw it to the ground. His mother would've scolded him for doing that, and he heard her voice now, frail and harsh simultaneously. But there was Janine to consider, and she was gone. Maybe long gone by this time.

"Hey, son," Manero heard a voice say. He shuddered, thinking it was the stranger with the deer, who had come back from somewhere. With Janine, or without her.

"Here, right behind you," the voice said.

Manero turned and found himself right in front of another car, this one turned off. Smoke exited the driver's side window though no indication that the smoke belonged to anything, let alone a person. "What do you want?" Manero asked. He'd had enough mystery tonight.

"I saw what happened."

The door opened and out stepped an old man who, for all the effort that it took him to dismount the truck, possessed an anxious hurriedness. A smile directed Manero's way suggested a fondness that was uniquely one-sided, for Manero couldn't remember if he'd ever met this man. But observing him now in plain sight—the illuminated spot of white hair, his wire frames bridging his nose, the slight limp—Manero knew who he was.

That Josef had aged since Manero last saw him was evident, but how much was contextual, like the bow of an old ship. He was in his late seventies and slight, and most in Holdam regarded him as an extension of the town itself, who knew its history as well as he did the name of every employer along Main Street. Maybe it was his diminutive body in front of his larger truck that made him think this, but Manero felt that Josef could blow away in the wind. His body appeared defenseless with regard to how it responded to stimuli: another passing car, the hollowness after it had passed.

"You're Alma's son, right?" Josef asked.

"Yes, sir," Manero said.

"Like I said," Josef said, "I saw it. And don't call me sir."

"How do you know—"

"That drunk son of a bitch."

"My mother? How do you know her?" Manero clarified.

"I saw her too, your friend," Josef said. "Pretty girl. Scared."

"Janine? Where is she?" Manero felt guilty for having already forgotten his friend.

They must be miles away by now.

"She ran off," he said. "Away from you it seems. What's the matter, no one ever taught you to fight?"

Manero shook his head no.

"A shame, really. Someone should teach you."

"Which way?"

"Maybe it's too late," Josef said.

"No, which way did she go?" Manero demanded.

"She's long gone," Josef said. He seemed content with the information he provided. "You really should have protected her, you know."

Manero stared down at his body, examined his own slightness and how the alcohol made him feel weaker, or at least how it made him reflect on himself as such.

"Come on, get in, we'll look for her," Josef said.

Manero pulled his cell phone from his pocket to see if Janine had called. If she had, she couldn't have been that mad at him, he thought. The phone was dead, its titanium slab cold to the touch.

"You coming?" Josef asked impatiently. He ambled back to the truck, his limp contradicting the hurriedness in his voice.

"What about the buck?" Manero asked, turning back to the road.

"What buck?" Josef asked.

"The dead deer, right there. Lying on the road. Didn't you see it?"

Josef shook his head. "Leave it," he said, refusing to look. "Lord knows there will be another."

Josef aimed his car toward the bog, where the water that briefly hoisted the cattails was a mirror of the sky, grey and flat and unanimated. The bog stretched southeast for fifty or sixty yards until it joined the bay, then interlocked with splitting inlets to connect to the Sound, which was a thrashing, a backwash, a background noise that one either chose to listen to or ignore. And in choosing to hear it, perhaps, Josef had kept his truck's windows open.

Beside him, Manero slept. If it had been his intoxicated state that sent him to sleep, he was now a casualty to the weather, shivering and sunken in the cloth seat.

Josef pulled into the parking lot adjacent to the bog and switched off the engine. "Wake up," Josef said over a soundtrack still playing. "Come on, wake up now."

Manero had passed between stages of sleep and lucidness, waking intermittently to see his hands and wrists illuminated by exterior light and the rest of his body dressed in shadows before the lull of the open road sent him back to dreams. They were strange dreams, too, the kind that accompany restlessness and expectation. Drunk dreams. Anxiety dreams. One where he was late to class because Jonathan hadn't allowed him to leave his kitchen, just kept plating sausages with ketchup until the plate was firebird red and the sausages muddy and derelict looking. When he finally got to school, it was empty save for a line of kids outside Nurse Liz' room. "There was a stabbing," one of the kids said.

"Who did it?" asked another.

The line advanced forward, Manero with it, until the whole of it was a swaddling mess of stab wounds and oozing pustules. The wound was nobody's and everybody's all at once, was, like the world, meaningless and yet full of meaning. Manero peered at his bleeding stomach, the hole of which was subsumed by another hole from one of his classmates, and so on and so forth.

"Wake up," Josef said in the truck. "I'm getting tired of waiting. Come on, wake up." The old man demanded at the same time he turned the stereo louder. A soul song with brass that was piercingly sincere.

"Ow," Manero said. "Shit, lower that. My head."

"You're a mess, son. Here, take this." Josef dropped two blue pills into Manero's hand, then reached below Manero's seat and fished out a flask. "And chase it." After a beat he said, "Don't worry, it's not poison. At least I don't think."

Manero took the pills in his mouth but gagged upon smelling the warm whiskey. He swallowed them dry. "Good boy," Josef said. "Good."

Josef let out expansive, struggling breaths, each with high-noted, compressed air at their tails. Like the end of breaths were the start of an exclamation.

"Why are we here?" Manero asked.

"You mean you don't recognize it?" Josef replied.

"It's dark. I can't see any—"

Josef clicked his brights into place, and Manero almost heard that sound too, like celluloid with breath siphoned into it. The concrete unfurled until it enmeshed with the bog, such that blacktop and sedge and standing water were indistinguishable; all were patterned with small rocks that shone like fragments of wedding bands. At the center of the portrait was a tree that was slagged down by the weight of one of its branches. In this lifetime, the branch would hit the stagnant water if some human or natural disaster didn't crush it first. One always did.

"So you see it now?"

He saw it. Where it was sometimes pristine, the low tide made it look spent, with fog that rose like steam from a subway grate; it was, as much as Manero could tell, a nightmare cloaked in gradations of nature.

Josef cleared his throat, took an awfully long time doing it. "Do you see her here?" Josef asked.

"See who?"

"Your girl," Josef said. "The one who ran away." Manero squinted. "Remember?"

"Janine," Manero answered, as if recalling her from a past life. He blinked his eyes wide, caught sight of a plastic bag fanning the big tree's leaves, stuck there. "Why would she be here?"

He searched his mind. It was here, in the parking lot beside the bog, where Janine had lost her virginity; in the same way one speaks to a priest with bated breath, Janine had confessed to Manero that she had done the deed one Saturday when her parents were out of town. The story was that she had met a college boy who was in town for a couple weeks, and that he had picked her up and drove her to the bog when it was late enough not to be noticed. She had told Manero this, sparing no details, because she was too nervous to get to the end of the story, the part where she had to explain, with trepidation, that it wasn't any good. What wasn't? Manero had asked dutifully. *Everything. It was just wrong.* She told him about their back-of-the-car rendezvous, of the baby seat that belonged to his sister that they had to move while they were in the process of undressing, about how they kept hitting their heads on the roof each time they lunged for each other. It had none of that sweet romance she had seen in the dozens of movies she watched with her parents as a kid, feigning disinterest every time a sex scene played but secretly wishing she could be like that girl in the movie. No, not *this one*, but one who didn't get her heart broken. Who made it all look easy. But nothing about that night was easy, she told him. It was awful. He couldn't even, you know, get it up. She didn't tell him that part. Rather, she told him how it was kind of awful and anti-climactic and full of apologies, from both of them, and how both had sat glumly inside his car, swollen with hurt pride. And after, how he had tried to be all sweet and rub her head for a considerate amount of time, until it felt like the sun was coming up and a new day was beginning and, holy hell, what would her parents think about all this? But he wasn't sweet, she said, not at all. He just used me.

Manero turned to face Josef, saw how the indents under his eyes looked like the Grand Canyon of Old Age. "No, she's not," Manero said finally.

"But you know what occurs here?" Josef asked. *Had Josef known? Was Janine's secret not a secret at all?*

"Yes. But she's—"

"Guilty," Josef said. "They're all guilty."

"I don't under—what are you saying?"

"You will, you...just give it time. Take your mother."

"My mother, you know her?"

"Of course." He didn't elaborate but let the words suspend there, become inflated.

"How?"

"We're friends, your mother and me. Your mother, now she is a woman. Alma is a woman!" Manero's previous remembrance morphed: it was no longer Janine struggling uncomfortably in the back of the college boy's car but his mother—Alma, a *woman*—or her being bent over some fallen log where the pavement opened up to woods, where the standing water pooled around her shoes; and there was Josef behind her, hunched like some cataclysmic saint of lost causes, portending the end of sex and of humanity as one knows it.

"She came to me, once, twice, for money," Josef said sternly.

"What?" *Nothing is sacred.*

"Because your father, well, never mind all that." He paused. "I gave it to her. She didn't even have to beg." He smiled. "Your mother, she's a woman though. A strong woman."

Manero couldn't shake the image. Did strong mean having to do sexual favors for people twice your age? Or did it mean having the gall to refuse them?

"I couldn't refuse her, you know. Once she told me the truth," Josef said.

"The truth?"

"That she never wanted you to see her struggle, to see yourselves as poor. No matter what it took. That you were too proud a family to have that happen. That you were too special." He touched the boy's shoulder.

Manero noticed that his headache hadn't subsided. "You make it sound so...so past," he said. "You said she came to you once or twice. When? When did she come ?" Josef struck a match and lit a cigarette that blew capriciously in the wind.

"The truth?" Josef asked.

"Sure, whatever, the truth."

"You're old enough to know, I suppose." Josef said. "Are you feeling okay?"

"What do you mean?"

"Your eyes, they're bloodshot."

There was a time he would often think about, as in moments like this, when he returned home after a night out with Janine and stumbled drunkenly into the box shrubs at the beginning of his driveway. For a few seconds, or minutes (it was hard to tell), with his head supported by the density of branches, he lay there unable to get up. And when he realized how stupid he appeared or scared himself into thinking that a passing car would've spotted him, or worse, called the cops on him, he tried to rise but found himself at the mercy of his muscles. They felt like glue stuck to the leaves, and that by getting up too fast he'd snap the elasticity. He liked being down there, felt at ease down there.

Then the light shone inside his mother's room, and he thought getting up too fast would attract her attention, so he stayed and tried to outlast her insomnia. But at some point, he had fallen asleep, and when he awoke it was significantly later and the sun a stone's throw from beginning its ascent. The birds were chirping louder than he had ever heard, and it was beautiful but also maddening once he thought about how lucky he was to have survived the night out there, with his legs halfway pitched in the middle of the street like they had been. He lit a cigarette and decompressed and then crept inside undetected. When he awoke hours later—he was in his bed and it was noon and the birds had been replaced by shouts of kids playing—his mother was there to greet him with tears lapping her eyes. Her anger, that came later. But her sadness was enough to make him feel guilty for having been out past his curfew; what he didn't forget—what he never would forget—was how she had stared at him, within him, and told him that his eyes looked like the devil's. Get some sleep, she said, we'll talk about this later. I'll have to think about what I want to do.

"I'm fine," Manero said to Josef back in the car. "It's been a long night."

"The nights are still long once you're old, just in a different way," Josef said. He exhaled his smoke, was brazen about where it went. Then it was true about second-hand smoke: that it never smelled or tasted as good as when you were smoking yourself. "She's been coming to me your whole life, son," Josef said. "Your mother."

Manero grabbed a smoke from the old man's pack. Only after lighting it did he realize he hadn't asked.

"It's funny our paths crossed at the very least, don't you think?" Josef asked. "Look, I can give you a job, if you want it. If you want to stop depending on your mother."

Manero needed work, ever since Jonathan had gone to California six months earlier and hadn't yet returned. Though his previous job helping out Jonathan on his farm didn't deliver a steady paycheck, it produced enough work to satisfy his wants and needs: cigarettes, tickets to the movies, and, lately, a film camera that he was saving up for. He had gotten the idea after reading an article in the paper about twins a town over who shot a film that was making the rounds at local festivals. The twins were being heralded as the next Coen Brothers, and the newspaper had even come up with a lovable name for them: The 'Camera'n Twins (their last name was Cameran, and the reporter was being cutesy, too cutesy Manero thought). He and Andre, after seeing the Cameran Twins at the pizza restaurant, couldn't stop staring at their table, in awe of them and the company they kept (read: their parents and siblings). After dinner, Manero mentioned the idea of procuring a camera in order to make a movie, and he told Andre that he would be the writer/director, and Andre, with his good looks, the actor. And Janine will star opposite you, Manero added, to which his cousin agreed. Since that conversation last fall, Manero had been putting whatever money he made into a clear jar that he kept in his desk drawer and measuring the progress.

"Do you want to know what I'm offering you or are you desperate enough to say yes on the spot?" Josef asked.

Manero thought for a while. There were stories, small-town stories such as they were though stories no less, about Josef slapping the asses of waitresses in the café or scaring kids away from their mothers on the sidewalks. The former he did because he couldn't keep his mind out of the gutter; the latter for pure enjoyment. He had amassed lots of wealth in his thirties—first by patenting some electrodes that went into building semiconductors at the behest of the United States government and then by coming into a heap of money after his father's death, and then by investing all of it. After money was no longer a worry, not that it had ever been, Josef wrote a novel for the heck of it, which, he learned, permanently dislodged any ambition of seeing himself as a professional, so he called himself a creative instead. It was just as well. For years, aimless and maybe bored, but with the boredom that only luxury could afford, he wandered Holdam and preoccupied himself with other people's business; and sometimes it wasn't their business at all but their charity, for he thought he was doing favors by putting neighbors to work on menial chores for pay. Usually, it was high school boys whom he employed at his home, so that at any point in the high months of summer or in early fall his house would look like a driver's ed course, with kids who barely had their licenses pulling in and out and parking and reversing. Coming and going.

There were rumors—because there were always rumors, and in this case, they weren't very surprising—that he was exploiting kids for cheap labor. These rumors were extinguished as soon as parents saw that their kids were coming home with bill folds larger than their own. But this led to different rumors, crueler and more sadistic ones, about Josef hiring only boys and, thus, having a proclivity for seeing these young men sweat as they pushed lawnmowers or rakes along his acreage, which needed all the help it could get by the way, and then inviting them in to wet their lips with some iced tea. One day, when some tough, bolts-and-all father tried to check Josef with this information, to call his bluff or catch him in a lie or, for the glory of the town never mind his own son's integrity, get the aging man arrested on some pedophilia charge, he had forgotten who he was talking to after all and had left the conversation with his own pride caught between his ass cheeks. For as defiant as the father was, Josef was as much so if not more honest: "You know, son," he had told the adult, "you're not the first person to question me on this, and I'm sure you won't be the last. But I'll tell you what I told the last person, and you can tell your friends this too so they can save a trip here. I hire young men because they're stronger, plain and simple, but if your wife would like to come down to help out, I'd gladly oblige taking her top off as well."

Manero wasn't strong, this he knew. His physique, such as he saw himself, was like sand that was walked upon—loose and capable of collapsing on itself.

"I have guys to do the heavy lifting," Josef said in the car. "That's not what I need you for. I need your intelligence instead."

"If you're asking me to do math problems, I'm not…"

"Books, Josef said. "Lots of 'em. A library full of 'em, from when I was younger and when I was in college and then after. Books from now. Those I've collected or pilfered from the library—you ever steal from the library?"

"Steal? No," Manero said.

"Never mind," Josef said again, placing his hand on the kid's shoulder.

Manero worried whatever Josef needed didn't require intelligence at all but company, time spent in dusty corners sorting fiction from nonfiction, and then nonfiction into its respective categories. Poring over copyright pages and examining book jackets for stains. Huddling over boxes and packing them, and then stopping while Josef reminisced about where he procured each book and what each meant to him. He imagined that the old man's collection wasn't all that different from the junk that his father presumably kept—the words stolen and procured synonyms for one another. This could take hours or days. And what if after cleaning and packing these books up Josef decided he wanted them back, all of them, put right back on the shelf? Hours, days. More unpacking.

"It'll be worth your time," Josef said. "State your price."

Days, and more money. Unpacking, and more money.

Perhaps it was the time of night or his drunkenness that compelled him to say yes, but Manero thought that, at the very least, this job would satisfy him long enough to make an impression on his mother. That he could—should he want to—forge his own path, which could prove to her, and to himself, that he wouldn't have to rely on anyone, even if it was Josef who was both providing the financial means to be self-reliant and, also, to be free. That if only by thinking it, the future could just happen, like that.

"Okay," he told Josef. "I'll do it." The old man smiled, which sent a chill through his toes. "Now I need to get back home."

"Don't you need to find your girl?" Josef asked.

"She's not my girl," Manero said with some pain. "Not yet at least."

"That's the spirit, my boy."

Josef reversed the truck, at which point it occurred to Manero that they might've attracted attention. But the wayward direction of the truck's wheels, and the heave of transmission, confirmed to him that they were indeed alone.

"Where are we going ?" Manero asked.

"Home," Josef said. "You said you need to go home."

Josef pointed the car east, where the road curved and the cedar trees abetting a road sign looked curiously out of season. They rounded the corner and then passed the bar, Sophie's, where, Manero reasoned, the man who'd hit the deer must've stumbled out of hours before. Manero squinted his eyes as they passed the parking lot in the hopes of detecting the make and model of the man's car, but he had already forgotten it. It didn't matter much anymore. He had been shown a sliver of the truth, but the truth no less. Did the truth matter if he couldn't find Janine, if he had no one with whom to share it?

Chapter Two

Janine awakened the next morning at seven o'clock to her father grumbling outside her bedroom door. Her mother was turning sixty the next day, and her father, feckless and inconsolable, was soliciting his daughter's help in trying to find a present for his wife. Janine tried ignoring him, but his bulbous head kept popping in from the hallway, each visit louder than the last. He reminded her of a dog scampering backwards with its head between its legs. And though he was a few years past sixty at this point—wise to the degree of bearing little common sense or at least very little self-respect for his role in keeping the family unit together all these years—he deferred to his wife who validated him very little and, yet, required a colony-sized amount of assistance. She was handicapped in the way women who come from money and live just slightly beneath their means for too long in middle-age become, predisposed to wanting that feeling of youthful Zen so much that they resort to indifference in daily matters of life. When her husband would suggest that the family go out to dinner to celebrate Janine's good grades, his wife would complain of migraines. If her husband wished for a glass of wine in the evening after a long day of teaching at the local college, she would reprimand him for setting a poor example around their daughter. But the opposite was true, as you might guess. Should she be invited out for a drink with the other wives from the yoga studio, she accepted without hesitation, and her migraine "disappeared" until it was a phantom feeling. What it left behind sunk her poor husband, which, in turn, made Janine resent her mother.

Her father stood obsequiously in the doorframe and cursed himself for having this "too big a problem," and too late, while Janine seethed at the idea of helping him, like treating her mother to something could somehow buy back her adoration. As if the woman needed more *stuff.*

"Give me a half hour," Janine finally said to her father. "And do some thinking in the meantime."

In the car forty-five minutes later, Janine's father turned the heat up and blew at his fingers when only cool air came out.

"Hon, where are we going?" he asked. Janine looked up. He had reversed out of the driveway and was now heading north, continuing straight until their road connected with Main. "I don't know, man," she said. "Wherever. I'm here for emotional support only."

"Okay, I'll keep driving then."

Janine's tone toward her father bordered on cynicism and crested whenever she was annoyed with him. "Watch out for deer," Janine cautioned.

"Roger that, man."

They passed the scene where twelve hours earlier Janine and Manero had run from the car with the Class of 1983 bumper sticker. She didn't forget that number. Though the stranger's face began to disappear from her memory (blame it on the unconscious forgetfulness that mild trauma brings on), the sticker shone like an exit sign above the doorframe of her mind.

"Janine, where are we going?" he asked.

"Shhhhh," she hissed. "Just drive…to Meme's."

Meme's was a clothing store a town northeast of them that boasted mannequins in high-waisted jeans and tight turtlenecks, the kind of place her mother would look into whenever they were in town together and wished she still had the body to pull off the mannequins' outfits. Curiously, as much as Janine rebuked the notion of shopping for her mother, she also reveled in the possibility of what clothes could do to a person, particularly a lady for whom material objects seemed of more import than her own children. Janine didn't come to this conclusion on her own: it had been suggested by her own father to her mother on countless occasions, most likely as a joke, but who could really tell?

"She'll like that store," her dad said. "It's expensive."

Janine's phone dinged, and she opened it to find a text from Manero. *Please tell me that you're home okay and that you don't think I'm an asshole…* He had inserted a sad face.

She began to type back but stopped when she saw that Manero had texted again. That he kept texting.

Speaking of assholes...I hope that guy didn't kill anything else on the way home. Other than that deer.

Thanks for getting me home safe. Thanks for standing up to that asshole. I'm sorry I couldn't.

I want to tell you something.

I'm sorry.

"Janine, look at that!" her father shouted. She dropped her phone into her lap and looked straight ahead. "No, there, on my side!"

Her father jolted the car to the shoulder, much to the ire of the truck trailing them. The truck screeched and made a hasty dash around them, punctuated by a few loud chortles of the horn. "Sorry, sorry," her dad said under his breath.

"Dad, what are you doing?" Janine shouted.

"Would you just look?"

Across the street, the fog had cleared just enough to reveal a couple news vans with a youngish female reporter outside of them. There were two cameramen facing her and an even younger female instructing the cameramen on where to shoot, her arms flapping wildly. Behind the reporters, where there used to be a universalist church, was now the fading remnants of the wood building. The small tower that stood adjacent to the steeple had collapsed while the steeple itself was a smoldering mess on the lawn, reduced to a wiry contraption with no beginning nor end. Three firetrucks remained on the premise, but no real fighting was being performed. The men, and one woman, were now congregating with spectators, enlightening them with their facts about the fire. Nearest them, yet so far away, the minister was pacing back and forth.

Janine recognized the minister, Mr. Leterno, whose son Owen was in her class. She had always thought Mr. Leterno too young and fresh-faced to be a minister; he was nothing like those hardened old men she had seen in Catholic mass when her father was going through his spat of religion, or as he called it, "reassignment." But she'd learn later that universalism was one of those sects that permitted a more nascent and puerile understanding of faith, and so it could stand that Mr. Leterno could be both spiritual and handsome, though boyish he remained. In his khakis and pressed black polo, he scanned the grounds for anything that was still standing. Nothing was except for the door and its framework, which should've been symbols for salvation but weren't.

"Holy shit," Janine said. "I wonder where Owen is." She scanned her phone for Owen's number, sorry that she didn't have it.

"Should we go? I mean, out there?" her father asked.

"No," she said into her coat. "Not right now." Her father rolled down his window and was immediately struck by the weight of air, an obtrusive, chalky smoke that filled the car with resignation.

"Close that!" Janine yelled, louder than intended.

"Sorry," he said. He fiddled with the radio in attempt to find a local AM station, and finding the channel listened in as a reporter ran through the weather. *Expect the clouds to remain through tomorrow and the wind to pick up through early evening.*

"They're not saying anything. Maybe it's not, not that bad?" Then realizing the twisted logic of this statement, her dad said, "Must've just happened. I think we should go out there."

"Dad, no," Janine said. "Can we just go?" She spotted a traffic cop approaching the opposite side of the road and locked into him. "Look, he's going to make us move. He's coming to talk to us," she said, not taking her eyes off the man.

She recognized the traffic cop, too. At twenty-nine, he'd still not made officer. It was rumored that a couple years ago, before Janine was in high school, he was dating a high school student and that the other kids would make fun of him for his crossing her on her way to class in the morning. Janine assumed that when a crossing guard was not crossing students, he was also setting up traffic cones on the highway or, apparently, assisting with a fire that, by now, had amassed its share of onlookers on both sides of the road. Cars and bodies and a few bikes huddled there, and though the windows of their car were closed, Janine thought she could hear the prolonged silence of trauma, like footsteps after a snowstorm. Or maybe she didn't hear anything at all, which felt worse.

"He's not doing anything!" her father said of the crossing guard. He wasn't wrong.

"But what are *we* going to do?" Janine asked. "You and me? What are we going to do by getting out of the car?"

"Emotional support," he offered. He glanced once more at the site and went solemn. Beside Mr. Leterno was his wife, wearing only her pajamas and a wool coat, and his seeing her there, a few minutes removed from sleep, shook him. "You're right," he said, "let's just go." He made a cross in the air awkwardly far from his shirt and said to Janine, "Say a prayer for them tonight. Poor woman."

Janine's manner of dealing with crises, be they hers or others, had its roots in the ancient philosophy of stoicism, though, more applicably, in the recommendations of her high school teachers who referred her to the Greeks of past, particularly Zeno of Citium. Her English teacher, Mr. Stabile—or was it history's Mrs. Rossum, with her medusa-like hair—had seen Janine poring over *Critique of Pure Reason* by Kant, aggressively marking the sides of the pages. Thinking, and quite correctly, that no regular teenager, unless she were lacking a moral compass or trying too hard to impress her peers, would understand such philosophy at her age, Mr. Stabile told her that her energy would be better spent ingesting a mindset that is effective. She'd research Zeno of Citium and then Marcus Aurelius and then Cicero, and a little Epictetus, and discover that the stoic mind was a saving grace in a world that continually disappointed her.
    It wasn't that this disappointment was a juvenile side effect of her age or worldview either; it was objectively real, was, as Kant said, "the age of criticism, to which everything must be subjected." And she observed that in the condescension of her classmates, and even her teachers, who rejected her intelligence and work ethic and financial means of achieving her successes, though what did Kant have to say about the upper class? Here is where she diverged from Philosophy 101 (she'd later take a course in college called Philosophy 102.3 – The Reason for Doubt, in which Kant would make a welcome cameo), and introduced herself to Zeno, who reminded her that her peers were mere obstacles on life's wavy river, were like shadows in the Battle of Valley Forge. There and then gone if she chose to look away, if she chose to slam the history book.
    She put up a façade. A strong—the boys would call it callous—front that took from life its disappointments, ingested them, and spat them out as productive coughs. This is what she imagined the Stoics did: took their failures and put them to work. All that writing that Marcus Aurelius had done, it hadn't come from nowhere, Janine reckoned. There was that time in ninth grade where she wrote furiously in the library for the entire afternoon. She remembered this because it took the verbal force of the librarian, Mrs. D., to shake her from her place after two bells had

rung, the first to get to class and the second to signify that it had started. And when Janine didn't budge, Mrs. D. snatched the paper she was writing and held it close to her bosom. That made Janine irate—not the snatching, she knew Mrs. D. was just trying to do her job, but the presumption that Janine wasn't doing any work by skipping class. On the contrary! She was writing up a storm. She was Marcus Aurelius channeling Zeno channeling Artemis, with those imperious hunting dogs in tow.

When that session ended, and another, she had written sixteen pages of punctilious cursive inside her notebook. Two hours of work. Two hours of classes skipped. Her kind of physicality bordered on obsession, and was, again, like Artemis with her quiver and bows, but what the ancient myth lacked was discussion of any work that Artemis must've done to excel in her ways; it all seemed to be within her all the time, uncomplicated. Janine, conversely, had to work. She had spent her time in the library with such hunger that when she looked down upon the pages she'd written, she was struck to see how many times she'd written a single name, one that produced grief and adoration simultaneously. *What you love is nothing of your own.*

The name she'd written was Andre Lockhard, and she loved him. Loved the sight of his name, the sturdy way the A and L stood there like sentries. Loved how the word 'hard' sounded like 'heart' if spoken quickly enough, and how 'lock' meant to hold it. Across the pages, As and Ls were dropped like landmines, and each time she wrote one or the other her knees buckled. She hadn't meant to write his name over and over, but somewhere amid constructing this self-narrative, his visage plagued her. Then she made herself hear the soft purposefulness of his voice, a pitch just below his older brother's, and sat with it for a while. She talked back to it, answered when it called (in her mind, but it was just as well). In real life, she couldn't recall a time she had ever spent genuine time with him or his name. She had only heard it in passing—in the hallways, among the bleachers, in conversations she overheard between him and his cousin, Manero. In her dreams.

But where did Andre go in real life? It wasn't a totally irrational question. One day he seemed to be hanging around Manero, and by proxy close enough to her, and the next, his popularity stretched over itself like wet yeast, kept folding her in deeper and deeper until she had dissolved into her own imaginations of what he'd become. But she had liked him from this moment—no, before this moment, back in ninth grade at the library—and continued liking him into her sophomore year, Andre's junior one. By then and much to her delight, although she didn't have a choice or agency in the matter, she had developed a body that most of her peers would have called well-endowed, if not still skinny. Hourglass shaped. And kids, plying their ego by way of name-calling, had also referred to her as Butterface, though that wasn't quite accurate either. She wasn't perfect in the facial features department, this much was true, but the lazy bottom lip and bug eyes that the students called 'ugly' would later come to define her inimitability. But in that school, she relied upon her figure to allure attention from the boys. This *did not* mean being slutty; no, high school abounded in that sad confusion (she'd be wise to point out how few female philosophers there were and even fewer who couldn't accurately distinguish between sexual liberty and repression). It meant having enough dignity, confidence, and self-respect to carry on the way she wanted. She could show her cleavage and masquerade her peek-a-boo eyes and expect attention that it begot to slope her way; and she could do that and still write about Stoics and get straight A's and swim competitively for the school team and revere everything about Andre Lockhard. The dialectic meant the pendulum swung both directions—that by attempting to attract Andre she would accidentally attract other kinds of attention.

She noticed that Henry Manero didn't seem to register interest in females whatsoever until one April afternoon in ninth grade, not long after her writing frenzy in the library, when he compared the branches of a tree in their school's yard to the legs of a woman. Janine pondered why natural imagery was always symbolically female, but nonetheless indulged him in his fantasy. Whose legs are you referring to, she asked, and could they indeed grow and then cleave like branches? Oh man. He looked across the grass where the girls' tennis team ran laps around the court, like a slow orbit of male passion, and centered his gaze on one girl, *the girl with legs*, Marissa Burke, whose body was like one line directed vertically, an inverted horizon.

"Her," he said, choosing not to use her name. "That is the girl with legs."

"Typical," she responded, because every boy said the same thing about Marissa, the walking magazine ad that she was. But Janine's curiosity was also piqued because though every boy had talked about Marissa, Manero never had.

"You like her too?" she asked. "Please tell me you're more original than that."

And he shook his head—was it yes or no or both? Directionless.

It took her a few months to realize that his fantasies were actually directed toward her, as opposed to Marissa, and that Marissa was simply a decoy along this littered path. Her proof? He had trouble holding eye contact with her, for instance. Or in settings in which they usually found comfort, like in the stands of the school's baseball diamond where they watched the night sky consecrate them as they smoked weed, she noticed how his movements felt stunted and peculiar, as if he had to give himself permission to inch closer or farther away. When passing the joint back and forth, he'd released his fingers quickly, and the joint would roll onto her lap before spilling into the grass. Shit, he'd say, I'm sorry, before staring at her waist. But she never questioned his clumsy intentions, for they were repressed so deep within him that to ask him such a surreptitious question felt like she was asking for a piece of his DNA. To pry this information and not return it in kind was a lesson in love's inequity that she was not yet ready to face. She might never be.

"You look sick, are you okay?" her father asked. His concern alarmed her, and in transitioning into the protective role that she was used to, she almost forgot the reason for her own disarmament. In the rearview mirror, the smoke 'was pigeon-grey and weakened her whenever she looked back at it. Then she looked at it: Manero's latest text.

I got home late and I felt like we'd been through something together, you know. The way they show in the movies. Maybe it was the way you stood up for me. Or that you stood up for us. And when I got home I had this crazy urge to kiss you, but you were no longer there. Did you feel that too?

She began typing a response. The click-click-click that she'd silenced on her phone sounded in her head. And then all vanished with a pause of her thumb. She didn't need to answer, did she? She didn't need to decide about how to answer. Because any response she could have given—be it passive nonchalance or a delighted recognition or silence, the worst kind of non-answer—put her in an uncomfortable position. But she *did* need to think about it, she reasoned. She couldn't let something like that go untouched.

Approaching the bog now, she thought of the college-aged boy and his physical demands and, oppositely, of what it would feel like to have been thought of with such adoration that one couldn't help but get nervous in the act. Like how it could be with Andre. In this way, she had changed her tune: love wasn't some bold, virile declaration but the confidence to be vulnerable. And for the first time in her short but prodigious life, she realized one thing: she had never been vulnerable in front of anyone. No, not even with her father, whose concerns about the fire wore into the contours of his face. She saw them, their ruinous lines, and briefly felt bad about having had her attention diverted by the sinful trappings of youth. Of sex. Because she really was a modest girl, and she shouldn't have been thinking about that, especially with him present, but she couldn't help it.

She had climaxed once or twice while her father was home, had felt bad about it but finished anyway. She had climaxed when her father was downstairs in the kitchen making bread, but never while her mother was there. Not even if her mother was outside in her garden or on the phone or distracted by a multitude of events. Not even if a hurricane had struck the house where her mother would be but had left the inside of the house intact. For if her mother had discovered her, Janine would not have been able to contend with the shame that would've rained down in the form of questions: *How dare you? Do you think you're invincible to rules? Who gave you permission to be sexual in this house?* All questions would have borne the subtext: *Who would want you?* Because whenever her image was concerned, her mother reprimanded her weight like it were a thing in control of its own destiny. It's getting out of hand, you're going to need to do something about it, her mother had said once at the dinner table, and Janine thought that commenting about one's food choices while eating was like telling a cop to withhold his gun after firing the kill shot. She ignored her mother's censure, but then, before bed, she looked up images online, dozens of teenage girls, like herself, except these girls had abs and cavernous navels and shrunken hips and some of them didn't wear clothing.

She was aware that her mother's vision of health was based on some unachievable ideal, worse than even the kind shown on the Internet, but imagining what it would be like if some boy touched her—if Andre touched her, the leviathan he was—she would've experienced the unfair sensation of her own body. So she scrolled and clicked and scrolled some more, and in doing so lost track of time; she could've fallen forward into the computer screen, lost to the world and to herself, if not for her father's voice. She would often hear her father rebuking his wife for suggesting that Janine needed to lose weight, that such comments were only going to make a girl "get a complex," and in between hearing her parents snap back and forth at each other and scanning the internet for pictures of skinny girls in bikinis, she found herself typing the word 'complex' into the search bar. But remembering that she was, beyond all, a smart and self-assured girl, she turned off her computer, slid her chair back, and crawled into bed and shut her eyes. The next morning, she'd do what any self-respecting, stoic woman would do: she'd go on living.

She hadn't planned what she was about to do. Planning had only disappointed her in the past, primarily in the form of her mother and her father, the latter of whom required an extravagant amount of thought to stave off what would surely be the end of his marriage. That's why they had been driving all this time anyway; that's why she had been ushered out of bed on a Saturday and forced to confront her father's fear. To plan. But when her father asked her what she would be doing the rest of the day, she told him she didn't know. The image of the recently burned church flashed in her mind and she imagined what it would have looked like had they arrived an hour earlier to find it burning. She saw flames spit out the windows and ride the sedentary pews like lightning, and she saw everyone inside burning, or barely escaping death, because amid her fantasy death was a reality from which there was no plan. The fact that anyone had escaped unscathed? That was truly a miracle.

 Her father turned the wheel into the lot behind the Arcade, choosing a spot farthest from the laundromat where a homeless man sat most days. When it was warm, like it was today, he never seemed to leave but insisted on new avenues of conversation with the same people who worked at the laundromat or who waited for their clothes to get done drying. He was like a windmill that chimed to the direction of one group and then to the other. Her father, it turned out, was in no mood to be stopped for idle conversation and, possibly, some spare change.

 He was already out of the car, walking in the opposite direction of the man, when Janine started typing her response to Manero. She hadn't planned on what she wanted to say concerning his wanting to kiss her, hadn't planned any of it, and so her response rolled off her fingers in a screed that she only later realized was half-intended, though which half was all about whose perspective you chose. If Janine were the only person who mattered—and she should've been, right?—her response would've been crystal clear to Manero. But communication meant that there was forever someone to answer to, one for whom there were no easy apologies but to whom she would always find herself offering them.

Chapter Three

Janine was to drive because that was her thing, driving Manero, and sometimes other boys, in her parents' car because she was almost a full moon older than him, which served her well when it came to driving but not, apparently, when it came to conveying what or whom she loved.

It was almost eight o'clock at night when she pulled up to his house, and Alma was once again at her place near the window eying the approaching car as if it were a seraphic vision. Janine flashed a misshapen smile from the car and waved with the hand that wasn't holding the wheel.

Manero came out carrying a book, a flimsy paperback, which struck Janine as weird—I mean, who reads in the dark and in someone else's presence? But in the car, he kept transferring it between hands, and it struck her that he was using it as a safety cushion to hide behind in case the conversation became too uncomfortable. They exchanged pleasantries and she drove through the clear night, keeping her hands on ten and two because she was nervous also.

Though why? She had drawn and outlined the scene in her mind and graciously accepted what she had put forth. She had decided on the place—the bay across town, the one closest to Benjamin's house, where there would likely be other cars and couples (except that these couples kissed) and where, if she supposed Manero looked, he would see his father, as big and as immovable as a bluff.

Earlier that afternoon, Benjamin Manero thought of a woman's face, the back of her hair laying over the couch and coming down in blonde rivulets; he thought of the back of her head, too, as in something he could grab, and then the vision became sexualized, although the difference between when it wasn't and when it was had become indistinguishable. Then his visions transformed to those of other girls, high school girls shimmering in pink lip gloss and holding secretive stares that he couldn't get behind because, well, he was old and they were not. Barely legal. He was not proud of these visions, even if he was the only one who acknowledged their existence. He thought of them sleeping there—sleeping over!—in heaps of blankets spread evenly on the floor like rows of Indiana corn, and it was this image, this unspoiled vision of safety, that made him justify their coming over. He'd clean everything up come morning, toss away the refuse into a dumpster and hide the key.

The parties had become more frequent and crowded since spring, with the cousins coming over as often as they wanted. Peter, Andre, and Sal signaled their arrivals with a honk of the horn or by forced entry, pushing Benjamin's door open with fanfare, and sprinting until they found the beer, warming inside cardboard boxes next to the refrigerator because Benjamin was too lazy to bend over and restock them. It took Andre's good-nature and Peter's distaste of warm beer to rectify this. When the boys invited girls over, which they had also begun to do with more abandon, they told Benjamin that these girls were "on the level," which their uncle took to mean they would keep their mouths shut. The less he had to worry about one of those girls going all-Judas and telling their mommies and daddies. Ruining the whole thing they had going, which, Benjamin reminded himself, shouldn't—*no, couldn't*—go on much longer. On mornings where he'd find puke on the lid of the toilet or a used tampon in the trash or a pair of sandals left in the backyard it was easy to convince himself that these transgressions were even beyond his self-imposed limits. And if he didn't want to get arrested or lose the privilege of seeing his one-and-only son again, he'd better stop hosting parties from which he didn't gain much except a headache come sunrise.

But he did get something in return, and that's how that old pendulum swung. Back and forth between uselessness and utility, between desperation and pride. He could've gone to the bar, sure. Could've spent his time and money sitting on a stool and chatting with strangers who would become his friends (Isn't that what friendship is in adulthood anyway? Petty conversations over drinks?). Could've gotten a lift home from the bartender when he was too drunk to drive or too drunk to not get caught by police. But that bar would've likely been Sophie's, where Alma or her friends went, or another bar, where Jonathan's friends congregated. Ever since the day Benjamin gave Jonathan the black eye, Benjamin feared retribution of the worst kind. He imagined this payback coming in the form of a late-night accosting at the front steps of the bar as he was retrieving his keys, missing the shadows that were plastered over the walls. Even though Jonathan was in California, had been for years following the fight, the tale of it had grown, and Benjamin was convinced that it was only a matter of time before he got a taste of his own medicine.

This is to say that Benjamin found comfort drinking in his own home, even if that meant having to keep a watchful eye on his nephews and discouraging them from inviting the entire school to the house at 565 Forsyth.

It was only natural, Benjamin convinced himself, that he had daydreamed of a teenage girl. It was like her being there had offered the filthiness that only boredom could make logic of.

Manero's turn to speak elapsed like steam from a kettle, dew from grass. And he made himself focus on a naturalistic image such as this if only to distract himself from the possibility that if someone was going to speak first it was not going to be him.

"It's Andre," she said.

"Where?" Manero asked. He clicked the window down and poked his head out. The warm air carried the sound of boys farther along the beach, their clinking bottles and cursing. "I don't see...where?"

"No, no," she said, "it's him. Who I like, who I've always liked."

"What?"

"That's why I didn't want to say anything. Cuz I knew you'd be mad."

"So you mean, all those times you –"

"Yeah."

Janine knew what Manero was getting at. That whenever he talked about Andre slipping out of their reaches and into the clutches of his brother Peter, she was also secretly mourning this loss.

"There's nothing you could've done," she said. It sounded so definitive, an ending to a movie of himself that he had been forced to watch.

"I feel like –"

"Don't," she said.

"Shit," he said. "Okay, I won't."

He sulked. Not in the gross way of children but like someone who thinks he deserves something. He turned his head away and unsnapped the seatbelt.

"Where are you going?" she asked.

"Nowhere." He hadn't intended to at least, but as soon as the idea was proposed he opened the door and announced his indolence by slamming it harder than usual.

Janine had told herself that she wouldn't chase after him if he reacted this way. She would be resolute in her denial. As Manero walked away and his shadows blended into those of oaks bending backward, Janine heard her CD still playing. It was Spiritualized, and it sounded atonal and unforgiving: something like love lost, never to be found.

Benjamin Manero shouldn't have thought of his inability to fall asleep in the dark, borne from the day he had to spend a night in the hallway as a child, as a talent. Like adults who can mold their hands into mini machines of labor or others can spin stories at the dinner table and leave kids amazed, Benjamin believed his restlessness a skill. He could sit in a chair only for a few moments before stretching his entire body out, neck to toes, as if filtering down the booze. It made him queasy, but the queasiness enlivened him and sent him to the bathroom where he'd turn on the light and throw his head into the sink and pour water onto his head. His entire head. He'd slick his hair back and reappear, looking like a washed-up actor or a European romantic, and walk out into rooms of his house where he'd find himself alone, with no one to show himself to. He'd travel through his house's interiors and not get anywhere, just collect dust in between his toes while misremembering time and place, and occasionally, when the mood got to be too low, he'd take his thoughts past the windows and into the wind where they might be free. He'd saddle up his boots, which he'd tuck into his long pajama pants, and put on the denim jacket he had had since high school and walk down the long gravel driveway to the road where a single streetlamp lit the black tar in a patterned spray of textures. The shadows gave the road the impression of depth, and he'd think to himself that there were puddles everywhere. He'd dodge these depths until deciding that the ground was solid and safe to walk on, and then would find room in his pockets and continue onward.

He'd check the air and its temperature like it could tell him stories of time. More specifically, people's stories of time and space, of what they did in their own homes while they thought no one was watching. His neighbors' lights would be off, most of their shades drawn, and the ones drawn in white would be inoculated to the rest of the neighborhood. They'd remind him that his front windows did not have shades at all and how the lack of them must've exposed him.

He'd continue down the hill, which came off a sharp turn and led to the bay on the right. The tall hedgerows on both sides of him would keep him confined to the road, and descending into darkness he'd find respite in the little flashes of light of the houses that intersected the hedgerows. He'd like these flashes, insofar as he could make out the outline of his hands and feet. But when he'd disappear again, he'd long for the light by continuing to feel around with trepidatious flails of his fingers. Finding nothing, he'd increase his pace and proceed down the hill.

He was afraid of the dark, remember. Though his childhood fear had eventually matured to a manageable one by which he could control darkness by turning on the lights in his house and not incur the wrath of his sleeping parents, he was still very much naive in his conquering of it. And going down the hill that surrounded him in green, which he could only experience as outlines of black, he'd picture himself inside his home again, though he'd see himself as a child sleeping between those scuffed walls, his parents so close he could hear them breathe.

Manero was crafting an apology on his phone, the white screen highlighting his bangs, when Janine found him on the beach. He'd wandered down the path, past the group of high school boys stationed there, and onto a wood plank that bridged a set of large rocks.

"I thought you left," he said and blackened his phone screen.

"You were the one who ran off," she said.

"Yeah." He turned away.

"Why don't you talk to me?" she asked. She paced around him, digging her shoes into the sand and bringing them up every few seconds to shake them out. He lit a cigarette, but his shakiness caused him to drop it into the sand.

"Leave it," he said. "Don't."

Moments passed. The boys several yards from them careened into a ball of hormones that pushed and pulled at opposite sides. The boy with the hat, who had made a mini sandcastle with extant beer bottles, spotted Janine's figure and called out to her. She ignored him, and when his embarrassment became evident before his group, he called to her again, louder. For some reason, Manero had evaded the boy's censure, but he now felt forced to act. If his drunkenness the previous night had caused him not to act, his soberness at this moment enlivened him. Seeing the way Manero clenched his two small hands, Janine cautioned him with her eyes. "Don't," she said, echoing his phrase.

"What's the matter, you and your boyfriend don't want to talk to us?" the boy yelled to Janine.

Neither he nor Janine recognized this group of boys, which made the danger feel more palpable. It was a similar sensation to having escaped the stranger the night before, with the prospect of him returning anonymously and with supposedly clearer intent. Manero wished for Andre to appear and shrink these boys down to size. He would've sacrificed his own jealousy of his cousin for a chance to see their scared faces.

"Just shut the fuck up already, all right?" Janine yelled back.

"Ooooooh, the balls on her," the same boy chirped. And then to Manero: "What happened, bitch? Girl steal your balls?"

Janine took Manero's arm and ushered him along the beach, away from them, and heard the howls of laughter that followed. When they peered back, they were relieved to find that the bodies hadn't moved where the voices had. Still, she could see that Manero was sizzling: that's what it looked like to her. A steak frying atop a stove, charred around the edges. He ran a clenched hand through his hair and matted it.

"Forget it," Janine said, facing him. "Look at me, Henry. Forget them."

He listened to her because he always had. "You're beautiful," he said. He couldn't help it.

"Stop," she said. "You can't say that."

"I can say what I want."

"Don't do that. You can't say that. I told you how I feel about—about this."

"That doesn't mean I can't say anything," he said.

She supposed he was right—nothing could stop him from thinking or even saying anything. But she also supposed she didn't have to accept it. She was tired of accepting it.

"I can't give you what you want," she said. "Or maybe you don't like what I can give you?"

"And what is that?"

"Friendship."

"That's it?"

"I'm sorry."

Across the bay, where the woods climbed the ridge and tucked their roots into earth, the moonlight pierced the overgrowth of night. If Janine were drawing a straight line from the ridge down to the water and back to herself, she would see the pieces of the sky divest and unburden themselves in the water. Everything might seem simpler if she could follow the path the ripples made. Instead, she watched as a few cars shone on the road that climbed the ridge, how they looked like ants with helmet-mounted lights making their way to the top of the hill. She watched and suspected she knew where these cars were heading because she recognized, she thought, the haloed lights on the jeep that belonged to Peter. And then the music that poured out: a rap song that rumbled the speakers and sent chills through her toes.

She turned back to face Manero, but he was halfway down the beach, running toward the group of boys.

Henry ran faster than she'd ever seen him run. Ran until his body folded into the darkness, became no more. But that is exactly the problem with history: that it's always tilted toward what's done versus what's not. In this sense, it could be reasoned that Manero's decision for acting was to impress upon Janine a moment, one that could will its way into history as she would one day interpret and remember it.

Manero was only thinking about the present when he launched his fist into the air and caught the cheek of one boy, who, being even smaller than him, fell backward and collapsed into the rocks and sand, which, historically, were older than boyhood and violence and anger itself.

"Henry, no!" Janine screamed, but he was already running ahead of the boys, who stood in disbelief that one of them had been struck and by no less than the person to whom they'd directed their insults moments before. Seconds after the shock of the strike wore off, the boys chased after Manero, swinging their half-empty bottles before freeing their hands by tossing the bottles into the bay.

Their chase continued from afar—Janine heard their shouts and then the truck doors slam, like the boys had made their way inside—until there were no sounds except the wake of the water and a couple hushed voices from neighbors who sounded like they were calling the police or simply commenting to each other, their tone hinting at caution and apprehension.

She checked her phone, believing news of Manero's safety would've flashed before her, thus signaling it was okay to make her way back to the car. But seeing nothing, she could only imagine him as he likely was: running on the concrete that was dark as night, darker, and looking back to see if the truck was close. He might've gotten a head start, sure. And believing that momentum and willpower were on his side, he might've even generated enough speed to elude them of his direction. He could be halfway home by now and not even out of breath. But then another picture emerged, and it was of the truck with its music turned down and windows open and the boys sniffing like dogs. Liquor would be passed around in the bottle, cigarettes would dangle from the boys' fingers, and the wind would push an ember onto one of the boy's arms and make him yell *Ow*, but it would be a minimal pain. Nothing like the kind that her best friend would experience once they caught up to him.

She moved quickly past the boy who had been bowled over but who was now sitting in the place where his friends had left him. Cruel to their own kind as well.

"Sorry," Janine mumbled to him as she passed. "About my friend. Seriously, I'm sorry." She barely managed the words before he grabbed her waist from behind and pulled her downward.

"Ow," she yelled. "What the fuck?"

"Shut the fuck up," he said. He slunk one of his hands over her wrist and pulled her the opposite direction from which she came. "I just want to talk to you."

"I said I'm sorry," she moaned. "What do you want me to do? I said I'm sorry. I didn't know he'd do that."

"My friends, they'll be back soon," he said.

"Your friends left you," she whispered.

"What?"

"They left you," she said forcefully. She looked to see if the neighbors were still out there, but they'd brought their conversations inside.

"They're looking for your dipshit friend," he said, squeezing her wrist harder.

They won't find him, she thought.

"Do you know where he went?" He tightened the hold on her wrist.

"Ow, you're hurting me," she said.

"Where *is* he?"

Janine scooped a pile of sand with her free hand and squeezed it. When he saw what she was attempting, he pulled down her arm. "They won't find him," she repeated mechanically. She resisted his pull on her and found it easier than she thought, because she lost her balance and landed shoulder first on the sand, her face parallel to it, or was it parallel to the waves that were far away but which now sounded so close? Then her eyes looked up at the ridgeline, which had gone dark without the presence of cars. On her pants, just above where they ended and her t-shirt rode up, she felt his fingers.

Andre had gotten out of Peter's car and was approaching Benjamin's front steps when the scream echoed across the bay and stopped him in his tracks. At first, he didn't think a human could yell that loud; its high pitch reminded him of a cat or of a child pretending to be a cat. He ignored it and looked at Benjamin, who welcomed the boys into his house, the outline of a figure behind him. But then the scream came again and accompanying it were words: *Help, please, stop!* Animals didn't verbalize pain so clearly.

Andre demanded that Peter drive them back down the hill to the bay, and seeing no other way around Andre's panic, Peter agreed. A minute later, the jeep sped down the hill.

Peter parked at the scene—that's what Andre referred to it as in his mind, a scene—and sprinted toward the path where it opened to the beach. He searched the sand for shoes, a t-shirt, a discarded purse, something to indicate that a struggle had taken place, and he was so intent on finding something that he hadn't realized he was hearing sobs from nearby. Sobs meant that someone was still alive; that she was perhaps okay.

"Hello?" Andre whispered, and then louder, "Are you okay? Where are you?"

"Go away," Janine said.

"No, you don't understand," he said. And then softly, modulating his panic: "It's okay. What happened?"

She sobbed a rhythm.

"Hold on, I'm coming," Andre said.

Had she been less upset she might've recognized the voice. How it both commanded and inquired, lifted and sank. He found his way to her by listening to her breaths after the sobs disappeared; he was so good at hide and seek and adept at navigating through the dark. When he crouched to her level, he once again expected to find tragedy, something like lacerations across her legs. That she seemed intact was surprising, like this whole thing had been a prank played on him by the universe. They met eyes and he couldn't help smirking upon recognizing her.

"Janine? I'm sorry, I didn't mean to smile. I just didn't expect to – what happened?"

"Andre?"

"Janine, what happened?"

It was as if she couldn't hold two thoughts at once: the pain of what just occurred and the surprise of his having come. "What are you doing?" she asked.

"No, what are you doing?" he shot back, worried. He lifted her up and dusted off her shirt.

"I think I freaked out," she said. "I'm not sure if he did it, if he did anything, but I just freaked."

She told him about what had occurred, how Manero had run away after landing a punch on one of the boys, of how they chased after him, and that the boy who was struck stayed behind and grabbed and threatened her, and when she couldn't speak, how he touched her and she blacked out momentarily.

"You scream loud," Andre told her. "That's a good thing. I'm glad you do." She shivered. "Where did he touch you? No, no, it doesn't matter. Never mind. I'm sorry, I wish I'd been here, earlier. If I had known. I'm sorry."

She laughed at his eagerness, if she could call it that.

"You sure you're okay?"

She told him what she had left out in the first telling: that Manero had revealed she liked him but that she didn't know how to respond. And lying between truth and untruth, like a bridge that spanned her conscience, was Andre. The boy from her notebook, reanimated.

His head swiveled as it surveyed the scene. From behind the trees, a car's headlights blinked on and off in their direction. He thought the boys could have returned, which startled him into telling her that they should be going. By the time he remembered the car belonged to his brother, he found himself gripping her hand. So close they could've fallen into a dance.

"Who is it?" she asked, suspicious. He examined her, thought he could feel her breath because her mouth was so close. He asked himself whether he found it alluring or ugly, or whether it could be both. Could he find beauty in imperfection? He stared a long time. He thought he could count her teeth in their imperfect rows, that he might be able to see their history.

"Who is it?" she repeated.

"Sorry," he said. "I got distracted. It's Peter. It's our ride." Recognizing that that might've been presumptuous, he followed with, "What if you came with me?"

"What if?" she echoed.

"Well, would you?"

"Depends where."

"A party." He paused and then smirked. "Sorry, I didn't think so."

"You make it like I've never been to a party," she said.

"Not there," Andre finished. His gaze fell upon the ridge and hers followed.

"No, not there," she said. Her face lowered.

"Would you, I mean you don't have to, but—?" His eye twinkled, then blinked away. "I'll tell you what. Peter's waiting for us. We'll get in the car and drive around and try to find Henry first. He can't be that far. You can call him on the way."

She had liked that Andre said *waiting for us*. As if she had been part of the plan. She didn't plan.

They walked back along the beach to the car where Peter, not willing to acknowledge her, asked Andre what had taken so long. "No one died I guess," he said sarcastically.

Once in the car, Andre turned toward Janine in the back seat and mouthed *I'm sorry*. "Here, take this," he said, and handed her a warm beer that he'd dug from under his seat. "You could use it."

"What happened to her?" Peter asked. "Are we going yard-selling?" He laughed.

"What my brother means," Andre said, "is, ah, fuck it, just drive."

Janine snapped the can and heard the foam like a wave pool. By the time the car was in drive and she had taken her third sip, she had forgotten about calling Manero. She hadn't even checked her phone.

Chapter Four

Andre had gotten drunk before he knew he was drunk and was now passed out in Benjamin Manero's basement. He'd excused himself upstairs twenty minutes before, when the saliva started forming in his mouth and he found it unpleasant and impossible to articulate to Janine, and the rest of the group the simple sentence, "I think I'm going to be sick."

He'd intended to text Claire, with whom he'd been flirting over the last few months, but thoughts of her coming over and seeing him this drunk racked him with anxiety, so he drank fast and without thought. The irony, of course, wasn't that the drunker Andre got the more he forgot his fears, but that the propulsive weight of his body wasn't enough to deter the low-alcohol beer he was drinking. It occurred to him while sitting alone in the basement that he was an impressive lightweight, and that despite being immersed in the culture that high school celebrated, he never really drank. This was a sharp contrast to Peter, who drank with the will of someone needing to prove something, and so it stood that the more will Peter had the more alcohol he could consume.

But Andre, sometime between forgetting and trying to remind himself that as Manero's cousin he had a duty to be kind to Janine, had fallen asleep with his phone in mid-text. The cursor blinked until the screen turned black.

Andre's sleep hadn't stopped the others from arriving upstairs; on the contrary, his friends arrived swiftly and without pretense. When they asked where Andre was, Janine tried her best not to look concerned for fear of their eyes resting upon her and judging her for being out of place. Peter, who each time the question was posed said he would look for him, chose not to look for him.

It was she who eventually searched, who ducked into the kitchen and dialed Andre's number and heard the ring echo in some lonely crevice of the house. She followed the ring until she arrived at the top of the basement steps, and Peter, seeing this a few feet away in the living room, volunteered to go down with her.

Andre, sleeping into his lap, wasn't awoken by Janine's sing-song hello but by the fist his brother delivered to his chest, an impact so centered it made him gasp.

"Let's go, pussy," Peter said.

Andre's eyes lurched forward, meeting Janine's. "Did I miss anything?" he asked.

"I'll get you a water," Janine said.

Upstairs, three girls, Claire among them, sat in a u-shaped formation and picked uncomfortably at the frayed hairs of the carpet. The party was young yet, and when Andre reappeared with Peter and Janine, the room erupted in celebration.

"We thought we lost you," one of the girls said.

"The prodigal nephew returns," Benjamin said. He was hovering over Franny, his newest girlfriend, his hands on her shoulders. She wore a thin sheen of lipstick that made her small lips look forced on, and above those lips—where the shade of the makeup tickled her skin—were faint hairs, visible now because the light hit them at such an angle that Andre thought of a dog's wet fur. There were a lot of them, now that he looked, and he wasn't sure if they were natural or if she made a point not to eliminate them.

Franny's eyes darted to the three girls beside her feet, to their painted toes, and, finally, to Claire, with the tattoo of a pepper showing on her ankle. Franny herself was without ink, which was surprising considering she had a nipple ring that Benjamin often liked to make mention of in their private conversations. But ink, these girls were too young for ink, she thought.

While Andre swayed in place, trying to regain his verve at the sight of Claire, Franny stared with such obvious intent that Andre saw this tattoo as well, how the stem of the red pepper shot up her leg like a pathway toward infinity and was cut off by her pant leg.

"What does that symbolize? Your tattoo," Franny asked. Claire uncrossed her legs and briefly lifted her one pant leg to reveal the stem, and Andre was disappointed to see that it ended so soon. "Every tattoo has meaning, so I hear?"

"Oh, it's silly," Claire said, obfuscating the pepper with her finger. "Most are when you get 'em that—"

"It's a tribute," she interrupted, "to my father. He has this garden in the backyard and would show me how to grow veggies when I was younger, and I was always fascinated by the peppers. They were always so colorful." She laughed before finding a need to say, "He's still alive, my father. Most people assume he's dead when I say that it's a tribute."

But it wasn't like Franny to assume that such a young girl would have the misfortune of losing her father; she was still caught on the fact Claire had shortened vegetables to veggies, and it annoyed her—the choppiness of the word, like she had regurgitated this response hundreds of times before and found a way to make it easier for herself.

"Well, I like it," Andre said. He had said it louder than he intended to, and the others in the room turned to face him.

Janine looked down upon her own legs.

"And I don't even like tattoos," Andre continued.

There was a knock at the door and Benjamin got up to answer it. He reappeared seconds later with four or five other kids from Andre's grade, including Martin Hladik. Since the knife-carving incident years before, Andre and Martin had gotten close, united around their opposite characteristics. Where Andre was reticent, Martin was bitter and sometimes resentful, and his tongue lashed out at others with the grace of a wet glove. He'd grown taller and more sinewy, with eyes that had trouble shutting at a regular rate, whereas Andre possessed the offhand sleepiness of Rodin's *The Thinker*, his eyes doubling in shadow and his brow dark and strong. Though together they made an awkward pair, it was Martin who was bold enough to call out Peter on his hostility. Martin had come from a large family of dissenters—his grandparents were first-generation Polish immigrants who were rebellious against the Leninist government and whose aim was to teach Martin the traditions that had, in their words, made them "cold-blooded snakes." It was meant as a compliment. From the time Martin was a child his parents had told him to "act the snake" if any kids were being cruel. And though kids were fond of making fun of his nose, of how it looked like a nail head that hadn't been hammered in, they all but stopped once Martin went "snake" on them and bit a kid in middle school. By the time Martin and the rest of the class graduated into high school, his reputation preceded him; and it was Peter, most of all, who would stay silent every time he saw Martin at a party or was resigned to working with him on a group assignment. Some things would never change. Martin would never not be aggressive, and Peter would always be condemnatory, but at least Andre could use Martin to deflect Peter's aggression.

"Where did this one come from?"

Andre heard Franny say this of Martin, and he felt defensive of his friend. Martin wore an oversized jacket that he kept his hands inside of for several minutes until Franny insisted that he take it off. "You're making me nervous," she said. "What's your name again?"

"Martin," Andre answered in unison with his friend.

"Martin's a Polack," Peter said.

"What's that?" Sal asked.

"A Pole. Polish," Peter said.

"I don't think you're supposed to say that," Claire said. "Right?"

"No, you're not. Actually, that's pretty fucking offensive," said Claire's friend Marisol.

"Hey Marisol," Martin said, beaming with delight. "What's up, you spic?"

"Half spic," Andre said. They laughed, and Andre was at last buoyed by the conversation, fished out from his malaise.

"Why don't you take a seat?" Benjamin said to Andre. His uncle came behind him and scooted a chair so close he had no choice but to sit. "Better, right?"

Now Martin was the only one standing, but used to being out of place, said, "Is this a party or a fucking séance?" He didn't mean it as a question, not really, and Peter, who understood Martin's aim (if there was one thing they could agree on, it was on the idea of getting salaciously and unapologetically drunk), stood up and rejoined by saying, "Yeah, let's fucking do something!" Then Sal stood and walked over to the sound system below the TV and turned Alice in Chains on loud.

Benjamin reveled in the possibility of what a night might offer. It wasn't enough to have had played host to these mysteries at his own house; he wanted to control their fates, too. This wasn't unlike theatre, where Benjamin had accompanied Franny weeks earlier to watch her middle schooler's performance of *Newsies*. But unlike the darkness of, say, his house, the theatre had a warm semblance of artifice, the feeling that the actors—and maybe even the audience—could deliver and take part in a fantasy. To him, it was the fantasy of the fake seeming real (that was obvious enough—he wasn't a savage, he understood plays!), but also the fantasy of what might happen sitting next to her. He felt it in his pants, that stirring, and reached over to touch her hand before feeling guilty that on the other side of Franny was her ten-year-old son, and so the magic was making this fantasy disappear just as quickly as it had come.

He didn't have to shy away from fantasy in his home. Standing behind Franny, gripping her shoulders as he would a barbell, he imagined the possibility of waking up with her in his bed, the two of them drinking coffee to outwit their hangovers, seeing what the other looked like when night's haze faded. And then making love again. No, fucking again. Making love is what teenagers who didn't know better did.

Teenagers like Janine. Benjamin looked around the room, like spinning a wheel at a game show, and stopped at her.

He stared at her long enough for her to regard him, for once, not as Benjamin Manero, the capricious adult whose house she was occupying but as Benjamin Manero, Henry's father. She saw then how much they resembled each other in the way their black eyes made them look disconsolate, or how his hair, which was greying but still much apportioned, was like Henry's mop.

"Who are you?" he asked.

"I told you, Uncle Ben," Andre started. "That's Janine, my friend. Henry's –"

"Girlfriend," Benjamin said. "You're the girl he always talks about."

"No," Janine said, turning her face away. "I mean, yes, we're friends, but –"

"You don't like my son?" he asked. His tone was bitter, and it made her detest him and think of instances in which Manero had also qualified his hate of his father, and between her own emotions and those flashing back, she experienced a guilt that stripped from her the wit that she was usually prone to. For the first time in close to an hour, she worried about Henry. She wondered where he'd run to and whether he'd made it; if he had made it, how she should've been there for him, *with* him. And if he hadn't, well then, how she was to blame. It was all her fault, she told herself. Her rejection of him had been too harsh. It was more of an erasure, like it never existed in the first place. Like it couldn't. And now she was—*how in the world*—in Benjamin Manero's house, face to face with him while he, of all people, tried to exculpate himself. While he tried to make her feel bad for not being a good enough friend. She should be the one defending him now. He wasn't there to do it himself.

"Are you blind, Ben?" Franny said aloud. "She likes Andre. Can't you see how she's been looking at him ever since they've shown up together?"

Everybody turned to face Franny, and her inability to recognize that she had crossed a line made her even more contemptible to Andre.

"I didn't notice," Benjamin said.

"You don't notice much," Janine said under her breath.

"What did you say?" Benjamin said.

"Nothing," she said.

"I was saying that my boy, my Henry, he has the hots for you. He'd tell me so whenever I picked him up for school, about how you're the only one who gets him."

"Gets him?" Janine asked.

"Are you denying that you like him? Just so I'm clear? Go on, you can say it," he smirked. "He's used to rejection."

"I want to understand what you mean by 'gets him?'"

The discomfort in the living room sent the others into the kitchen for more alcohol, and left there were Benjamin, Franny, Andre, and Janine. Even Peter had excused himself.

"He means Henry is shy," Franny offered.

"Let him talk, my uncle," Andre said. Franny offered a half-smile but rolled her eyes.

"You want me to spell it out?" Benjamin asked.

"What?"

"This is what you want? Fine." Benjamin slammed his hand on a desk, one of the three mismatched ones that were taking up space in the room. "My son has hated me ever since I cheated on his mother, and he would've hated me if I hadn't. It was his mother's mission to make sure he hated me. All I was saying, all I meant is that I'm glad Henry's got someone to help displace that anger. Does that make sense? Maybe you're too young to understand this. Maybe you have to be a parent."

But Janine wasn't too young to understand. She knew Henry, even if she could never love him.

"Do you hate him?" Janine asked.

"Do I hate him? Do I hate my own son? Give me a break, bitch," he said. "Franny, will you top off this whiskey?" Franny stood frozen for a second, and then walked automatically to the kitchen.

"Janine, come on. Let's go," Andre said. "Let's go get a drink."

"No, no, no. We're adults here," Benjamin said. "Right Janine? Is that your name?"

"That's right," Janine said coldly. "Janine." Two syllables.

"Then let's talk. As adults," he said.

"Then answer," she said.

"Do I hate my son?" He pondered the question aloud. "Do I hate my son?" He laughed and pulled at the collar of his t-shirt. "Do you love your mommy? Is the sky blue? What balls you have."

"Thank you," she said.

"Come on, Uncle Ben. Get off it," Andre said.

Franny returned with Benjamin's drink. The ice cubes clanked in the glass. Behind her, in the kitchen, the long, tall shadow of Martin bobbed and weaved. Peter was acting out a scene from an action movie and mowed down Martin.

"Here you go, baby," Franny said, handing Benjamin the drink. "Now what did I miss?"

"Oh nothing," Benjamin said and took a long, forceful sip. When he exhaled, Janine could smell the rank of cigar and peanuts.

"Nothing," Janine said.

"That's right," Benjamin went on. "She wasn't saying anything important." He turned away and stared at an unknown spot on the wall.

"Do you know about his hand?" Janine asked. "That he once punched a grave over and over and cursed your name? And that it bled. And he was screaming and crying at the same time over you?" Janine hadn't moved, but it felt as though her words had marched toward Benjamin and tipped him over. His glass was almost empty. "That you can favor your nephews over your son," she continued. "That you never paid him any attention even when he begged you to. Andre saw Manero's hand, he saw how hard he punched that grave. He was there."

Andre couldn't deny that. He remembered questioning how and why his cousin had punched the graves to begin with, why someone would do something that stupid. Why someone would walk into a cemetery to begin with. Stay there awhile.

And Manero had told Andre the same he'd told Janine after that event occurred. The one of how a classmate had gone with his mom to Benjamin's yard the weekend prior to look for used furniture for her husband's office and had spotted Manero's collection of baseball cards—a binder full of them—on sale. Some had been taken out of their sleeves to be sold individually, while others sat in the binder that had Henry's name written in red permanent ink on the front. Benjamin hadn't even bothered to get a new binder. When the classmate inquired about the baseball cards, Benjamin referred him to a pile of other "kid's stuff"—his words—all of which were Manero's belongings. A book with Michael Jordan's very bald face on it. Two or three video games without their console. A pile of books with their wings torn. The classmate, after seeing this and asking his mom if he could have money for video games, wisely called Alma's home and asked to speak with Manero about the console. Was that for sale, too? Manero hadn't a clue about what the boy was talking about and raised the issue with Alma, who, frustrated with Jonathan having left or still very much confused by it, hissed at him to go take it up with his dad. If it means so much to you, she said, then go get it. I can't fight every battle for you, Henry. If you want it back, go get it.

It wasn't that he still wanted it; he was too mature and uninterested in these items to have sentimental attachment to them. But he was vindictive to have had the privilege of knowing stripped from him. So he called Janine to meet up with him—of course he called Janine—and complained to her. And yelled some. And when he wasn't satisfied with her trying to assuage him, he punched the grave. Once. Twice. A third time, and then one more time for good measure. Because that's where they happened to be walking. Because that was the cut-through to town that they always used. Because the dead wouldn't pay any mind to his tantrum.

"And do you know who he wished for? Who he wanted in that moment?" Janine was facing Benjamin and Franny. Even Andre, who was beside her, seemed to be opposite her. Like the universe tipped unevenly away. Nobody answered Janine's question because nobody knew to whom she addressed it.

"I remember," Andre said.

"Tell me who," Benjamin said. He sounded corrosive. "Tell me, Andre."

"Jonathan Bartlett," Janine said.

"Jonathan," Andre said.

"Jonathan Bartlett," Janine echoed.

Benjamin's cheeks welled up, like the whiskey was being siphoned from them. His fingers trembled at his side, and he grabbed onto his shirt ends to steady them.

"Hon," Franny said, "we should step out for a second." She pulled out a pack of cigarettes from her purse and put one to her lips. When Benjamin didn't move, she withdrew it.

"Andre, who is this bitch?" Benjamin asked his nephew.

"My name's Janine," she said.

"And you brought her here, so I'll tell you what, son. Either this bitch is going to leave right now or you're gonna have to explain to your brothers why you have a piece of your skull missing." At that moment, Peter and Sal came into the living room laughing at something one of them had said. Sal tapped Peter and signaled for him to shut up.

"That's some threat," Janine said.

"Andre, I'm warning you," Benjamin said. Peter, Sal, and Franny had instinctually backed up, but Andre hadn't.

"What's it gonna be?" Benjamin asked.

Andre turned around to face Janine—perhaps to ask for her silent approval to strike him—but she was gone, the tail of her shirt escaping through the hallway. The front door slammed.

"Go on," Benjamin said. "Go on. And when you regain your senses, you come on back now."

Andre and Janine walked down the hill to the bay where her car was parked. He had offered to accompany her, now that the night was dark. Dark, still, and disquieted. They didn't say much—there was nothing to say, she thought, in her anger about their leaving—and he felt humiliated for having to apologize to her for his family. So he didn't: he stayed quieter than the moon song.

They got to her car at the docks and she fished her keys from her pocket, conveniently and swiftly like she had been planning on an escape. She clicked the unlock button and the taillights blinked awake.

"Are you okay to drive?" he asked. "I'm so sorry."

"Fine, yeah. Only had a few beers." She jangled her keys, and Andre thought of Benjamin's ice cubes in his whiskey. Then he considered his own drunkenness, how Benjamin's ire had sobered him up, or at least that's how he felt. The split-image of the world had become one again; Janine's eyes were the symmetry of taillights. Of someone going.

"Me too," he said, laughing. "I wish."

"Hey, thanks for standing up for me," she said. She looked tearful, or just on the verge.

"I'm sorry I didn't do more," he said. "I didn't know what else to say."

"You did what you could."

"I stood by you, I guess." He hiccupped and swallowed. "I stood there at the very least."

Just like they were now. Within inches of each other's face. And she felt the urge to let him kiss her, if that's what he wanted to do. Did he want to? He felt brazen enough to, but then the single image became two again, briefly, before dissolving back into her face. It was this temporary interruption that made him realize he couldn't be in two places at once. If he were here, he couldn't be back there, at Benjamin's, where Claire was waiting.

He hugged her. "You be careful," he said. "And again, I'm sorry."

"Nothing to be sorry for," she said. "It was my fault for coming. I should have known what would happen if I did. I shouldn't have left Henry."

Henry. Where was he now? She pulled out her phone and saw a message from him sitting there unread. She walked to the front door of the car, got in, and turned on the engine.

His message was raw like the chipped edges of a seashell.

Outran them. I hope you have a good night.

Where are you? she texted back.

I'm okay, I'm all right.

She waited a few minutes at the docks to see if he'd say anything else, but when no message came, she reversed the car. Andre had retreated up the hill—she could no longer see his shadow illuminated under the single streetlight that guided the road—and she felt like it was finally time to leave. The night needed a rest, as did she.

But she didn't want to go home. Not yet. It was early still and her parents would be up when she got home, her father watching TV on the couch in his Pink Floyd t-shirt and her mother reading the newspaper in the adjacent office. Though only separated by a few feet, their silence would've seemed grandiose, and she couldn't deal with that. She would be the reason for their breaking their vow of awkwardness, and she feared the questions would come without relent. And after they stopped, if they stopped, her father would try to appeal to her soft side by begging her to watch a movie with him, some classic film starring Carole Lombard; he'd say, come on, it's not like we spend that much time together anymore.

She drove. To the bog where she had lost her virginity. And maybe she needed the affirmation of someone who, for instance, wouldn't be afraid to kiss her, no matter the embarrassment her presence had caused his family. Or maybe she needed the memory.

The ferns in and around the bog looked like moles coming out of a translucent face, and when Janine got out of her car she saw the empty water bottles and candy wrappers that swirled in the shallow water. Kids, she thought. Kids must come here and tell each other stories about the kinds of things that happen at night.

But outside was silent, like a scene from a film that was happening off-screen and far away. She thought of what might be occurring at Benjamin's house now that she was gone: Peter and Sal in a screaming match to get their uncle's attention and Andre sitting stone-faced and drunk, using his eyes to flirt with any pretty girl who took his silence as contemplative thought. Suddenly, all of love seemed to be happening off-screen and far away, and that's how it always was, right? Love breaking your heart right behind your back.

She thought, too, of her fellow students finding rooms in Benjamin's house like in the cavities of a whale's stomach, pulsing in and out of them until they decided one was safe enough to burrow into and take off their clothes. Nothing quotidian happened in her fantasy: each and every image was, by its nature, extreme and stark enough to be its own mini movie. There were a hundred, no, a thousand movies occurring at one time, and Benjamin was the star of each one. He was the Charlie Chaplin of serving underage drinkers. Nobody talked about Olga Edna Purviance, Chaplin's co-star in most of his early films. They only talked about Charlie. By the party's end, would anybody even remember Franny? Janine thought of her as a parasite kissing the hand of Benjamin, bringing him to his knees then dying off.

There were insects in the trees, louder than they should've been, she thought. She saw them, too. Earwigs with their hellish pinchers that climbed around the bark of a faded tree trunk. She itched herself and recalled a time in which bugs weren't a nuisance but a wonder. Much like boys.

Manero texted her again—her phone lit up—and she slipped it into her pocket. To be truly alone was to be disconnected; and to be disconnected was to not need to think about a response. All she had to do was breathe. Breathe, she told herself. Two more years of school, and she'd rid herself of this place. Douse her clothes in oil and set fire to the past.

As this image formed in her brain—not of a raging fire either, but one slow and warming as of a candle—a car, with its radio blasting, sped to the edge of the grass nearest her own car and screeched to a stop. Standing at the edge of the bog, within feet from the cars, she was startled by the noise. In a second, as if she had blinked it true, the car shut its headlights and radio, and both front doors opened, then closed, simultaneously. The blinding headlights one minute and the returning darkness the next strained her vision, and she couldn't make out the two figures approaching. One broader and one shorter. By the time they reached her, the two figures collapsed in on each other, and she didn't have time to blink and see them as they truly were.

She could only scream. Scream but not hear herself scream. There was pain, and then, on the ground, so many insects.

Part Three
The Longitude of Grief

Five Years Later

Chapter One

I had figured by now Josef was ignoring my calls. And why shouldn't he? A man in his eighties has every right to ignore what he wants — especially things as cryptic and droning as phone calls. Which reminds me: have you ever met an old man in good shape, with exertive mental capacity who, in the midst of talking, says something completely off color but with such conviction that he believes it to be true? Pretend it's midsummer and the conversation is baseball and the unpredictability of the third base position, and he says something like, What we need is a quarterback. Not even a great one, but a competent one.

And you say, A quarterback? Weren't we talking about baseball?

And he says, Yes, but football was on the other night and it got me thinking.

You: The other night? Football won't be on for another two months.

He: Yes, I know that. It was a re-run of last year. Don't you think I know what season it is? You: I know, I'm sorry.

And you are actually sorry, because maybe it's true that the old man had seen a re-run of a game, but part of you knows he's slipping. And you say, Oh sure, we desperately need a quarterback. And he says, Oh, but there's time. What we need now is for fucking Ramirez to start planting his feet on that bag.

What bag? you say.

And he says, Third base. You listening at all?

All is right. In the end, all is right. Maybe he's not sick but distracted. And that's because distraction, or, rather, having nothing on which to focus anymore, is a good thing in old age. Hell, this man is eighty-something and talking about baseball. Good for him.

So, Josef, why should he answer? I had even tried relaying to him in my voicemails that calling me back wasn't a priority, that I know he's a busy man and has other things to do than respond to my appeals for creative acknowledgment, which is why I was calling, wasn't it? But the utter lack of response (Imagine white noise here, like the noise of two dozen airplanes taking off and landing) was getting me down, but I knew better than to be tortured by it. What could I do? Maybe Josef had gone on a trip to a place where people call him Joey and hadn't returned home to receive my voicemails yet and was more concerned with people calling him the right name than responding to my pleas. Have some respect after all.

Then it was a Sunday and a week had gone by and Mom showed up at my door. She asked why I hadn't called Josef yet, and I was surprised and a little vexed to hear her say this. He's been asking about you all week, she said. He misses you.

All week? Where have you seen him? I asked.

Everywhere, Josef is everywhere! she said. At the bagel place, by the auto mechanic, on the bus stop, he is there, he is out there! Why haven't you called?

I've been calling all week, I cried, and in my attempt to remain calm I sounded desperate, like a child again, and having Mom there validated this feeling. I couldn't do anything about it—about this childish symptom or Josef—so I said, That's okay, I'll go find him.

Try the bank, Mom said, I just saw him at the bank! He is out there!

I was even more exasperated to hear that she had seen him minutes earlier, but I just said, Fine, I'll go find Josef.

He wasn't at the bank. I smelled the pine-scented vestiges of his cologne in the vestibule and immediately recalled what he had said once about the trail of dust that settles all problems or something about finding the clues or putting the clues together, and I was enlivened to think that I was getting closer.

I had an urgent need to run, and I chased the sound of a barking dog through the path that cuts behind the church and ran into Father Kelly, who was planting spring flowers, his fingers clutching them at awkward angles, like he was too weak to clutch them. Have you seen Josef? I asked him, short of breath.

Henry, my boy, what a rush you're in, he said. Slow down, it's Sunday.

I thought about what Sundays meant or what they hadn't meant in a very long time, and realized I hadn't eaten anything all day, combined with the fact that Sundays used to mean pasta and fresh garlic and meat sauce (the kind Benjamin used to make when I was a kid, where the meat dissolved in clusters and we'd routinely dip the bread to check the consistency) and that it had been a lifetime since Sundays were Sundays.

Is Josef in trouble? Father interrupted my reverie.

Oh, no, nothing's happened, I said, I just need his advice on something.

Josef is a busy man, Father said.

I know, I said. But then I thought: how was it that Josef could be seen around town, in perpetual dalliance with nothing at all, and still be busy?

You've been running around a lot, Father said. Slow down. I only see you as a blur these days. Why don't you come inside the church? Mary Ann is cooking rosemary chicken.

As if a sign of God (food!) presented itself outside this House of God (the church was like a chicken roaster most days), my eyes lit up. But I still said, No, thanks, that's nice of you, but Mom is waiting for me back at home.

Father was still holding the tray of flowers and wasn't going to do anything with them, I decided. I took it from his hands and placed it next to the empty ones on the ground.

Thanks, he said wistfully. You'll have to stay for dinner with me and Mary Ann one night, he said. Makes the best chicken, Mary Ann does.

Next time, I said.

And if you find Josef, he said, tell him I've been asking for him. He's become, as we like to call it, spiteful of God. Maybe spiteful isn't the right word, I don't know.

I told Father I knew what he meant, though I didn't, and then thanked him and continued running: north through the cemetery, next to the crooked headstones, and out through the gate where the cars blinked wildly in the sun. I looked both directions several times, thinking Josef would appear in the middle of the street as a mirage, his stumped (was it spiteful?) body moving between the cars, hardly noticing them. And this pursuit would continue through the long, unbridled streets where I could witness just where Josef goes until he'd turn, and then I'd turn more slowly, onto the block where he lives. And I'd approach him, ragged but keeping it together, as he'd walk the slow trek up the slope to his door, and I'd say: Josef, you bastard, there you are! And he'd turn and face me and say: Henry, my son!

But there was no sign of Josef on the street, only cars that were speeding to get somewhere, just as I was. I settled on the idea of calling Josef early the next morning and ran back home. And in the short run to Bernard Street, I heard a pulse in my head that was slightly more fragmented than a song, and it sounded like all the new pop songs do: too much beat and lacking any soul, and I asked it questions, like: What does it mean to be spiteful to God and how many times do you have to reach out in order to get an answer and why has everyone become so damn tyrannical lately and where the hell was Josef?

Chapter Two

Fathers are larger than life and fatter by the day. Or that's what I thought when Jonathan returned from California wearing a vest a size too small with wine stains on it. I had never seen the man drink to excess, not in front of my mother at least, but the proof had settled into the rivulets of his clothing. He wore a large-brimmed baseball cap that said SOUTHERN in block letters.

California, he said. Cali-fucking-fornia.

I thought of the stress one puts upon one's body in a lifetime and then imagined Jonathan Bartlett sending his weight through the fields and valleys of California, going Buddhist with the whole thing. Waking at dawn and going...where is it he went?

We were seated next to each other at Sophie's while the rain pounded the windows and the whole place went slack with inactivity. Jonathan was bronze in the fading light of the day. Bronze but spray tanned.

When did you get back? I asked.

I've been looking for you, he said. For your mom, too. I don't think she wants to see me. And if she does, well she's been...busy.

I haven't seen her either, I said. I'm not lying.

I realized how that clarification made it sound like a lie, like how saying "I swear" often negates the point.

Then where is she? Jonathan asked. If you haven't seen her, you must've talked to her.

No, I said. I haven't done that either.

What do you mean? he asked.

We had a fight, I said. About this dickhead guy she's seeing.

Oh, I didn't know, he said. That makes sense.

I shot him a confused look.

Not that she's dating a dickhead, he said. I meant why she wouldn't be answering my calls.

How long have you been back? I asked.

I already knew the answer: driving home from the library last week, I saw Jonathan coming out of the grocery store carrying a loaf of bread. I tried to pull into the parking lot in an attempt to get to him before he got to his car but was blocked by traffic going the other way. I called his name but my window was still up, and feeling slightly embarrassed (though who would've been watching anyway?), I continued back to Bernard Street. To my home.

About a week, Jonathan said. A week and a day.

Who are you staying with?

With my friend Jack. You know, the plumber. What makes that guy a dickhead?

Two younger women walked in, and I think Jonathan sensed a change of rhythm because his body performed that sway whenever his mind was moving faster than it wanted to.

Tommy righted his posture behind the bar and set out two napkins on the wood, a suggestion that the women should sit there.

For starters, he's been married three times, I said. And Josef says the dickhead had killed someone, years ago. Sounds worse than it is, maybe. He was drunk and bringing a boat back to dock and crashed into it and killed the woman on the boat. I think he was sleeping with the woman at the time.

It's just as bad as it sounds, Jonathan said. Fuck.

Yeah, I said. Got off because his ex-wife, his first ex-wife, is a lawyer.

No justice, Jonathan said.

None, I repeated.

What's his name?

Seamus, I said.

Fuck.

What?

That name, he said. I hate him and I don't even know him. That name. I hate that stupid name.

I doubled over laughing because I had thought the same thing when I first heard it. Seamus. Like the name of a poet. Seamus, like the name of a seafaring god, except this one got drunk and crashed boats into docks and killed young women. And then the image crystallized for me: Seamus, with his fiery red hair and weak jaw—the real Seamus—kissing my mother in the space of her house where the kitchen met the living room. That awkward space, as if I wouldn't have been able to see them. Seamus was neither a poet nor a seafaring adventurer, but sometimes he was a stutterer, a disorder carried over from youth and reactivated whenever he got nervous. Especially when that meant asking me for permission to go out with my mom. I thought it incomprehensible that Seamus had not only landed an eligible bachelorette but brought about her death, although I guess death was the easy part. There's nothing extraordinary about living fairly.

Fortunately, or unfortunately, depending on which side of morality you favored, Seamus had tried to get close to his young lover's family after her death, even forsaking his own dignity to mourn with them. According to Josef, this had two effects: the first was that the young woman's family, as expected, rejected him wholesale. They cursed him straight to hell and told him that all the repentance in the world would only make them hate him more. But seeing that her family was also not rich with money nor, as it turned out, joy any longer, Seamus tried to buy their happiness. Not two months after she had gone into the ground, Seamus sent an undisclosed amount of cash to the family through a mutual friend that visited them during their time of grief. This should have given the impression of complicating the messy affair that already existed, but Seamus figured that the messenger would diffuse the animosity that would've occurred had Seamus shown up himself. But the messenger was on a mission to explain Seamus' magnanimousness. Seamus, he has a lot of money and a lot of guilt, he might've said. That much was obvious to the woman's family, but the messenger had also added, You can't refuse his money forever. At some point, common sense will outlast your hatred.

This could've been read as a petty threat, but the young woman's father was also sensible (as sensible as one could be given the loss of a daughter) and had already made the decision not to bash Seamus' skull in with his son's metal bat. That left only the money and his own pride to decide between. And seeing that his pride was close to shattered given his choice not to take violence out on Seamus, he chose the money.

Jonathan took delight in my telling of this story. He bared his teeth and raised his eyelids during the dramatic turns, and his good humor almost made me forget that was the reason for my mom ending up with Seamus.

I told him as much, said, You know she loved you, right? You never told her why you left. She hates you now.

Get me two shots, he told Tommy.

Tommy poured two shots of Tullamore Dew, didn't even have to ask Jonathan for his flavor.

We celebrating something? I asked.

Yes and no, he said.

Then what are we cheersing to? I asked.

Your mother's love, he said and tipped back his head and threw down the shot. I followed him, and jerking my head felt like coming up from underwater. Day-drinking does that to you.

One more, Jonathan said. You in?

I'm good, I said.

Jonathan slid the single shot closer to him but didn't take it. Not yet. He palmed the glass, wiped the beads of sweat forming above his lip, and said, I loved her, too. I did. But I had to go. I knew you wouldn't understand then, but maybe now? I love her too. Present tense.

The women beside us had ordered their drinks and were taking their time, the ice cubes melting at a rapacious rate given the heat inside the bar. They looked to be Peter's age or just older, but the amount of makeup they wore precluded any way of knowing. Jonathan was looking at them while talking to me.

I want to make it up to you, kid, he said. This time he knocked back the shot and hit the bar, louder than he'd intended. Hotdog! he yelled. Tommy turned away from the golf match on TV and sent a warning with his eyes. Jonathan laughed, like this were a skit they had played before.

I fucking love this kid! Jonathan shouted, taking me by the shoulders and forcing me forward so that I had to hop off my stool in order to prevent being dumped over the bar. If it was to get the women's attention, it had worked because they asked if I was his son. And then one of them said to Jonathan, You look familiar. Are you from here?

Jonathan got off his stool and positioned his body between me and the women, and since he was a big man, one who never ceased expanding, he blocked whatever chance I had of joining the conversation even though I heard my name spoken liberally. Henry this, and Henry that. I knew him when he was just a boy. Look at him now. I'm so proud of him, of Henry. And the women poked their heads around him to look at me and smiled endearingly.

He looks familiar, too, one of them said. She didn't bother addressing me directly.

Jonathan turned. How old are you, Henry? And then to the girls: Maybe you know his cousin, Peter? How old are you girls? Ah, mhmm, I see.

Jonathan turned back to me, winked, and mouthed something I couldn't make out. By the time I had realized what he'd said he was asking the women what they wanted to drink.

We're fine for now, I heard them say. Maybe later.

I went outside for a cigarette and through Sophie's big windows saw that Jonathan had taken my seat. His hat was off, placed on the bar with the brim pointing toward me. Between the rain and the fog I read that stupid hat again—wondering what SOUTHERN meant, whether it was a direction or an attitude—and ducked under a tree in order to keep from getting wetter. Then I recited what Jonathan had mouthed to me, in his voice as he would've intended them. Full of force and bravado. Full of insolence. *Don't tell your mother.*

Chapter Three

Sometimes you couldn't see where he came from. You'd watch people excuse themselves on the middle of the sidewalk to allow him to pass; would hear them say, "Josef, good morning," as he'd emerge from the debris of coats and wave a cursory hand before continuing onward.

Where was he going? East usually, to the park along the main road with its gazebo and benches and not much else, where no one sat during the day except he, who sat there contentedly and without complaint. He drank his tea and opened a book, though he never seemed to be reading it, and watched the cars along Main Street. Sometimes he'd wave at someone he thought he knew, and they in turn waved back, but it was equally the case that he didn't know who he was waving to at all.

It's not that he was without his faculties; it's that they were hidden in plain sight. Those who knew him talked about how sharp he was, about how his mind formed the collective memory of the town. But at eighty-two years old, Josef had remained—blissfully, ignorantly—in town, and though the town had changed, he had not. Not that anyone would know this, though. Most of Josef's peers were dead and gone, and those who knew him, and who were younger, could only assume his personality was baked in like weathering skin. They accepted his general aloofness and its occasional turn to disappointment.

But how could he not be disappointed? He had lived by himself since his wife passed in the late '70s, a passing he later found out was caused by her hanging around the train yard with her father when she was a child. She had a bad habit of getting too close to the men, which inevitably meant she got too close to the steam fitting and the smoke and the dust. Nobody could've seen it coming. When she later took up smoking as a teenager, which continued until her premature death, everyone figured, the doctors included, that she'd smoked her lungs to black hell.

She died like a man's supposed to die, her father had said to Josef at the funeral, puffing his own cigarette, the irony lost on him.

What does that mean? Josef had asked. He felt defensive of his late wife. She had been in the ground not five minutes and he was convinced she could still hear them talking. And she would not come back, and he could no longer rescind any of his statements. Whatever he put into the ether would live there, unheard or not.

The smoking, her father responded. She lived like one of the boys since she was little. She could never stay away from the yard. That's how she picked up the habit, I think.

Josef would inquire more about this yard when they got back to his house for coffee and tea and walnuts. She was Italian and had made a tradition of having walnuts on the kitchen table, no matter the season. Spring walnuts and summer walnuts and fall. It was fall, perhaps the most appropriate season for walnuts, and the tragedy felt unburdened by the commotion of hands cracking, splitting, placing. It looked like the father's hands were never idle, a lesson he likely had bestowed on his late daughter. Smoking and cracking walnuts. Chewing walnuts and picking the shells from his teeth. Josef asked him about this train yard and listened to the explanation in between the spitting of shells.

She loved the wheels, her father told him, loved how small they looked compared to the rest of the hunk of metal. You should've seen her next to the other boys, next to the train. She'd get right in there too, wasn't afraid of anything. The boys would try to shoo her away, but by the end of the day she'd be dirtier than them. God, her mother would have such a fit.

Josef heard this and sweat. He was certain of late wife's handiness, how she could tell him the tool to use before he even knew what needed to be fixed, but in all their years together she never went into detail about her time at the yard.

Excuse me, Josef said. He went into the living room to find a seat on one of the chairs, but they were occupied by the dispassionate guests. Sit down, Josef, they all seemed to say in unison. Cryptically, mechanically. He sat on the arm of a chair instead and insisted that his young nephew not move from his place. I'm okay, Josef said, though no one asked if he was not. Josef's daughter put a hand upon his shoulder and rubbed it, and the small talk restarted around him. His attention went to the kitchen where his father-in-law was prattling on.

She'd look like she was sucking one of those exhaust pipes, he heard his father-in-law say. She'd peer down the exhaust pipe of the train and try to talk to the person on the other end, thinking someone would be there to answer her. He snorted and then it hit Josef: it was that yard; it was her father who had introduced her to the dangerous world of men.

Josef imagined him there encouraging his daughter, egging her on, and he felt sick. He rose and walked to the bathroom, and he thought he could feel the eyes of his family following him. Inside the bathroom, the sun cast the window in a dusty façade, and Josef felt compelled to rid it of its filth. All of it. The window and the counters, the shower liner that still had her dirt smeared across its plastic. He wanted to remain busy, if only because it kept the image of her alive. No idle hands.

He opened the window and experienced a burst of dirt and ash. A couple of her cigarettes that had been left there rolled into their silent wakes.

That's what he was saddled with. That's what made him so resentful of it all, he told me.

Chapter Four

Before he disappeared for a few weeks, Josef showed me a painting by Caravaggio, the Italian baroque artist who painted scenes of saints and beheadings and political scandals, sometimes all at once. Among his famous paintings is *David with the Head of Goliath*, which depicts David, his body a pasty glow, holding Goliath's monster of a head by the hair. What I enjoyed about Caravaggio was the way he painted the heads, how they seemed just a little too big or too small for his subjects' bodies and how they would tilt to the side like they were propped up by loose, tiny screws.

So, Josef, he had said, You should think like Caravaggio, you should see the world through his eyes. And it was settled. I would spend every afternoon I could in the library studying his paintings or studying those who had studied him, and one day I came across the word *askance* in an essay about religious iconography. Askance, meaning "in a way that shows a lack of trust or approval," but I also imagined it was the way people tilted their heads to evoke a manner of genuine questioning, like how David tilts his head to the side while holding Goliath's, as if saying, *Look what you made me do*, and then, turning to himself, stating matter-of-factly with self-denial, *I can't believe it's come to this*.

That's when I started titling my head in conversations, and it became a sort of game to see how far and how long I could tilt until people noticed. And it was always Josef who noticed, who would say to me, Why do you look askance, son? What's wrong with you? And I'd reply, I'm seeing the world through Caravaggio's eyes. And he'd shake his head like he was mocking me and say, No, no, you're doing it all wrong. You have to feel it.

That's how I knew Josef was serious about all of this. About Caravaggio.

Then one day Josef told me that Goliath's head was really Caravaggio's head, and that the painting is a self-portrait made to represent Caravaggio's fear with which he fled the country on a murder charge. Caravaggio had sent the painting to a Cardinal who had the power to pardon him, and it was supposed to mean that he, like Goliath, was being repressed into the shadows, or worse, killed, with all his blood and guts streaming to the floor. It really is a graphic painting. Is it coincidence or with intention that Goliath and Caravaggio looked the same in real life?

This felt desperate to me. What Caravaggio did by sending the painting to the Cardinal, I mean. And I told Josef this, suspecting he would slap me upside the head or reproach me (which is like the verbal way of being askance), but instead he said, Hmmm, maybe you're right, son. Maybe that *was* desperate. And he tilted his head and I tilted mine, like what we were trying to figure out could be figured out by feigning the act. I did this until my neck grew sore and I had to straighten my head again, but Josef's was still pitched low, balancing on his shoulder. He might've been asleep for all I knew. But then he said, Son, whose head is tilted in the painting? David's, I said. And who's doing the killing? he asked. David, I said, he's done the killing. It's over with. Right, he said, and for all we know he's been keeping the head as a souvenir for a week. Huh? I said. So you tell me, he said, if David's done the killing and his head is askance and his face is half-lit and half-dark and he's looking at the severed head with a pitied look, who's really the desperate one? David or Goliath? David or Caravaggio? The cardinal, the Church, the State, Italy, or Caravaggio? It's so dangerous to stick by your instincts, Josef said. Especially when you know they're right. What do you mean? I asked. He breathed hard and looked out the window, where the moon turned his eyes light and spiritual-gazing. I think you're right, he said. It was desperate. But it was necessary, too.

After a few months, I put Caravaggio in the shadows of my mind, like how he put his subjects in the shadows, but sometimes I would think about the blood. Like I couldn't help it. I had moved on to Rembrandt, whom, I thought, did a better job with the heads, but still maintained their mysterious qualities.

By that time, Josef had left me a message that said something or other about why he had been ignoring me—that his mind was bad, that he had family stuff to attend to, that I couldn't really learn anything worthwhile from someone like him. This was unfortunate, because by the time I received the message I had convinced myself that there was nothing desperate about my trying to find him.

Chapter Five

My mother never dared invite Seamus to dinner at her house whenever I was over, but his traces were impossible to ignore. They seemed to follow their own pattern of elusiveness, like shoeprints on recently vacuumed carpet. Most evident was a pair of tickets to a Fleetwood Mac reunion show that he had bought her and that my mother displayed proudly on the refrigerator.

It was a Tuesday when I went over, and Stevie Nicks was singing "Edge of Seventeen" when Mom brought out the salad and stuffed peppers. As the music climaxed, I thought about how I could never be as honest as Stevie. Not in a million years. All that coked-up confessing.

The peppers look good, I said.

Do you remember how you used to hate them? she asked. You would always eat the breadcrumbs and cheese on top and leave the peppers. Do you remember that?

I nodded.

And then one day Jonathan made them like I asked him to, she said, except they weren't at all like I asked him to, because you know him. Oh my god, he put so much cheese inside. They were like stuffed cheese balls. And you ate all of them.

She laughed and scooped a serving onto my plate, three peppers that bowled into each other and collapsed under the weight of their toppings.

I made them like he would, she said. For you. So you'd be happy.

I thought about how Jonathan Bartlett reminded me a lot of a stuffed pepper. Firm and sweaty on the outside, and ribbed and gooey inside. Well-meaning but stuffed with sentiment.

Do you like Stevie? Mom asked.

What's not to like? I said, she's the best.

Do you mean that? she asked. Or are you just trying to make me smile?

"Edge of Seventeen" ended and another song came on, and it wasn't Stevie or Bruce or Tom or Bob or Mark, such was the usual rotation she played whenever I came over, but somebody whose song I couldn't place. Someone without a first name I recognized.

We ate in silence for what felt like a while and I thought about how no singer worth a dime was ever named Seamus, but that some were named Jonathan or John.

Jonathan Richman. John Lennon. John Mayer, even if he sucked.

I appreciate you coming here, Henry. I really do, she said. I know you don't approve of him, so it means a lot that you would come see me. That you'd swallow your pride.

That's one way to put it, I said.

What?

That I'd have to swallow my pride, I mean.

That's not what I meant.

That's what you said.

Sorry.

She had barely touched the peppers and instead kept mixing the salad on the plate, trying to dig up the tomatoes from the bottom. When she recovered them, she brought the fork up to her face instinctively before dropping it back down.

You know, a lot of what they say is untrue, she said. About Seamus.

You don't need to say his name, I said. I know who you're talking about.

Sorry, she said. She pushed away her plate, and though it was only an inch it felt like a deafening protest.

I'm assuming he got you those tickets, too? I asked, gesturing toward the kitchen. Fleetwood Mac?

Maybe it was because Stevie was gone, outplayed on the stereo by some dude with tenor-range theatrics and church harmonies behind him (another John, John Legend), that I brought up the tickets. Like I wished she'd come back.

I won't go if you don't want me to, she said.

No, go. I don't care. You should go. I don't care, really.

It's not for another five months. Who knows what will happen between that time, she said.

I fantasized about Alma and Seamus parting the away adults do—bitterly and slowly over time—but perhaps I was thinking about Stevie, too. Parting the way rock stars do. Suddenly and with so much left to live for.

Maybe they'll break up by then, I told her.

Who? Stevie? Lindsay? Mick? Christine? Not a chance. They've tried before. They're like the, well I don't know what they're like. Like the Fleetwood Mac of break-ups.

Isn't every song of theirs a break-up song? I asked.

Alma shook her head wildly, like she was the queen of heartbreak. The resident fan of Stevie Nicks' hall of songwriting. Yes, yes, yes, she yelled. Ha!

Go Your Own Way? I asked. You can't get more obvious than that.

Yes!

Mom began poking at her salad again, this time with the intention of eating it, while I moved on to my second pepper. The music changed again, this time to Bruce moaning about an ice cream cone.

Tell me you know how to dance, she said.

I don't know how to dance, I said.

Then I'm teaching you.

To this?

To Stevie!

She leapt from the table, came around to my side, and lifted me by the collar. No excuses, she said. Nuh-uh-uh.

I stood with my hands in my pockets, the peppers' juices still rolling around my tongue, while Mom changed the song. And there came Stevie on full blast: the lightning, black-laced goddess that she was belting out "Rhiannon," yet another name, though male or female or first or last name I couldn't tell. The way Stevie sang it made my staying feel so urgent.

Do you know this one? Mom asked.

I nodded.

She's singing about a girl who gets possessed by a spirit, she said. Like this. Mom convulsed with the energy of a theatre director, her arms hiccupping this way and that way as she sang toward the ceiling. *Rhiannon. Rhiannon.* She grabbed me and forced me into her unpredictable rhythm. For a second—maybe longer than a second—I forgot all about the pepper standing solitary on my plate. And I forgot all about what I imagined Mom would say if she knew Jonathan was back in town. If she realized I had decided to keep that dirty secret.

We were each other's dates for the night; we danced.

Chapter Six

Josef finally called and said that he had watched my film and read the short poem that accompanied it and asked if I could please come over. He said nothing about liking it, nor did he sound thrilled to be calling. When I asked where he'd gone, he acted confused, like he didn't understand what I was saying. If you want my advice, he said, come see me.

The film was seven minutes and twenty-two seconds long, just short enough to get me and Andre accepted into the Under-8-At-8 Festival, which was held every July in the county's capital. Andre and I had worked the previous summer on writing a script and through the fall and winter on casting and scouting locations and through the spring on, eventually, shooting.

The plot was simple: an old man wakes up on the first anniversary of his youngest son's brutal murder and tries his best to honor his memory. He makes pancakes and sets an empty placemat and silverware. He packs a lunch—ham and Swiss with those spicy deli pickles—and places it in his son's backpack. He laces shoes belonging to no feet. After, he waves goodbye to his son as a school bus appears, ready to cart the ghost away. (Since we didn't exactly have a budget to rent a bus, the bus shots were of an actual school bus en route). Then the old man goes about his business while a creepy organ sounds in the background. He calls his other two sons on the phone and says to them, "I really miss him today. I just—I just blame myself," the idea being that the old man has something—*plot twist*—to do with his son's murder. Later that evening, he sits on the couch with the TV on mute. A commercial for anxiety medicine plays, featuring a playground and kids running through a hose. The old man swallows a pill.

He wakes up. He is on the couch, yes, but now the couch is in the woods (we found an abandoned couch in the woods by Andre's house) and the sun is going down. The old man is confused as to how he got here and when. He checks his watch, but there's nothing around his wrist. A beard that wasn't there in the first sequence now straggles his face. The trees shroud any sight of road or escape. He wonders how long he's been here—has it been hours or is this a continuous, never-ending dream? (We struggled with how to show this without making the old man say something to himself, thus making it feel too expositional). He takes another pill, swallows it bitterly.

We fade to black and then fade into a static TV, which makes the viewer think we're back in the old man's living room. Except we're not. The TV is now in the woods, unplugged but running (this required adding graphics in editing, which cost Josef extra money, though he never complained, nor did he see the bill). The sky darkens; the second pill he's taken makes him feint and he passes out.

When he wakes up, he is back in his living room where leaves cover the carpet. It is Christmas, except the Christmas tree is not decorated with ornaments but with photos from his life. Of his life. The old man and his family. The old man, younger and shirtless, planting lilacs in his garden. The old man shopping for eggs. And finally, the old man alone in the woods. When the camera pans out, we reveal the old man playing with his three boys, the youngest one covered in blood. Before the camera cuts away, for a final time, it finds the old man. The old man stares back at his boy. Their communion is one of animosity and distrust. The screen goes black. A poem sounds, it's Josef's voice:

It is easier to break bread than to draw straws
and easier to die than to live

We had cast Josef as the old man and three kids from the neighborhood to play his sons. The kid who was cast as the deceased son had a natural lazy eye, which made his final stare-down with Josef feel spectral. To pay them, we bought them all ice cream after shooting. This included Josef.

I had apologized to Josef about not being able to pay him after he'd given us cash to make it—the budget to purchase the fake blood, print the photographs, and to download an editing program that could deliver effects as needed. If you don't become famous, he said, you'll just have to find another way to pay me back.

Andre and I were convinced we had a good chance of receiving an award for this film after watching our first cut, but I was not confident upon getting Josef's phone call. I called Andre and complained about what Josef had said, or rather about what he had not said. Isn't it strange, I asked, that a man who funded and starred in the movie has absolutely nothing to say about it? Andre told me I was being paranoid.

He accompanied me to Josef's house for moral support only, he insisted, because it was no surprise that he felt weird around the old man. Andre's reticence had started years before when I began working odd jobs for Josef and continued through the filming, whereby he always took stock of his belongings whenever Josef was around. His camera bag, which was full of additional lenses and a tripod, was usually strung on his shoulder or kept at his feet during filming. When I asked why, Andre said it was because Josef stole things. What do you mean? I asked. What do you mean what do I mean? he said. Andre explained that during the planning stages for filming, in which we met Josef for a coffee at Centurion Café in anticipation of the following week, Josef snagged Andre's pocket-sized notebook that was propped open in front of him on the table. Andre had gotten up to use the bathroom and found the notebook gone. When he inquired about its loss, Josef pretended he didn't even know what Andre was talking about. I had been writing in it for an hour straight, Andre told me. Later, as we were about to leave, Andre swore he could see the metal spirals sticking out of Josef's khakis. I was going to lose it, Andre confessed to me: But what could've I done? Punch him? The guy's like a hundred years old.

Now, anything that Andre carried he left in the car, including his hat and a bag where he kept his computer. Lock it, he said, before we marched to Josef's steps. I don't trust this son of a bitch.

The house itself wasn't anything remarkable: a two-story brick ranch that was dated compared to the development in which he lived. A Virgin Mary statue idled in the bed nearest the steps and had become a dumping ground for birds. Though it was June, the grass surrounding the large acreage came up in crabby sprigs, like thyme left out to dry. It usually took five men with throbbing muscles and an insatiable appetite for work to keep up the property; the boys that had previously done so had graduated into adulthood and had either gone to college or realized the extent to which their going there was questioned and mocked. Accepting the fact that his home was an eyesore, or instead ignoring that completely, Josef had begun putting miniature statues within the beds as artistic expressions. But that only convinced his neighbors, and Andre it appeared, that he was losing his mind.

That derision persisted through Andre's censure of me, and walking up the hazardous stairs, gripping the handrail that had no purpose as a rail except as a vestige to its past, Andre said, I don't get what you do for this guy all day.

I said, Does it matter so much as that he pays me?

And he said, Yes. Actually it does, cos.

Fair enough, I said.

Most days we sit. We sit and talk and I bring him stuff from his study—stuff to write letters with or checks to pay his bills. And I run his errands for him, and once in a while he reads what I write and gives me feedback on it. He once struck it famous as a writer, back in the '70s, I said.

What did he write? Andre asked. Fiction or nonfiction?

A little bit of both, I said. And hey, don't forget that he helped us with our movie.

He nodded but didn't say anything.

We knocked several times, rang the bell that only sometimes worked, and knocked again. Andre sighed, and I have to admit I was relieved too. Relieved because I could delay having to hear what Josef would say about the film, if anything. Because right there, with the sun shining and the yard making everything look so big and open, I don't think I could've held that kind of embarrassment. I had a sudden urge to run—through the field and out past the far gate of the backyard that connected to a patch of reeds and eventually to home—and destroy the film and any chances we had of showing the public, but then I heard the pitter-patter of Josef's cane making its way down the steps, and any prior notion we had had of leaving was supplanted by Josef swinging open the door and yelling, You assholes woke me from my nap. Come inside. Quick. The AC's on.

I don't know if Andre had ever seen something as magnificent as Josef's house in his four years at college down in Florida, but what he encountered made him stop in his tracks. Josef was a collector: of junk, sure, but also of antiques whose value was unquantifiable by virtue of the amount of stuff there. And I mean it was everywhere—vintage signs tacked to wood door frames, glass cabinets full of miniature figurines, carpets rolled or stacked on top of each other and inhabiting various corners. And yet—this was the craziest part —almost everything was clean, dusted, and polished, so that the space resembled the interiors of a museum rather than that of a garage. When I started working for Josef, I encountered a boy whose only job was to dust the bottom floor from head to toe. I don't know if he showed up with a lambswool duster or if it was gifted it by Josef, but I never saw him without it. Even when it came time to eat lunch—I never found out the boy's name, for he was too shy to look in my direction never mind say hello—he lay the duster at his feet until the crumbs on his plate were swept clean and began work punctually a half hour later.

Andre took in this sight and remarked the way most people do, the same way Mom had when she first accompanied me here when I was in high school. Holy shit, he said. This is Art.

See what I mean? I said. Andre stuck his hands in his pocket, afraid to touch anything.

Josef put his hand on the small of Andre's back, which made him jump. Andre, let me ask you a question, Josef said. You went to college, right? Can you tell me the meaning of this? He plucked a gold-framed painting that was balancing on a velvet couch and turned it around so that it faced Andre, then positioned his body as an easel. Please, Andre, tell me what the fuck this is! Huh, college boy?

The painting was of a young woman with blonde hair, blue eyes, and an aquamarine nose whose neck was boiling with blisters and whose sternum, before it dipped down below her paisley dress, began scaling like a lizard's skin. Her legs were cross-legged at an impossible angle on a bed of flowers. Above her was an advertisement written in old timey font that said *Mrs. Aitken's Eggs and Chicken Emporium.*

Andre shook his head and winced.

Nobody has been able to figure it out, Josef said. Not even smart folks with college degrees. Henry here doesn't have a shot. What did you study, Andre?

Film production, Andre said.

Ah, Josef replied dubiously.

Andre turned back to me and made a face that suggested he didn't know how to take Josef's response. I started thinking about our film and reflected the same face back at him.

Boys, let's sit in here, Josef said. He led us into the study, where I had spent countless hours organizing Josef's books chronologically and then, when he changed his mind, alphabetically, and I took my spot on my bench nearest the far window where a comet of light punctured the glass. Andre sat opposite me in a wooden chair that squeaked under his weight. Josef remained standing and said, Boys, I can't finance this film if I'm not happy with it. Heck, I can't support this film if I'm not happy with it.

What's wrong? I asked. Andre shot me that look again.

The casting, he said, it's all wrong. I'm too old to be in a movie like this. I'm too old to have a young kid who I'd be grieving over. Consider this: I'm old enough in real life to have seen all my friends die. Most of them have. I'm used to this kind of pain. But your character, he—I mean, me—when I see myself on the screen, I can't help but think the emotional pain is dishonest. His pain is dishonest.

Then what do we do? I asked annoyed. The film is shot. Edited. Submitted. The screening is in a month. It's too late.

You wanted my opinion, right? Josef asked. He was blocking my view of Andre, whose reaction I could assume was pure aggravation. After all, he was the one who begged me not to use Josef, to use anybody but him.

I wanted your opinion, yeah, I said.

Then take it, he said. Take it and don't get defensive.

Josef, perhaps detecting his own exasperation or realizing that there was another witness present, walked himself backward. Literally. He kept moving backward until he nearly landed in Andre's lap.

Look, he said. I didn't mean it that way. I lost a kid too. Maybe I'm just reflecting on that.

I had been at the funeral for his youngest son, Charlie, had seen how Josef had disguised his pain under a hat. Noticed how whenever we were filming the scene of the film where the old man was supposed to call a family member, Josef wanted to make a real phone call. At one point, we had to prevent him from doing so because he would carry on a real conversation with his daughter. They'd talk as the sun was setting and our opportunity for light was diminishing.

I'm sorry, Andre said to Josef. About your son. Manero told me.

That was years ago now, Josef said ungratefully. Now, about your work. Excuse me, your film. Movie. Whatever.

That's when I saw Andre's eyes light up: not because of what Josef was about to say—he was mentally tougher than I was—but because Josef withdrew a notebook, *Andre's notebook*, from the front pocket of his jeans and started reading off notes.

Hey, hey, hey, Andre said. What the fuck.

It's real amateur stuff, Josef said, but it has heart. I'll give you boys that. Lots of carnivorous blood and guts. The mental kind I mean. But let me ask you this: why does he take a pill? Why does he keep taking pills?

Andre set his focus on the notebook. Couldn't take his eyes off the damn thing. He wiped at his chin the way one might scrub off bacon grease.

It's supposed to be symbolic of a distorted reality, I offered. It does two things, though. One, the old man—I mean you, your character—he takes the pill because he is sad and it's an anti-anxiety medication of sorts, and two, it makes the viewer believe that the pill somehow alters his reality. What is up or down? Day or night? Is he in the living room or has he been in the woods for years?

Have you ever taken a pill? Josef said. He addressed the room like he was on stage. Then he walked to the desk, opened the top drawer, and pulled out a pill bottle that had some indescribable markings. Like this, he said. See?

I shook my head. Andre shook his.

This little thing right here, this 50 mg capsule, is supposed to take me back to reality, not away from it, see? At least that's the point. So when I take the pill in the movie—excuse me, when your character takes the pill in the movie—shouldn't he be more aware, profoundly aware, of his loss?

I don't understand your logic, I told him. It felt like my tower of creativity was falling over, being deconstructed brick by brick, and that Josef was bulldozing it to create a mega mall.

He looked down at his notes in Andre's notebook. And one more thing, he said.

That's it, Andre said, now standing, his presence looming over the old man's. That's it. Look man, I know you're trying to help and all, but this is our movie. Film.

I'm just trying to help, Josef said. He sunk his head.

I get it, but we've heard enough, Andre said. I'm sorry. Now give me back my fucking notebook.

There's one more thing…

No, Andre said.

Josef handed over the notebook, then jiggled the pill bottle in his hand. I think you should leave, he said. He was looking at Andre when he said it, but I could only infer he meant both of us.

As I followed Andre out, I couldn't help but wonder what Josef's last piece of advice was. I turned around to see if he would offer it, to see if anything would come of the silence between us, but he said nothing. He popped a pill and rolled back his eyes.

Chapter Seven

If nothing else, Josef said, we must interpret these women. We must discover their values.

Three days later, we were standing in his kitchen facing a computer that broadcasted a Hispanic woman, fifty or so, with gigantic tits. She was muted, but whenever she smiled, he smiled back.

You know she can't see you, right? I said.

He looked on nervously like he didn't understand.

Take this girl here, he said. Woman, excuse me. Hell of a body, tits that don't look a day old, perfect skin tone, swollen lips. You know?

I nodded.

Now let's look at where she's going.

We watched her pick up her laptop and do a POV-walk to her kitchen where she lay it on a marble counter and climbed in front of it. Meanwhile, Josef was building himself a colossal of a sandwich, dipping his butter knife into a variety of spreads as if painting a watercolor.

The woman took a banana from her fruit basket and teased it around the area where her thigh barely hid her genitals.

Take a look at that, Josef whispered, as if not to disturb what she was about to do. That reminds me, he said. Bananas. I forgot to pick up bananas.

We watched for a couple minutes, expecting her to finish. When she didn't, when she grabbed another fruit, Josef took a bite of his sandwich. It's the anticipation that kills men, Josef said. Then he yelled at the screen: What's with all the fucking teasing? Let's go already.

I reminded him a second time that he was one of five hundred or so sex-crazed men (or women or otherwise) who were watching the same scene, and that the woman not only didn't see him but she didn't even know he existed. She wants your money, I said. That's all she wants.

I have money, he said.

You need a credit card, a password, a log-in. You'll need to pay.

Then I'll pay.

No, that's okay, I said. I'm supposed to be fixing you—

Shhh, he said.

We watched. The slow crawl of her legs across the counter, the sun that came through the blinds and reflected off the knives near her sink, the glass saltshaker shaped like a bird. We watched, waiting for something to happen, maybe for someone to appear in the kitchen—a husband or a kid—and ask for food, so that we could watch her make it, and Josef, he would stare as a tomato seeped out of his mouth, amazed at the skill and concentration with which she could touch herself and then, moments later, make food. But then her phone rang and she got up to answer it off-screen. She came back to the screen every minute or so to blow us (strangers) kisses, but the touching languished and so did our excitement, and Josef had already eaten his sandwich. I was starving, but having seen Josef eat while we watched the woman touch herself in the kitchen turned me off (I mean, how could it not?), and so I just drank the whiskey Josef had provided, telling myself with every sip that I was certainly going to throw up.

Where's the girl I watched last time? Josef said. The one with the birthmark under her breast?

I took over the computer and searched for the one he was talking about: Brownsissy02, the Asian woman whose birthmark looked like an extension of her tit. Admittedly, she was my favorite too. She also wasn't online, and this disappointed me. I scrolled some more. Dozens of boxes appeared per page, with previews of each one's live broadcast. Josef's eyes darted up and down, this way and that. There was a multitude of ages, nationalities, years of experience on the site, and stats counting viewers. Some women had gold stars attached to their previews. These were for the women who earned the most tips. I clicked to the last page, page nine, where only a few preview boxes existed. I told Josef that this was where the derelicts hung out, the bottom of the barrel, the orphans of the porn world. Click on that one, he said intrigued, pointing to the last box. I clicked. A black box opened to grey walls, in front of which were yellow patterned blankets, nobody on top or under them. Just like watching the woman in the kitchen, we waited for something to happen, not knowing what we'd find (*it's the anticipation that kills men*).

And then something happened. Someone pulsated up and down underneath the blankets, like an animal scurrying away from its capturer, until the blankets went flat again. Josef turned to me. What do you think is there? he said. Zoom in.

I told him that wasn't an option, that the who or what would have to be waited on. Come out little thing, he said. He threw a fistful of pistachios into his mouth and licked the salt around his lips. A couple of them fell to the floor. Come on little thing, he teased.

Josef's phone rang, and just like that the guilt-ridden feeling rose in my chest (as big as an eclipse) and I thought about Mom, about what she would say if she knew I was here condoning this—even though it wasn't my idea but Josef's, though I had on one occasion mentioned the site and on a different occasion showed him how to use the internet and on another "stayed in the room" while he perused the site and on others explained to him the intricacies of the webcam world and the greater world wide web itself, and finally had shown him the wildly entertaining girl with the birthmark under her tit; and oh what would Mom say and how would I explain myself and would she be more disappointed in me or in Josef?

But Josef answered the phone, and it was clear that it wasn't my mom but his daughter, whom he told not to forget to buy the strawberries he likes before hanging up. Eager to get back to the cam but looking poised, he slow-walked to the computer with his ambling limp that looked half put-on and said, Did she come out yet?

Not yet, I said.

He got closer to the screen, his nose about to touch it, while its light reflected harshly off his dark eyes. He didn't look healthy. Come out, he said.

The sheets on screen moved a little, and the tiny bump underneath them that could've been a hand or a knee took a bigger form, like the whole picture was slowly coming alive.

She wants to come out, Josef said.

He clicked the volume louder until we could make out faint music coming from her room, and it was something poppy and light but not at all offensive and I wanted to hear more of it, if only to break the awkwardness that existed inside Josef's kitchen. But overwhelming the music was the sound of deep, staged-like moaning from under her blankets that were becoming more and more animated. Josef's breathing along with it. They co-existed, rising to long, drawn-out exhales and smaller inhales, and Josef looked at me like what was occurring was a movie in which the viewer was also the participant, and I nodded along (to Josef or to the music or to the moaning, I'm not sure). And then Josef said, If I could just rip off the sheets, and I said, Yeah, I know, but I didn't mean it. I didn't know anything. The woman's moaning grew louder and more percussive, her exhales erupting through Josef's cheap computer speakers, and he was even closer to the screen now, his pants rubbing against the base of his counter.

It was too much, of course, and way too dirty. I wished for the phone to ring or for his daughter to show up and, with a remonstrative tone, ask what the hell her father was doing, and then look at me with complete disgust (like all of this could be my fault!), while I watched Josef's mouth quiver as a few sandwich bits still fell from his beard and considered that the woman underneath the sheets, the one who had caused all this commotion to begin with, better come out soon, to make all of this worth it.

I felt hard all of a sudden, imagining her. How she would feel or sound, and thought about her body as one enveloping voice, with mine underneath it, begging for help. Getting smothered by a voice, that was a new one. But it was not to be. The voice wouldn't show itself, and the sheets flattened out like the person below them had been plucked from midair.

Then the room went silent, much like the scene. My vision went soft, the contours of the computer screen now blurry, which required me to invent what was going to happen next. But before I could come up with a logical conclusion to this saga, Josef flipped down the lid of the laptop and came closer to me. Your trouble with Janine, he said touching my shoulder, is just like this.

Chapter Eight

During our senior year of high school, Janine was bitten by a Lonestar tick and contracted Lyme disease, the symptoms of which she hid from everyone until one day in early June, right before graduation, she discovered she had trouble swimming. She had done her laps at the YMCA in her usual time and even lifted weights after but noticed that her strokes felt heavier in the water. That every time she went under the surface and kicked her legs toward the wall to prepare for the next lap, she experienced a moment's hesitation, like how a donkey's ears flick a second too late with the invasion of a fly.

She wouldn't have noticed this slight disruption, especially after coming out of a delayed spring due to the long winter, but Janine was a champion swimmer who was awarded a college scholarship to compete the following semester and was hyper-aware of any changes in her performance.

In school that morning—and I remember this because I wasn't feeling well either—she told me the details of her morning routine and how she had begun to feel chills shortly after. *Is it cold in here too or something?* When I told her that it was the opposite and that I was burning up, she said, Well, shit, I don't know what's going on.

I said that she was likely swimming herself sick, which was true: every time I'd ask her to hang out, she'd tell me she was training. And when I'd tell her, Sure, that's fine, let's just hang out after, she'd respond that she needed rest. I'll admit that her unavailability disappointed me and that maybe I was being unfair to her, but the waning days of school made me yearn for more time. Or maybe it was that school felt so dull and that there was really nothing but time, but, either way, I knew she would be leaving soon, and I needed to see her. While the rest of the senior class began wearing the t-shirts of their chosen college and speaking in terms of the future, I opted for clothes that better represented my mood: dark blue sweatshirts with hoods that covered my hair.

And that's the funny thing about time, right? That when Janine and I were sitting in the classroom and she was complaining of chills and I was burning up from a possible fever, I couldn't see then that everything was in jeopardy; that her diagnosis of Lyme's was a few weeks away, and that the tests she'd take would make her more nervous, and, in turn, the nerves would make her blood feel thin and the thinness would make her feel weak. And the weakness would make all her days feel prolonged.

But then school ended and summer officially came, and with it the warm weather of invincibility. I would stay up late into the night listening to music, and before bed I'd have this urge to text Janine. Sometimes her response caused me to sit up in bed, and I'd pry the covers from my body in the hope that her next text would say something about wanting to hang out, but when it didn't—or there was a lack of response—I once again got under the covers and prepared myself for sleep. But sleep hardly came, not when I thought about her leaving and maybe never coming back. Or Andre leaving for college again and never coming back. And so, I'd text my cousin and ask him if he'd want to smoke one down, for old time's sake. We were seeing each other less and less those days.

In the dark of the car, his voice felt like a bass drum and mine the accompanying cymbal crash, the high percussive alarm that missed Janine. She's not dead, you know, Andre would say with that slow roar of his, and I'd tell him, No, she's not, but that damn tick has changed her. And we'd laugh at the ridiculous idea that a tick could also have a personality and apparently a name, whom we called Doc. Doc as in the character in *Back to the Future*, which, like him, we imagined had grey hair and frantic energy. But this Doc, our Doc, was a messenger for evil, and it was at his will that Janine suffered.

When we were high, I thought I could feel the itchy sensation of Doc among us, and I'd scratch and scratch until realizing I was scratching at nothing. I asked Andre if he thought Doc was capable of changing from evil to good, you know, like if he were to undergo one of those experiments?

And he said, Are you asking if I think she can get better?

Andre, who looked like he was tracing an invisible bug across the steering wheel, said, I think he can be convinced. Then he slapped my thigh and said, Let's go get her.

She's sleeping, I said. I felt protective of her, ready to lie if it meant respecting her privacy.

Nonsense, Andre said. Doc doesn't sleep. He lives in a garage, remember?

It was also true that Janine was in possession of such a garage, which her father had spruced up for her after years of its lying dormant. It was to be her room upon her return from Hanover during breaks, but Janine had also spent time occupying it over the last year, sleeping among the books and musical instruments and extra furniture of her youth in the space that permanently let in a cold draft. She had taken to setting up her art studio there too, which contained pieces from senior year's advanced studio art class. In all the works she showcased, not a single one contained water (I pointed this out to her). She told me that it's hard to paint something you're so immersed in. You lose perspective. Water becomes shapeless.

Andre drove while the outside world was transformed by the shadows the trees cast on the dashboard. Maybe they, too, looked like water, which made me think again of Doc. Drowning him. But Doc always came back, like he could adjust to water and its myriad dangers. Like he could grow wings.

We arrived outside Janine's house, at which point my high had transformed into a ravenous hunger. I could feel my eyes in the dark, and I rubbed them with the trepidation of someone who had to show them to someone. Then Andre turned on the interior car light and opened the middle compartment and pulled out the lighter and bowl. Might as well, he said. When he turned off the light, I felt relief and closed my eyes and breathed in the smoke that had escaped his mouth, and felt it enter my pores. Nothing felt itchy this time.

I must've slept for a minute—or it felt like I slept—because when I reopened my eyes a figure was making its way across the grass. The way it hunched and stalked made me think Janine's father was coming, and in a panic I tried to sit upright and flush the red from my eyes, but when it neared the car the figure was cut in half and the body shone translucent.

Janine, I said. The window was closed, and she palmed the glass then scratched at it like a deranged house pet.

I just texted her, Andre said, laughing. And then mumbling to himself said, Here, I'll let you in. He flipped the lock and Janine piled into the backseat and in the dark vanished momentarily. She clapped her sandals together and shuffled them until they found room behind me. Manero! she said, putting her hands on my neck in a playful choke hold. They felt both cold and warm to the touch, and I would have moved my head to embrace them, but the seat backing prevented my doing so. Andre, hi, she said, and slipped her skinny wrist through the middle of the car until her hand dangled precariously next to his right leg.

I should have noticed then that everything people say about barriers is correct—that unless you physically traverse them, no amount of mental strength will do the trick. And I should have realized that my barrier was a car seat—or maybe it was the car itself and who was driving it—but at that point I thought the barrier was an invisible voice inside Janine that consistently misinformed her. That it was Doc, who could not be seen nor reached.

I'm glad you boys came for me, she said. My heroes.

Across the yard the oak's giant branches created a maze of arms across the driveway. What are you guys doing anyway? she said. You guys look baked.

Manero wanted to see you, Andre said, smiling.

It's true, what can I say? I said. But what I really wanted to ask was why she hadn't returned my texts to hang out. I wanted to know why it took Andre, and him alone, to will her from her shadow over the last few weeks. Because now it was July and the deer had gone back into hiding and the tourists had brought with them the scent of foreign money. But it was without her that I also experienced our town as a half-stranger, watching the boats flirt with the dock, or, more specifically, the older women aboard flirt with the dockhands, prying from their purses the tips which secured their boats for the day. And at night, I saw little kids with ice cream cones dripping flavors into their fingers as their dads cleaned away their accidents. I thought how simple life looked from afar, from my vantage point atop the library stairs where I used to go with Mom as she'd lecture me about the importance of reading—Books! she'd say. Henry, you need to read books!—though I never saw her reading any herself. And it was atop these same stairs where we'd see Josef, noting how, even back then, he lumbered without any place to go, and she'd tell me that he was the smartest person she'd ever met: smarter than your cousin Andre, smarter than your dear mother, and lord knows how much smarter than your father. You should learn from him, she'd say. From his mistakes, too. I wasn't keen enough to know what she meant by mistakes, but I assume it had something to do with loneliness, and that is what I thought about when I saw those ice cream cones melting down like the reverse pyramids they were. How the things we love go away—how we release them unwittingly away.

 Yeah, Manero? Wanted to see me? Janine asked.

 I didn't respond.

 Damn, it's cold in here, she said. Can you turn that air conditioner down?

 Andre turned the dial, which made the pot smoke balloon over our heads.

 I'll crack the window, Andre said, and the three of us turned to watch the smoke billow out.

 That part always makes me laugh, Janine said. Sometimes I wish I smoked just so I could watch it do that. What do you call it?

 Hotboxing, Andre and I said together.

 The doctor said I can't, she said. She laughed at herself before turning inward again. Fucking doctors.

 Doc, I said.

 What?

 Nothing.

 Doc, Andre said. You mean Doc. He turned to me and smirked.

 I guess, she said, confused. She shook her hair and a couple strands reached the back of my neck.

 I lost the scholarship, you know, she said.

 Andre and I turned to face her, but she had squeezed her body against the window, the reflection from which created two Janines.

 They called my mother, she said. Told her on the phone. I wasn't even there when they told her. I was swimming. Fucking traitors.

 I'm sorry, I said. I didn't know. You should've told me.

 I'm telling you now, she said.

 Then who told your coach? I asked.

 My mother, she said. Not really my coach anymore.

 She broke down, told us of how her mother was worried about how much she was working over the last few months in order to get her times down. That she was losing weight and still her swim times weren't coming down; that even when she got a time she was halfway proud of, her body would ache as recompense. Then she wasn't eating—and it wasn't like she could eat all the foods she could have before the disease—but now, now she was being really selective, which carried its own kind of stress. Her mother had called the coach and told him that she didn't think her daughter should be competing until she got better; and given the news was a complete surprise to the coach, he reprimanded her mom for not telling him sooner before offering up a half-fast apology. He said they'll give it a year and see how she feels as a sophomore.

I'm useless without swimming, she said. I have nothing.

I told her I knew what she meant. After all those years of beating her body into submission, until it was dense and waterlogged, what did it matter if she couldn't compete? If she couldn't get what she wanted?

It's only temporary, I said. Maybe it's your body telling you that it needs a break.

God is saying this to you, Andre said sleepily.

Fuck God, she said.

Yeah, fuck him, I repeated.

All of us harmonized, Fuck him! Because the way I saw it, God had done nothing except given me a small hand and Janine a body she could no longer steer toward perfection and Andre a charmed life, and it was God that made Janine answer his text and God that kept her in his car long after he'd driven me back home that night.

Chapter Nine

I was also in high school when Mom and I stood around the grave and watched the coffin drop into its forever place in the dirt. It was hot, so hot it makes one wonder if all the inanimate objects that surround us are also capable of feeling heat. Then the coffin was dropped and the dirt was laid over it and I thought, selfishly, how relaxing it must feel to mix with some of the colder earth, to hide from the sun. Josef's son was dead, and all anyone could whisper between prayers was that it was so sad a man so old could lose a son so young.

Mom wore black like the other mourners, which is also what she wore whenever she we went out, and it was black she had worn when she met Jonathan at the Town Hall meeting all those years ago and black she had put on for my school functions. She had spent time with her makeup too—she told me this, making a joke about how long women have to spend doing their hair and skin just to see the dead—but the makeup ran from her eyes like fresh squid ink, and she and the other mourners formed a black mass around the grave, tugging at their blouses and wiping sweat and makeup from their cheeks. Even Josef had chosen to dress for the occasion, ditching his usual denim shirt and beige pants and selecting a periwinkle suit that brought out his eyes, Mom said. I had never realized how blue Josef's eyes were until they were kissed by the sun, until each of us in attendance was forced to absorb his sadness by looking into them with compassion and understanding.

But I couldn't understand, not then at least. I hadn't experienced loss of this kind, and I hadn't ever met his son. And when Mom told me that he had suffered a seizure as a result of a drug overdose, I was more concerned with the flailing image of a body recoiling from drugs than the personality inside that body. I asked how a person—by whom I meant Josef—could allow someone to go so far astray that a death was the event that reunited them. But Mom asked me, Who said they weren't close? And I said, I don't know, I just figured. And she said, It's not your job to make conclusions about things you don't know, Henry. It's your job to be there for our friend.

Our friend.

I bounced the phrase inside the walls of my mind and played out the image of Josef attending school with me and my cousins—wearing his periwinkle suit to graduation with those stupid hats they insist on, his tassel torn to shreds and, below, those ugly boots with the lifts that keep older people's feet padded. Smoking a cigarette on stage.

Or worse, I thought, being Mom's friend for all those years. Like an invisible shadow that followed her and paid her bills. Who owned her.

Josef was smoking a cigarette when he tossed into the grave what appeared to be a souvenir belonging to his son. I asked Mom, Are you even allowed to smoke in a cemetery? And she said, Today you are. But not you, Henry. Why don't you throw in a flower? Show your support, come on now. Be here.

There was a line of people being supplied flowers, a troupe of black now decorated with red and white petals, and I waited until the line thinned out so I could say to Mom, I can't go now. I'd feel weird. She just sighed as if to say whatever, so be it. But then Josef got on the back of the line where a few dozen flowers were still idling after all the other guests had taken their turn; as opposed to them, he held his head strangely high. Approaching the funeral director, he said, I'll take them all. The director looked confused at first and suggested that she could just put the remaining flowers in the car for him to take home, but he austerely said, No, I want them all. All in. Then he turned to the mass of us, who were still trying to understand what he was attempting, and said, Do we have any other takers? Before I part with them?

Mom nudged me forward and I turned to her and gave her the eyes that said *don't you dare*, but when I turned back to the flowers, I had made eyes with Josef and knew I'd been caught.

Come here my friend, he said. His smile ended at the word *friend* and defaulted to solemnity, so that whatever resilience I thought he had mustered fell under a cloak of frailty. He was still clutching the dozens of flowers, but they wilted under the heat (he was choking them nearest their blooms).

Come, come, son. I need your help.

I turned back to Mom, but she was at least three feet behind me. I couldn't tell if I'd moved forward or she back, but, either way, I was fixed at a location too close to Josef and too far from retreat. That's how lovers must feel, I reasoned later, when they're in pursuit of a romance about which they're still unsure.

Waiting. Then Josef approached me and handed me most of the flowers, leaving himself with only one or two. You look able-bodied, he said. You can handle this, right? He laughed and spit into the dirt and turned back to face the grave. Come, he said.

He waited for me to match his steps, and together we went to the hole. The flowers that had been dropped in by friends and family moments before looked pale under the weight of the dirt, and beside them was the souvenir Josef had also left. I could see it was a small notebook that, I learned later, was on his son's person when they discovered his body in his apartment.

The sun that shone into the hole and onto the notebook reflected a manual pain that the flowers didn't, and at that moment I thought about the mysteries the notebook contained, but it wasn't my place to ask nor wonder about that which is sacred to the dead, and plus I had a job to do.

This, he said.

Josef threw a flower into the hole, which didn't fall as fast as I thought it would but moved slowly through the heat. And then he threw another, this time away from the first spot. Your turn, he said.

I threw mine closest to his, and he followed by throwing another, and I followed him, and so it went. But after three or four of my throws, I noticed that he didn't have any flowers left and that I was throwing to his non-throwing. His arms were moving to a rhythm as if he were.

Once my hands were empty, I wiped the excess dirt on my slacks and turned back to face Mom, who was now under a tree hiding from the heat. But somewhere out there—was she twenty feet away, thirty?—I could detect her pride, a mother's pride, so biased and singular that you seem guilty for reaping it.

You did good, son. Josef put his hands on my shoulder. You did great.

He turned away and watched the workers throw additional scoops of dirt on the coffin. And when I tried to get his attention, he turned further until I saw only the slope of his back and a single flower peeking out from the front of his coat pocket.

Chapter Ten

Janine couldn't leave the bog alone, the way, say, one might leave behind a case of bad dreams. She couldn't sleep it off nor wake up having forgotten about it. She couldn't chalk it up to imagination or a night of partying or latent puberty. The emotional scar of that night during sophomore year stayed with her long after the event, and now, at Sophie's, she was fingering the literal scar as she sipped her beer.

Does that still hurt? I asked.

No, she said. Ever hear of a phantom limb?

Sure, I said.

It's kind of like that, she said. Except it itches.

So it's nothing like that, I said. A phantom limb is something that isn't there. Hence the phantom. I'm looking at yours.

You're a genius, Henry Manero. She laughed and clinked my glass.

I still think it makes you look tough, I said.

The scar ran horizontally across the top right quarter or her forehead and disappeared into her hair line. When her hair was parted, it gave the appearance of an errant hair or a smudge mark. Once, when Andre was kissing her, I saw him accidentally try to brush it aside, and, embarrassed that he had made this mistake I watched him throw his hands frustratingly to his side before she brought them up again.

In years since the incident—what she called it was *that night*—the scar seemed to double in size, though that of course was only in her mind. There were other things, too: the way she sometimes thought she smelled grass, she told me, whenever she scratched at the scar long enough. How it smelled like the basement of a forest, water-logged and sun-kissed. And whenever she ran her finger along the edge, where the tissue had coalesced into a ridge, she felt her toes go numb, momentarily, as if shot frozen. What the heck is with that? she'd ask. I mean, is that even possible?

The psychosomatic relationship between trauma and the body is still little understood, but I think that if scientists were to cut open Janine's brain many years from now, long after our time on this planet, they'd find pieces of *that night* littered among her parietal lobe; that no matter how hard she tried to clean them up, they'd found a way to penetrate her.

She stopped trusting men, specifically. Older men like Benjamin. Or men like the kind who came to Sophie's and played pool with the side door cracked open so they could enjoy their cigarettes at the same time. Men like the kind who itched at their crotches and used toothpicks to fetch chicken bits from their teeth and who—now that I stared long enough—resembled the one who had hit the deer and accosted me and Janine all those years ago.

His collared shirt was tucked into his t-shirt underneath, like a tongue hiding beneath gums. His hair was greased and rehearsed, and he swirled his beer and then peered into it after taking each sip. He was chasing a reflection of himself, and each subsequent sip was bringing him further from it. In the light of the bar, he did not look as old as he had five years ago. Or maybe it was that he was not yet that drunk. Either way, all my studying his face had backfired because he caught me looking, and that's when I realized that he had not been peering at himself through the glass but at me, looking at him.

Janine was already three tequila sodas in and looked so intent during our conversation that I didn't want to bring attention to the fact that the bar was filling up, which would've signaled in her a panic like a tiny alarm. She would've reflected on the fact that Andre was not yet here—that it was his choice to come here, not hers, and why did she have to bear the stupidity of townies just so he could get a few free drinks at the bar? So, I sat stone-faced and silent and bit my lip and didn't say anything, which proved to be the exact wrong thing to do because Janine noticed me doing so and said, You okay?

I imagined my insides being flushed out. And then it felt like my eyes and my body were in two different places, one being stretched toward her while trying to remain present and the other peering into the past. I looked at the man—was it even him?—and hated him. Hated everything about him.

What are you looking at? she asked.

Nothing, I said. Which gave it all away. Like being caught by Mom with internet search history when I was using her computer all those years ago. I had been looking at naked pictures of women, women much older than I was, and when Mom took back her computer later in the day, I had forgotten to clear some of the browser history. She asked what I had been looking at and I said nothing. As in everything that I shouldn't tell you. Nothing at all.

Janine turned around, and I expected her to shudder or for the ice in her drink to tremble, as in the movies, but she took stock of the bar and then resumed facing me. It was as if she had stared at the man but hadn't seen him, or that seeing him lacked specific context. If only there had been a car. If we had been outside. If there had been a high school football bumper sticker and a dead buck. If the man had called her a cunt.

He approached us, but it was Janine whom he addressed. Swarmed, got uncomfortably close.

Is this your boyfriend? he asked.

No, she said. Why?

Because he's been looking at me, so I wanted to ask you in order to give him the benefit of the doubt: do we have a problem here?

What's he talking about? Janine asked.

No idea, I said.

In this light, the man looked worse for wear. A wrinkle ran vertically between his eyes; his chin sagged a couple levels below his mouth, as if the puppeteer holding up his jawline had fallen asleep and gone slack with the rope.

Why the fuck are you looking at me then? he said. Huh? Want me to teach you not to look at people?

That's when it hit Janine, or I assume that's when it hit her because her expression turned sour, and she grabbed my arm and led me outside through the side door. Behind us, I could hear the man laughing, a shrill that didn't shut off until we got into her car. By then, she had put her radio on and locked the doors and dialed Andre, cursing with each unanswered ring.

Where the hell is he? she asked. Where is he when you actually need him, you know?

On the radio, a DJ fielded a listener's request and joked that he hadn't heard that song since he was a boy. Janine fingered her scar.

She called Andre again and again.

Holy shit, she said to me. We found him. I mean, I think we found him, right? Was that him?

I think, I said. You think?

What I didn't say: What does it matter if we can't do anything about it? If too much time has passed.

Chapter Eleven

The invitation to Peter and his girlfriend Mariah's baby shower was pinned to my refrigerator, flapping next to takeout menus and a sticker of a car towing company left over by the previous tenant. On the invitation was a note from Benjamin that read: *Henry, would love to have you there.*

A month earlier, Franny had stopped me in the supermarket next to the toiletry aisle, and I don't know if it was the scent that enlivened me, that made me pause when she called my name, but we had come face to face. The way she balanced items in her hand, even though she could have used a cart, told me that she had come here alone, and I thought of Mom all those years ago balancing the toilet paper in the cart while she struggled to control me in her arms, though maybe it wasn't a memory at all but what Mom had told me life had been like.

Franny and I stared awkwardly, each waiting for the other to speak. I've been meaning to call you, she said. I didn't have your number though.

I thought of how sorry of an excuse that sounded and then said, I can give it to you.

I'm glad I ran into you, she said. I wanted to invite you to this.

She didn't have the invitation with her, but she handed me a couple of yogurts in order to free up a hand and take out a polaroid of Peter posing with his girlfriend Mariah. Mariah's stomach jutted out and Peter positioned one arm around her shoulder and one arm on her stomach. They were in Benjamin's living room, in front of the fireplace where a sole stocking still hung, and it looked like the Christmas tree had been plucked out of the picture, and with it any sweet affection I had for either of them.

She's big, I know, Franny snickered. And don't tell Peter this, but he hasn't grown since high school.

I looked again at the photo and noticed how uneasy Peter looked. How he appeared to be itching to get away. Or that he was asking himself: How did I get in this position, what with a baby and all?

The pregnancy wasn't planned, and everyone knew it. Peter and Mariah weren't married, hadn't even been dating for longer than six months, and when they were seen together (Josef attested to this fact), they wore the stigma of having made some kind of accident together. Not that it was the baby's fault—nothing unborn could have any effect on the living—but Peter got drunk on most weeknights and passed out in his car with the keys still in the ignition, and Mariah was three years younger and still sang karaoke with her friends and worked as a hostess at the Italian restaurant and was perfectly fine if not for having much else going for her, but that was the thing: despite the fact that they were of an age where people could have kids and even raise them, nobody believed that these two were choice candidates to do so. Especially since neither had a home to call their own.

Josef had a theory that the lack of a home—by which he meant splitting homes between Peter's mom and Mariah's parents—would be best for the young child since. Let's face it he said, neither is prepared to take on this child. Let's pray that adults can rescue them from this disaster.

I told him that that makes no sense. What are they going to do? Wake up and be thirty-five years old, and still living at their parents?

And he said, Exactly.

You know, Benjamin is going to be the godfather. This was Franny talking, in the supermarket. She took back her yogurt and then the photo.

I nodded.

He wants you to be there, she said.

Where? I said. What is it?

He wants you to come, she said.

She waited a few seconds for me to answer, but when it appeared to her that I wasn't, she sighed and said, You really don't have to. I mean, I get it.

In Benjamin's front yard were relics from other people's homes—maybe Alma's home—that had price tags affixed to them. I imagined he got up in the morning and appraised what he had and realized that the conversion from memory to sensibility to monetary value was only a point of view.

So that's where he greeted me—in his yard, among all that stuff—and signaled that I should approach. And I was hesitant at first, unsure whether those relics would come alive or run away and leave only him and me there with nothing between us. I was afraid of the silence.

Son, he said. Son, you've gotten so big.

I wanted to tell him, like I'd told Josef, that I wasn't his son, that I didn't belong to anyone, but the gift I was holding—wrapped in green cellophane and secured with a bow—reminded me that I wasn't out to make enemies today.

Today was about Peter. I gripped the present tighter and approached.

Benjamin, thank you, I said. For inviting me here.

Why so formal, kid? What, because you have a beard, you call me Benjamin now?

(I hadn't been at Benjamin's house since I called him Dad. Hadn't called him Dad since I couldn't remember when).

He took my face in his palms and burrowed his nails in. I heard them scrape against my skin, and at the point of resistance tick against the grain until they landed near my eyelids. He hugged me and I fell into it but didn't return the action, which felt like slow dancing with no one.

How long has it been now? he asked. Huh?

Too long! a voice yelled. It was Franny, who, by the look of it, was on her second or third drink. Our eyes crossed while I was still in Benjamin's arms, and she got uncomfortably close like she was going to join, and then she said, Hold on, let me get my camera. She stumbled backward and disappeared as quickly as she had come.

Benjamin emptied me from his embrace and said, Come on, let's go to the back before she starts taking pictures. He led me around the house, past a swing set that had since been usurped by weeds, and to the patio where a few tables stood with umbrellas propped on top of them. A portable stereo that was playing music was being tuned by Mariah, whose belly blocked the food spread adjacent to her. Seated, with their backs to us, were Peter and Sal who were involved in a conversation. Andre and Janine were farther down on the lawn, their heads protruding from where she was picking flowers. They were holding hands; I didn't take my eyes off that.

Ladies and gentlemen, Mr. Henry Manero, Benjamin announced.

I wasn't prepared for the public declaration or Andre and Janine to wave and make their way back to me or Peter and Sal's heads to turn concurrently like a car's front wheels. Nor did I expect Mariah, the frontloaded presence that she was, to make her way over to me so quickly and, with a stained smile, plant a kiss on my cheek.

Oh my God, I've heard so much about you, she said.

This, of course, sent Peter up from his chair to rise and greet me, first with a handshake and then a hug as awkward or worse than Benjamin's because there was no closing of the circle, no excuse to feel as though it was worth anything more than a cursory favor.

I hadn't talked to Peter regularly in years, not since Andre had confronted him about what had gone awry at Benjamin's house, in which Janine had been present (though he nor Janine wouldn't tell me what exactly had happened). That was one way to put it: what had gone awry. But that was the image I conjured whenever I thought of the cousins—taking their sins downstairs to the basement and hiding them from the rest of the world. Sin was Mom's word choice, not mine. When she had quit drinking and then started again and then quit, until stopping and starting was as impulsive a line as her self-image, she told me that it was useless trying to stop a sinner once he reaches a certain age. She was talking about Benjamin of course. But she also said that Benjamin's influence was like watching a game show in which you know all of the answers: you should be wise enough to stop watching, but you can't because it's fun to see someone awash in stupidity, in their own stubborn ways. And that was what my cousins were doing: watching their uncle fall deeper into his own destructive patterns, wise enough to know better but young enough to fall prey to repeating the same mistakes.

The news had come down fast and hard on me during my senior year. First, rumors about what might have occurred at Benjamin's—those involving Peter and Andre and a myriad of women and one or two even involving Sal—and then certain photo evidence: snapshots of Benjamin shooting liquor with girls my age, one of Peter making out in Benjamin's basement, with the grandfather clock faded into the distance, and one of Sal, blurry but flipping a knife next to a table with cards on it. He looked so young in that photo, and even now, with stubble on cheeks that constantly filled out, with arm hair that crept up his shoulders and formed the back of his neck, I recalled that photo. I thought of whether that knife was his or was Peter's from all those years earlier. When I asked questions of these rumors, I was met by the same curious stare, followed by an astounded response from my classmates, some of whom I knew and others who were like passing cars: It occurred to them that I hadn't been there at any of those parties, for any of that time. And staring back at them, wishing I could speed up time or dissolve from the edges of the conversation, I'd say nothing. There was nothing to say. To ask about Peter or Sal or, god forbid, Andre was to learn the truth. Anything could be true if enough people had witnessed it. And if not, just believing it was good enough.

    Josef had told me that. Even back then, when I was blinding myself to the truth, Josef was taking share in gossip like a neighborhood barber. Shaving the heads of kids for knowledge. Shaking split ends loose.

    I heard your cousin Peter abused a girl.

    That's the way he said it, too. We were seated at the café where the child waitress was pouring us coffee, and he let it fly like he was telling me about the latest movie he watched. I looked at the waitress, who was dead set on Josef, like she had never heard someone say that with such deadpan expression, and then turned back to Josef, who was cutting into his pancakes the way an old cowboy might. Josef, what the fuck? I said. And the child waitress with the snap bracelets—I couldn't believe it—but she said, Don't worry, I've heard much worse. Then she walked away. What confused me, and still does, was her intention: did she mean she had heard much worse about Peter or that she had heard worse things in general? Did she mean both?

    I watched the waitress back behind the wall where she was retrieving the rest of our food, and then I said to Josef, You can't say that shit, not in public.

    He said, Would the story change if I told you in private?

    Guess not, I said.

    Then you see?

    But I didn't, not then. Disbelief hadn't come over me yet and I ate in silence and avoided conversation and eye contact with Josef. When the waitress returned to ask me if I needed something, I said yes, but I couldn't remember what it was.

    Peter's aptitude for violence—and for the reputation it produced—was alleviated by his physique. He had grown skinnier over the years, like he had matured into it, and the façade of toughness he had once carried dropped with his weight. And watching him standing next to Mariah, who was crowding me with love, I almost felt that he was incapable of having conducted the kind of violence that the school, that the entire town, that Josef, figured him guilty for. Even his voice seemed unsure of itself. He paused mid-sentence, swallowed his words, said, Henry I'm so—thank you—thanks for coming.

But his uncertainty, which carried its own kind of guilt, reminded me that, if the rumors were true, he was only a step away from doing something so unspeakable that to think of it was to be guilty by association. That my being here was like standing in for some type of violence being committed by the star of the show.

I couldn't ask Peter about it, not now, not with Mariah standing there with their baby on the way, and the baby decorations in white and blue and pink flapping like sails on a mast and the celebrating occurring behind us. I heard them: Sal snapping a fresh can of beer open and exhaling every time he took a sip; and Benjamin asking for a fresh one himself, and, in front of us, Andre and Janine, awkward and not nearly as drunk, having their own quiet conversation that seemed just out of reach, even if I smiled at Janine. Even if I let her know that I wanted in. She returned that smile, as wide and as genuine as I had ever seen, and gestured for me to come over there. Where? On the other side of the gate that seemed to be her and Andre's domain, far enough from the other guests and from Benjamin. And as I excused myself from the clutches of Mariah, Sal burst out open the screen door and demanded that I meet him inside for a celebratory shot.

Mariah rolled her eyes and Peter said, Isn't it too early for that? It was enough of a warning for Mariah, for she waved her hand at Peter and quietly said, It's okay. Go. Enjoy.

Sal yelled once more. Andre? Janine? You joining?

They maintained their distance behind the fence. Janine had put one of the flowers she was holding behind her ear. Go ahead without us, Andre said flatly. We're fine.

Behind the screen, pixelated by a web of shadow and light, were Sal and Benjamin, and behind them Franny, whose voice I heard say, Not the good stuff now, please. Sal, not the good stuff. The kitchen had an order to it that I didn't expect, either due to Franny's expectations for a clean household or Benjamin's desire to spruce it up for the party. But the chaos that he preserved around his house was reduced to a lonely pile in one corner and otherwise tucked into cabinets and rows above them. Just as Josef's antiques were on display over every surface of his estate, Benjamin kept empty bottles in the space between the cabinets and the ceiling. He passed out in corners of the house and left traces of their disease.

Sal took out a bottle of Buffalo Trace—it's not the good stuff, he told Franny—and planted it in the middle of the table, then poured six shots.

Just four, I think, I said. Andre and Janine are out.

What's new? Sal asked. Two more for me, I guess.

Slow down, son, Benjamin said.

This warning came on strong and unexpected. Sal threw up his hands in a defensive *What?*

Fine, he said. One more for me and one more for Pete.

Oh, fine, Benjamin said.

Eh, Peter said.

Oh, you'll drink it, Sal said. You'll regret not taking it once that baby shows up.

Peter considered, drew in his lips and shook his head like a dog letting loose of water.

I won't tell, Sal said.

Me neither, Benjamin said.

Me neither, I said.

Oh, you fuckers are on your own, Franny said, and we all laughed.

To loyalty, Sal said, and lifted up his glass.

Is that what we're calling it? Peter joked.

To family, Benjamin said, which Sal repeated, and we all clinked glasses and raised our heads back.

Not five seconds later, Sal took his second, and slid Peter's toward him.

Nuh uh, Peter said. I'm gifting mine to Manero.

Are you allowed to do that? Sal asked nobody.

He can do anything he wants, Benjamin said. Henry, do your cousin the honor.

Shouldn't the godfather do that? I asked. (Was it meant sarcastically? I wasn't sure).

Benjamin walked to the cabinet and withdrew another shot glass. He poured himself a shot, of the good stuff this time, and said, Now you have no excuse.

Sal laughed. Bottoms up, he said, and we all raised our heads back.

When we finished, Franny kissed Benjamin's neck, but Sal, being next to him, was transposed into this image, and the reality of who was kissing whom was temporarily dislocated. Then Sal reached across the table to slap my shoulder and said, You've been underground too long, cos.

Underground?

You know, away. Far away. Right, Uncle Ben?

But Benjamin and Franny had already left the table, and Sal was left having to talk to me. He said, You heard I'm becoming a cop, right? He cracked open another beer, and this time I witnessed it fizzle and wash its own torso clean.

Seriously?

You surprised? he asked. Another semester of college credits and I can take the exam. The exam is the easy part—some bullshit P.E. test. The college credits are harder. They're making me take biology. For fucking what, you know? Biology? Do cops cut people open?

Yeah, I said. Yeah, that sucks.

You were a good student, he said. Why didn't you go to college?

I was okay, I said.

My ass, he said. We used to call you Steve Jobs behind your back. We thought you'd be the one to get rich.

Really? I said.

Oh fuck off, Manero. You were such a suck up, he said. And in a phrase, his playfulness had turned mean, like his brother's had in the shed so many years before. I saw it again, the photograph of Sal turning the knife in the basement.

We were surprised you never left, he said. That's all I'm saying.

Yeah, I wanted to stay close—

To Alma, he said.

Yeah, I said.

To mommy, he said laughing.

I swallowed. The kind where you feel yourself swallowing and think about all the swallowing you do all day and never pay attention to. Then I noticed the swatch of fat that hung around Sal's Adam's apple and considered how much saliva he must keep in there. He'd get older and the gills on his neck would slope and he'd become the type of person who had saliva forever coating the sides of his lips. And he'd be a cop, so fat in his unoriginality.

You work for that guy, that old guy, right? Sal asked.

Josef, I said.

Yeah, I've heard things, he said. Some of them involve you.

People talk, I said.

What I didn't tell him was that I too had heard things about him, from no other than Josef, who had said that Sal had failed the police physical. Not once, but twice. Twice at his age? Can you believe that Josef had said? And then—get this—after he had failed the test, his mom had to pick him up because his car had broken down and all the captains watched him get picked up by mom and drive away with tears in his eye. I told Josef there was no way that was true. Josef told me I was entitled to believe what I want.

I studied Sal's eyes, and he said, What the fuck is wrong with you? Why are you looking at me like that?

And I said, I don't know, I don't think I'm looking. Maybe I'm just hungry.

Well, we're going to have to change that, he said. He poured himself another shot. For the road, he said.

We walked outside where the blinding light emboldened the yard, made the trash littering outside the cans feel homely, the stains covering the barbeque lived in. That's where Benjamin was, turning over steaks and burgers as a flame rolled in front of him.

By this time, Andre and Janine had made their way into the yard but hadn't joined Peter and Mariah at their table. Sal, balancing the shot in his hand, walked over to Andre and said something that I couldn't quite make out.

Benjamin's burgers sizzled and a shot of oil landed on his wrist. He cried out. I really was hungry.

Then I watched Janine's face change. I didn't need to hear anything to know that Sal had said something unpleasant. Right there, I saw her in high school again, in the cafeteria, biting into a sour apple. I saw her at the edge of the beach where I had told her I loved her and where she had replied in a similar way—like what? With a face that communicated her awkwardness without her having to say it. She could have written a thesis with her expressions.

Then their voices got louder, and Andre positioned himself in front of his girlfriend while Sal slammed the shot and threw the glass on the grass where it landed without shattering. Benjamin didn't turn, for nothing had smashed. Franny was setting up a row of condiments next to him.

Get the fuck over it, Sal said. It's been years.

Hey, Peter said, trying to calm them. Hey!

It's fine, brother. I got this, Sal said.

I didn't ask if you got this, Peter said. I told you to calm the fuck down.

That's when Benjamin turned. He cooled his flame with a turn of his wrist.

How long have you been going out now? Sal asked Andre. And you can't even sit the fuck down with our family like normal people? You come over here with this attitude, like you can't be bothered, and yeah, I get it. We're not good enough.

Then he turned to Janine. We're trash, right? This family is trash. That's what you think.

Had Janine been wearing a long-sleeved shirt or a jacket, she would've cocooned herself inside and never come out. But seeing that she only had on a dress, she could only turn her back. And that's what she did, turned her back and walked to the gate, and stepped out to the other side of it.

Yeah, Sal said. Walk away.

Andre stepped forward so that he and Sal were nose to nose, though Sal's nose ended where Andre's neck stretched upward. You're fucking drunk, Andre said. Don't do something stupid.

Boys! Benjamin said. Boys, what in the hell happened?

Everyone turned. Benjamin's age commanded attention. The smoke billowed behind him and traveled to the far side of the roof before exiting around the corner.

Nothing, was just leaving, Andre said.

Benjamin approached him, spatula in hand. Son, he said.

No, I'm going, he said.

Andre joined Janine on the other side of the gate and the two of them hurried away, she still holding the bouquet of flowers she had picked for herself. When she got to the end of the driveway, Andre took them from her and crumpled them into potpourri. Then he turned back around.

Manero! he called. Manero, you coming?

My stomach churned. I heard Sal say something indistinguishable, could only guess that it was directed at me. Saw Benjamin shake his head and Franny purse her lips, like what she was thinking could be kissed off. She said, Don't go, honey.

Benjamin said, Don't go, Henry.

Then Sal, this time clear as a bell, said, Go, Henry. You're not wanted here either.

Sal, slow down, Benjamin said. Let's all just calm down here.

I don't know how long I stood there or when the idea of standing there felt like I had been the sole cause of the argument that had broken out or when feeling that way felt like a recapitulation of the grief I'd expected to encounter by simply showing up, but it must've been a while. And I know this because by the time I regained awareness, the sun had forfeited itself behind clouds, and Andre and Janine had left, and I had discovered that I wasn't hungry anymore, that the ketchup and mustard stains on my plate had revealed my true motivation, and that I was staring at the cellophane wrapping for the present I had brought and which Mariah was now opening. We were inside the kitchen surrounding the island. The island was so far from reality.

What was inside was as good as a guess for me as it was for her, since Mom had done the purchasing and wrapping, and as I waited, not so much anticipating as watching, Sal whispered in my ear. His words were heavy and slurred, but he spared no time in repeating them again.

She ever tell you how she got that scar? he asked. Janine I mean? *The night at the bog? The creep with the bumper sticker?*

I know who did it, he continued.

What?

We all know who did it, he said. He searched for someone and landed at Peter, before his eyes went slack with inactivity.

Sal, what are you saying? Peter asked. You're drunk. Sit the fuck down. You don't know anything.

What did he know that I didn't?

Sal burped into his mouth and slinked his body past mine, hitting my shoulder on the way.

Don't be an asshole, Peter said to Sal.

Sal left the room and Peter was resigned to let him go. Don't listen to him, Peter said to me. He farts out bullshit when he's drunk. I think he drinks too much, honestly.

Meanwhile, Mariah held the blue blanket that she had withdrawn from the box; its stains from overuse contradicted the shiny, new objects also around him.

My blanket, Benjamin said. From when I was a kid. How in the world did you get that, Henry?

Henry, thank you, Mariah said, and rubbed her stomach. This is so sweet of you.

I felt Benjamin's eyes on me. I heard my mother laughing someplace offscreen.

In another room, Sal's anger had turned to weak sobs.

Chapter Twelve

Jonathan Bartlett, now he's going to do something about these taxes, I overheard a woman say to her friend in the bagel shop a week later.

Still sleepy, I thought that what I was hearing was either a hoax or that I must've still been dreaming (a cliché, Josef would say), but suddenly the past dug in its heels and it felt as though all of morning was a giant reclamation song conducted by Jonathan Bartlett, the fat—I mean husky—political pretender who called himself a Republican simply because Ulysses S. Grant did, but who cared little about political parties, especially now, given one convenient fact: Jonathan Bartlett was a rich, rich man.

Once I heard this exchange between the women at the bagel shop, I realized that this is what Jonathan himself had intended to tell me at the bar when I saw him weeks ago, just before he was distracted by the two girls. That he was rich and that, man, there's nothing better than being rich after coming from nothing. (That is not what he told me, but one can only assume). And though he hadn't told me this at the bar, I thought back and now could see it everywhere: in the smoothness of his cheeks and the clarity of his teeth and on the vest, though wine-stained, as expensive a brand as I had ever seen. And the biggest giveaway? The brashness with which he excused himself to talk to the women.

It didn't take me long to find Jonathan Bartlett the way it had to find Josef after our time with Caravaggio. His face was plastered on a telephone pole, and upon closer inspection I saw his face many times over, stapled on white paper on every side. But it was a new Jonathan—his hair parted, though mostly grey, and having ditched the farm clothes for a blue suit (he had even printed the flyers in color). On them he had called for an unofficial meeting at his "estate" where he was to "talk through the biggest issues facing taxpayers today." Below his picture he listed his experience, which included "Local farmer, businessowner, political strategist, and family man." And below that, smartly I must add, he had written, "Booze, beer, wine, and food is complimentary. Bring a friend."

I called the number that was listed on the flyer, let it ring. And again. Then I hung up. I was already late to see Josef and getting into a conversation with Jonathan would've only made me later, so I decided that my confusion would have to suspend itself.

But he called back immediately, and though I recognized the number as the one I had dialed, seeing an unsaved number made me feel like I was in trouble. Shoving the phone in my pocket would've saved me from this disastrous turn of events, but I answered instead.

Jonathan, hello.
He said, Henry Manero.
How did you know it was me?
I have my ways, Henry.
Andre? When did you see him?
Is this an interrogation?
No.
Are you sure?
I don't know.
Did you just call?
No.
You're a liar, Henry Manero. He laughed heartily and then sighed.

I was only a block away from Josef's and could feel the anxiety slink through my fingers. Josef didn't like anyone being late: he thought that it sent shock waves through the rest of the day, made the rest of the hours feel off-balanced and neutered. He used that word, too. Neutered. Like the dick of the day had been cut off and was bleeding out.

I saw your posters, I said.
Yeah? You like that?
They're all over, I said. You're considering running again?
No! Well, not exactly. I lost last time. I don't think I could stand that kind of defeat again.
Why?
Have you ever lost in your life, Henry?
This felt like a trick question, and I didn't answer.

I couldn't take that defeat, he said again. This isn't the reason you called.

No, I said. It's about your family.

What do you mean?

It says family man! On the flyer. Family man? I said that more defensively than I should have.

Although I had still not obtained the answers to how Jonathan made his money, I found it hard to believe that he would call himself a family man. Was it possible—and what wasn't possible I thought—that Jonathan could have had a family in California, which is why he relocated there in the first place? My face burned with embarrassment—for my mother, for the belief she had held on for too long that he was coming back. For the fact that I had too.

Well yeah, he said.

What does that even mean? I asked. I heard him breathe into the phone, like breathing more deeply could save him from his embarrassment.

I guess that is a stretch, he said. I don't know if I was ever considered, if you –

Did you have a family in California? I asked. That's what I wanted to know after all. That's how I should have begun. I heard Josef's voice ringing in my head: *Art is authority. It's demanding what you want from yourself and from the viewer.*

Ah, California, he said. Cali-fucking-fornia.

Did you?

No! he said. I was talking about you. About your mom. About your cousins. And yes, even Peter and Sal. Speaking of: what are those devious bastards up to?

Family man, I repeated.

Maybe that's a stretch, he said.

Yeah, maybe, I said. Could he hear that I was angry?

The old Jonathan Bartlett might have cried at his own sentiment, but this Jonathan—this boisterous, excitable, wealthy one at the other end of the line—laughed and laughed and in between laughter said, What can I say? Holdam treasures a good family man.

We met at the shed an hour later. After all this time, Jonathan Bartlett had held onto his land like a toy in a child's memory, though now that we were on it, I felt long out of place. As we walked the fields, the dirt from the previous rain soft against our steps, Jonathan stopped to inspect areas that had overgrown or gone slack with carelessness. This included most of the land: though he had kept a staff employed to harvest before the freeze, his being gone had permitted a sort of nonchalance when it came to tending to the organization and preservation. The house was further neglected, with several of its shingles gone and its siding growing green and yellow with mold. He told me that he had employed someone to watch over the house every winter, to make sure the pipes didn't freeze or that the mice hadn't overtaken the walls, things like that.

When Jonathan talked—which he did a lot of—he didn't gesture or make a scene with his mouth the way he had years ago. His lips didn't curl or button or stretch but remained mostly stationary despite the constant flow from them. But talk he did, and the narrative, insofar as I could track it, followed him from California, where he had found work producing wine at a popular vineyard in Santa Barbara, to discovering that one of his brothers, who he had gone to see in the first place, was dying. This wasn't a sad story, though. Not in Jonathan's telling. For the brother and he had had a sort of spiritual awakening after Jonathan had "borrowed" him from the hospital and taken him out to wine country where they spent an entire day drinking in the field, the field where he worked, and then passed out under the stars. When they awoke at dawn, their sleeping bags several yards from each other as if they had rolled away during the night, they both saw a migrant mother and her child at the far end of the vineyard picking apples at the adjoining farm and walking away with the bounty in a backpack. Jonathan's brother told him that he had a dream about this mother and son, but when Jonathan affirmed that he had seen the same image, the brother said that must've been a sign. A sign for what? Jonathan asked. That I must give back— will you do me a favor, he asked Jonathan? He told Jonathan that he wanted to give him half of his inheritance when he passed—tens of millions of dollars—but that he had to promise to build a farm that would feed the poor forever. It was very Edenic. And Jonathan promised, and they both went back to sleep.

When Jonathan awoke again several hours later, the brother was gone. Not dead, not yet, but gone as in back to the hospital. Around Jonathan's limp sleep, the migrants had started their daily work and laughed at what in the hell this fat man was doing in a sleeping bag with wine bottles laid at his feet.

There was more to that story, Jonathan told me, but this isn't what you came here to know.

We had walked so much that by the time we came to the shed, my feet were pulsing and the dirt that had gotten into my sneakers and onto my leg, forming a ring around my sock line.

And he was right. I hadn't come to learn about the romanticism of getting blissfully drunk in a field and swatting fruit flies. I hadn't intended to even inquire about his wealth, but suddenly it was everywhere: this was no longer Jonathan Bartlett walking the fields but a stranger for whom fields should seem foreign. He belonged in a bank or in a high-rise that propped up the city millionaires and dumped them into our town for the summer.

At Sophie's, where I first ran into him, he had shown his hand in the form of twenties laid on the bar like fanned fingers. Expensive fingers. They were crisp and not weathered by the kind of stress that middleclass men put upon their wallets, as if their money and cards were an extension of their minds. His was clean, orderly, virgin.

The shed on the farm had a lock on it, but Jonathan was intent on trying to see what was inside. Though he was tall enough to peek into the windows, I was not. I craned my neck to see what he was seeing, imagining the room my cousins and I had inhabited so many years before, but Jonathan, returning from taking a glance, reported that there was nothing there except a pile of boxes. Shit, he said. I guess my boys store the equipment inside.

I craned my neck some more.

Don't worry, he said. Nothing really to see.

You know, Andre and I used to come here in high school. We broke in a couple times, I said.

Broke in? You make it sound like you're strangers, he said. But you aren't. You were never strangers. It's your house too.

I fixated on the word 'house,' on all the ways it could've been a house but wasn't. How even then, when Jonathan had installed the cot and desk and storage compartment in which Peter's knife lay, the presence of Jonathan's actual house several yards away precluded any possibility of that little home ever feeling real.

Jonathan's house looked pale and small against the sun. It had never felt so unlived in. Jonathan caught me looking at it and said, I'm sorry I never asked you and your mom to move in.

And I said, I never knew that was a possibility.

He said, I know, that's what I'm saying.

I said, It's not like we didn't have our own place. I remember you coming over there.

You do?

Yeah, I said. At first I thought it was Benjamin—the first time you stayed over I mean—but then I'd come downstairs and see your shoes. I'd smell the pancakes you were making. Hear you and my mom in the kitchen talking quietly. And I knew.

Knew?

It's not important, I said. For what it's worth, I think my mom would've said yes, if you asked her back then I mean.

Yeah? His eyes lit up. He stroked an invisible beard and thought on it. What do you think she'd say now? If I asked her?

It was what he had wanted to know at Sophie's, before he struck up with the younger women next to him. Before his attraction to them had gone on its own joy ride.

I don't know, I said. There's Seamus.

Ah, the infamous Seamus, he said. Is this Seamus a wealthy man?

Doubt it, I said. Seems like he would've spent most of his money on court fees.

I thought you said his ex-wife represented him, he said.

I didn't say she did it pro-bono. We laughed.

Son of a bitch, he said. So she's dating a poor murderer? he asked. I thought she had better taste than that.

Me too, I said. Me too.

You thirsty? he asked. Need a drink? I don't know what he meant by a drink, but he led the way to his back porch where we had begun our journey and where the lack of breeze kept everything still and sticky. A rocking chair that used to hold his body now held ballast to a rake and a shovel, two metal figures burning in midday.

Does she know I'm back? he asked once we got there. He didn't wait for my answer but went inside and returned not ten seconds later with a warm bottle of whiskey and two cups, no ice.

Let's do as the farmers do, he said, and poured two shots. He didn't toast nor slug it down. He drank it slow like a long yawn.

Do you think she'll see me? he asked again.

His need for permission—or was it validation?—surprised me. He winced, expecting me to say no, but I said, You'll have to ask her yourself.

And he asked, perhaps appropriately, Wouldn't that mean I'd have to see her first?

I said, Not necessarily.

What do you mean? He asked this, but I asked myself it too. *What did I mean by that?*

A meeting, I said. And since he still didn't understand, and maybe neither did I, I said the first thing I thought.

I can arrange a meeting—with her, with Seamus—and you show up. I mean, that's the point, right? That you're gonna see her. Except this way, it's accidental. Or incidental. Coincidental? The point is…

I think he understood the point—even if I still didn't—because he nodded wildly, and I followed the folds of his chin up and down, up and down.

That's brilliant, he said. A meeting. We'll just have to make it special. Henry Manero, what if I'm able to save your mom from Seamus, from herself? Henry Manero, you might be a genius.

I nodded and said, I'll think on it.

You do that, he said.

I had begun to think. Right there and then, too, sitting on the porch and observing the crops in their sloppy rows. I thought not just about the supposed meeting but also about the reason I had come to see Jonathan in the first place, which was the same reason I called. It was about wanting to know what Jonathan had meant about being a family man and if the title could be true if such a person also had gone away and returned only when it was easier to justify. When he was no longer looking at a boy but a young man. Years ago, he could've given a thousand excuses to the boy in front of him and come up emptyhanded. Now he could give me a thousand dollars and not one excuse. But all he had to say now what we were both thinking anyway: What's good for you is also good for me.

Chapter Thirteen

The problem with supermarkets is that when you go on a full stomach, you wish the apples would rot to shit. That the eggs would spill out from their baby cradles and die quick deaths.

I wasn't hungry when I went shopping for Josef—he gave me 100 dollars for three items and told me to keep the change—which meant that I was both bored and bound by duty. It's funny how a chore can feel enjoyable one minute and then painfully dull the next, and by the time I got to the aisle stocking the toothpaste and skin creams, I felt that there was no greater sin than getting old. I finally understood why Josef sent me on these errand runs: it wasn't because he couldn't do it but because he didn't want to accept the fact that every week for nearly fifty years he had been going to the same store to stop at the same aisle to pick out the same brand of methyl cream and to turn out of the same parking lot to take the same route back to his house. Shopping wasn't a chore so much as getting old was; shopping was optional and aging not.

I held the package of cream in my hand, which felt like every packaged tube I had bought for him up to then. Cold and scentless, though the memory of it being opened in front of me suffused into the store and suddenly the entire aisle felt medicinal and cold. Then I read the packaging information—bottled and shipped from a plant in New Jersey—and the scent was neutralized.

It was true that Josef had many sores and that each time I came back with a new bottle of Bengay the sores had solidified with a shellac that could've only been the medicinal cream doing its work. And the application of more cream—done as soon as I came back from the store, though I disappointed him once or twice by saying that I would not apply it on him—could've only been considered gratuitous, for the entire house felt like the plant in New Jersey must've before the bottles were capped and packaged, packaged and shipped, and then sent to a store where ivory soaps smelled stronger than Josef's favorite item.

Since the only items in my hands were this package of Bengay and a family size package of sunflower seeds—again, I wasn't hungry, not in the least—Franny should've known when she saw me that I was shopping for Josef. (I should mention that Josef preferred the salty texture of sunflower seeds, though he didn't actually get to the seeds. He had told me that as a kid he never learned how to properly get to the seed, so he would suck on the shells until the salt expired and then spit them into the dirt. He continued this habit and was convinced that a human could get an adequate amount of salt—and never too much—from sucking on a couple handfuls a day). But Franny eyed me curiously as I had just grabbed the third item—eggs, this being the most normal of the three—and it was the sensation of feeling eyes on your back before you know where they're coming from. When I turned around, she was a static, smiling ball.

Why is it that we're always running into each other here? she said. Your father hates those, by the way.

I mentally juggled the items in my hand and decided she was talking about either eggs or sunflower seeds.

I once put a few on his salad and he thought the devil himself was trying to poison him, she said.

Eggs or sunflower seeds.

He likes that, she said, pointing to the Bengay.

Oh, it's not mine, I said.

Don't you think I know that? she said.

You never know, I said. I could be a walking muscle ache. I could be a hundred years old.

I thought of what it would be like to be walk around being Josef. Did he experience these aches all day? Or were they a side effect of his slowing down, sores that popped up like flowers on the side of the road if he ever stopped long enough to look?

You've got so much time to get old yet, she said. So much time. Not that that's a bad thing either. Isn't it glamorous? She did a curtsy of sorts, devoid of anything in her hands, and almost bumped into a litter of kids who were fighting over who would get to wheel the cart.

It doesn't look that bad, I joked.

Well, thanks. That's the nicest thing I've heard all year. If only your father—

And then she stopped. Didn't say anything for a second. She watched the kids with the cart careen into the frozen food section.

She tried again. If only Benjamin...he was so glad you came to the barbeque. Even if all of us drank too much.

I'm sorry about that, I said.

You? Sorry? You have nothing to be sorry about. You weren't the one passed out in a plate of corn salad. Gosh, that kid was a mess.

Sal had taken a nosedive into his plate as Benjamin was building the fire pit. When he came to, his face was red with embarrassment or sun, it was hard to tell. And Benjamin, who had usually plied Sal with the brazenness to be who he wanted, whenever he wanted, had told the kid to go inside and get to bed. On his way in, Sal fingered his forehead where an imaginary scar might lie, where Janine's real scar did.

He was drunk, I said to Franny. More so than usual, I guess.

For once it wasn't Benjamin, she laughed. You're not much of a drinker. That's good.

I have my moments, I said. And there were traces of them over the years—like streaks of debris across a lawn or contrails in the sky— mostly involving Andre and some involving Janine and once, when I was fifteen, when Mom came home and found me on the back porch smoking cigarettes, which I had since given up.

You're not like them, she said. Even Andre. He's a good kid, I suppose, but there's an edge there, you know? I don't know how to describe it. It's been hard to break in with them. They respect you though, I see how they're competitive with you.

Respect?

I don't know if I said it aloud, but confirmation wringed inside her hand and then exploded once she touched my shoulder.

Of course, they respect you, she said. They know you're going to be the first one to leave. To get out of here and do something real with yourself. They don't say it—they don't want to—but they know.

Andre went to college, I said. Andre got out.

Andre got an education, she said. Doesn't mean he got out.

Outside the giant window of the IGA, the cars jammed inside the small parking lot offered no escape nor did the checkout lines that were growing bigger. Next weekend was July 4th and families were stockpiling on food. Josef, who said fireworks were like guns for sociopaths, would simply treat it like another weekend.

I should let you get on, she said.

No, no, it's okay. I was just thinking about what else I needed, if I forgot—

Where would you go? she asked. If you did go somewhere, where would you go?

I pictured California, with its rivers of gold or wine—or were they blood red and biblical—and saw Jonathan Bartlett whistling songs like a dodo bird. But I also saw Hollywood, with its staged sets and fluorescent actors, and thought maybe I'd want to go there.

To Hollywood, I said. I want to make movies.

That's beautiful, she said. I wanted to be an actress once. You'll never believe this, but when I was eighteen or nineteen, I was on my way to Hollywood, was actually at the airport, when I called my mother from a pay phone to give her the address of a friend I was staying with, and she picked up and was frantically shouting. It turned out my father had a heart attack five or so minutes before I called, and while the ambulance was on the way to get him my mother had sat next to him on the bathroom floor. That's when I reached her, while she was waiting. And that changed everything for me. I rushed home to be with my father and my mother. I never got to go to California. He died three days later. Call it God's Comic.

I'm so sorry, I said.

That was so long ago, she said. The lesson is this: don't call your mother when you're at the airport. Matter of fact don't even bring a phone. I'm serious, she laughed.

I know, I think mine's preoccupied anyway. My mother I mean.

She looked away. How's your movie coming along? I'm looking forward to seeing it. Andre said there was an issue you wanted to resolve first?

That's right, I said, but we can't agree on what the issue is.

Too many cooks in the kitchen, she said.

Too many small actors with roles that aren't small, I laughed.

Too many opinions, she said.

Too many wrong opinions, I answered.

She nodded her head like she understood. In Hollywood, they're taller and even more opinionated, she said, which is infinitely worse.

You'll figure it out, I'm sure. Well, I wish you luck Henry. Whenever it is you do leave. Promise me you'll go.

I'll try, I said. I'll let Hollywood know you're still waiting for their call.

You're sweet, honey, so sweet. She leaned in to kiss my cheek as I stood with the eggs, cream, and sunflower seeds. Then she held my wrist and covered one hand with the other. A silver diamond band choked her ring finger and swelled to a glittering orb. It looked like my mother's had, but Franny looked nothing like my mom.

Chapter Fourteen

Sometimes the living, knowing that they only have a few years left before they buy the farm, congregate on the second floor of the library and host an informal meeting called The Liar's Club. Josef, who is reigning secretary of the meeting, runs through the minutes and the items for discussions, of which one, and only one, is of chief importance: *Tell the truth. Any lies that you had told at A.A. an hour ago, you are free to absolve now.*

The meeting is an informal continuation of A.A. that is held at Father Kelly's church every Sunday morning, in which the group meets before being booted out for the 7:00 morning mass. Then, a third of the group continues to the library where they go upstairs and conspire. They are quieter there—for Jean, the librarian, will have no part of any yelling or epithets or slurs that the church is witness to—but they are also respectful of Jean's generosity in letting them gather. Without Jean, they'd be forced to brave the cold winters or find a place that would permit their staying there for hours without buying a single thing. And in summers, where they'd sweat just thinking about how much they'd sweat through their truth-telling, the library was kept as cold as a meat locker.

That was the key: storytelling as a form for absolution. Revealing things that members of the group were afraid to say in the church. Things about their daughters and sons and ex-wives and their own drinking, which they had sometimes relapsed into but were embarrassed to admit in front of Father Kelly. Because it was a small town. Because their daughters and sons and ex-wives were people the other church members knew. Because Father Kelly, whose own reckless drinking had helped him find God years ago, didn't tolerate slipping back into drinking for fear that it harmed the reputation of the church. So, Alcoholics Anonymous wasn't anonymous so much as it was acknowledged repentance.

This meant that Josef and his convoy of three friends went to Jean's floor—she supplied the coffee and the Tollhouse cookies and could be civil while also demanding quietude on behalf of the library—and lied their asses off. Or, rather, they told the truth. They corrected half-truths they had told during A.A., and I suppose the lies they told—to speak nothing of the way they had ripped off a famous book by that title—were instances where they convinced themselves that they were going to get better. They knew that given their age and the ways they had repelled previous solipsistic attempts of making themselves whole again, they were only fooling themselves. Sometimes, Josef recorded these lies in a book—in a notebook resembling Andre's but couldn't be—and under each half-truth or truth-bearing exercise or whatever you want to label it, he wrote *Full of shit.*

It was on one of these mornings that Josef called me from the library to say that there had been an emergency. No time to explain, he said. Just come.

I rode my bike (Mom had to use my car for the week while hers was in the shop) and weaved in and out of cars and pedestrians in my rabbit-like pursuit of the truth. I had barely parked the bike by the front ramp when I saw Josef's Liars, as I had come to refer to his makeshift group, walking out of the library with their paper cups still steaming and the bullshit streaming from their lips. They looked giddy, and when I asked one of them—the youngest one, and therefore the most approachable—where Josef was, they told me that he was still upstairs. He said something about an emergency, I inquired, with the same desperation I had used with Mom when I couldn't find Josef for some time. Well, that's a lie, the man said, and laughed. The others joined him, although their laughter was delayed, like a piano key that's stuck, and when I stared dumbfounded, the man simply said, I'm sure everything is okay. He's upstairs talking to Jean.

When I got upstairs, Jean was at her desk fiddling with one of those transparent shelving units that hold magazines, trying to rid the dirt without removing all the contents. Have you seen Josef? I said from across the room, perhaps too loudly because Jean shushed me without looking up. Bathroom, she muttered. I think he's locked himself in. Dumbass, he is.

I passed the short stack of books, manuals on home repair and electricity, and approached the bathroom. I couldn't detect whether the smell of mildew was coming from the bathroom or from the carpet underneath my feet.

I tried opening the door, but it was locked. I expected Josef on the other side of the door—if he was there—to remark on my lack of manners. To say that it would've been proper to knock first and then attempt to open it if I hadn't heard anything, but not a second later, before I had a chance to call out his name, Josef opened. His belt was still unfastened, but he didn't look the least concerned. Not about Jean. Not about the college student two rows over checking items off on her syllabus. Not about me.

You came, he said tearfully. But I didn't notice a single tear. It was as if the welling had stopped at his eyes and exited through his throat.

You told me it was an emergency, I said. What happened?

He didn't say anything, just looked around the room like he was expecting someone to come around the corner. From where we were standing, we could see the rough edge of Jean's wooden desk, could still hear her shuffling with the magazine rack. Then, after several beats, he asked, You haven't seen her yet, right?

Who? Jean?

My daughter. She called me.

His daughter's name was Lucy, but I only remembered this after the fact. He named her after a poet or a poem's dedicatee in a famous poem, I couldn't recall. I knew one thing: Josef was getting sicker.

He had once told me that if his daughter was coming to visit it was because someone he knew had died and she was coming to take him home on the other side of the country, to a state that sounded like Missouri but wasn't. She'd be picking him up and carrying him to a burial, and then keeping him with her until his own demise. Then she'd take him to another burial, his last. When that day came, Josef said, it was safe to assume that I'd be out of a job, but, then again, so would he.

But it was also true (and this is the first thing I thought as we were standing there) that Josef could've been imagining this phone call. I recalled our conversation about baseball—or was it football?—from weeks ago and how perplexed he seemed about a simple television broadcast, and then I thought about the logistics of such a call. If he didn't have a cell phone (which he didn't), when and where did this call take place? And furthermore, if he had just taken part in The Liar's Club, would it have even been feasible that he could've answered a call, even if he had had a cell phone on his person?

When did she call? I asked.

Does it matter? he said. She's coming. Tomorrow. Or next week. I can't remember exactly when, but she's coming. I'm dead. That's it, I'm gone.

As if I needed confirmation, Josef's forgetfulness presented itself loud and clear, and I wanted to yell at him, to listen to my words sail across the room and land at Jean's desk where even her shushing would've proven ineffective against my urgency. But then his dry tears turned real and he started sobbing into the valley of his sleeves. We exited the bathroom, Josef's cane rapping against the doorframe.

Shhhhh, Jean said.

Shhhh, I said, quietly back to her, or to him. It's okay, it's okay. Let's go for a walk.

You don't understand, he said.

And he was right, I didn't. I'm trying, I said.

It's not just the going away, he said. That's the easy part—the going. All those latitudes and longitudes and roads to drive down. That's easy. The hardest part? Well, that's what I'm not ready for yet.

The hardest part?

Aren't you listening, son?

Shhh, Jean snapped. Josef, didn't your group end a half hour ago?

Sorry, he said, but not loud enough for her to hear. Then he looked at me, wiped a tear from with his sleeve, and with an expression that I'll never forget—one so filled with self-pity that I swore he could've redeemed a lifetime of lies with it—said, It's this feeling of disappearing that I'm scared of. The never-ending wall of never-enough. The longitude of grief. Man, what the fuck am I going on about? Just follow me.

He led me past Jean, down the stairs, and into the fiction stacks where the letter 'B' peppered the spines. Bending down, but not without toil, he withdrew *The Collected Stories of Jorge Luis Borges*. See this? he asked. They've got three copies of this shit, and do you know why? Man has never told a lie in his life. You read these stories and you realize what it takes to be a man of your word. Borges was blind, you know. Which means that people naturally distrusted him, expected him to distort the truth. If Borges had said he saw three foxes jump into his neighbor's land and tear apart a litter of cats, who would believe him, right? A blind man?

No one. That's why it was so important for him to try, even in his fiction, never to lie. He couldn't.

I shook my head. Yes and no. No because I hadn't read him, and yes because what he was saying seemed to make sense. I worried about forgetfulness, too, though a different kind: the feeling of never having started anything worthwhile in my entire life.

You don't seem satisfied, he said.

No, it's not that, I said.

I looked past him where the window onto the sidewalk showed images as reflective shards. I watched a bike, though not my own, whiz past halfway from somewhere to nowhere.

Then Josef, still facing me, backed up several inches until his fingers grazed the shelf where the letters BU began. He looked like he had done this a thousand times; in one second he was without a book and in the next he was holding his own.

See this? he asked.

Your book, I said, with as much enthusiasm as I could muster.

That's right, he said. Read me the title.

Oh come on.

Read it, he said.

Low and Behold, I read.

That's right, he said. Do you know how many copies of this they have?

I knew the answer. *One.*

And do you know how many people have read this in the past year? he asked. He flipped to the back cover where a mustard yellow library card barely clawed on to the surface. Read me the names, he said. Read me the dates.

I read them, beginning with three years before (when the card was first reissued) until now, but after three or four dates the names took on the sound of a computerized voice in my head. All of them, in blue ink, were the same name: *Josef, Josef, Josef, Josef.* There were no exceptions to the rule. It was as though by seeing only his name, every other possible one had disappeared. Worse, they had never existed.

Chapter Fifteen

What I'm about to say is graphic.

In the middle of the day, Josef, who is sick, who, due to Alzheimer's, forgets sometimes he is dying, takes to sucking candies and spitting them into a plastic cup. It's the noise I hate: his mouth vacuuming the saliva or the candies themselves as they smack against his molars, until the whole carnal act is forfeited by the release of a single wet object into filmy plastic.

Here comes the graphic part, though. The TV next to him reports on beheadings, how in this town in Syria the terrorists are playing soccer with the severed heads, that there are more soccer balls than players.

Josef says that maybe if they'd show the carnage, the act of it, well then we'd be fed up enough to actually do something about it.

I'm busy watching the scar on Josef's throat, how it contracts into the folds of his wrinkles every time he speaks. I think about the juices from the candies that are swishing under his skin. I wonder what Josef would look like with no head and all body as another candy drops into the cup.

Would you believe that most of these fucks wouldn't know who Caravaggio is? Josef says. And then I remember it's been months since we've talked about Caravaggio's painting of *David With the Head of Goliath*, and, as if a tailwind of inspiration lifts me, I realize I've known the truth about the painting all along: that it is David who is the desperate one, the way he proudly displays Goliath's severed, gigantic head, with as much audacity as there are tendons in his neck.

Most of these fucks wouldn't know who Goliath is, I tell Josef.

Then you *have* learned something, he says.

About the candies: they are multicolored ovular lozenges of which Josef can hardly tell the difference. He's convinced the red ones are orange-flavored and the yellow ones are cherry. But they're doctor prescribed, and it's my job to make sure he doesn't choke on them. When the saliva gets to be too much, he spits into the cup.

These, he says, you can't even taste them anymore.

I tell him that his lack of taste is sort of like my relationship with Janine. Things get confused, diluted, distended. We barely talk anymore, I tell him.

He makes the sound and holds it a second too long. The lozenge falls from his mouth, misses the cup and sticks immediately to the ground. I'll get it, he says, and does so. Sticks it in the cup instead of his mouth, thank god.

Your mother. Is she still seeing that guy with the poet's name?

Seamus, I say, yeah.

Jonathan is selling the farm, he says. This wasn't a question. He says it as fact.

Selling? I just saw him the other day. We were at the shed.

Poof. All of it, Josef says. He wants to start developing land. Building houses and shit like that. Maybe a multiplex.

A multiplex?

A movie theatre, he says.

How do you know all of this?

I was at that little party of his, which wasn't very little at all. He even had little women serving finger foods on trays. Do you believe that? Jonathan Bartlett classing it up!

He's become one of them, I say.

One of what?

Those people who are from out of town and come here to change what they don't like.

But Jonathan is from here, he says. He's a hometown success story.

Josef spits a lozenge into the cup.

I want to spit my own, but my mouth is bone-dry. I had fooled myself into thinking that Jonathan's party was about political strategy and family (or the strategy of navigating family) when, really, it was a call-to-action. It was about getting enough support to fund his money-grubbing ambitions. I remembered Jonathan's strategy for reaching out to my mom, too, which we had finalized after our meeting at the shed. It would involve a "chance meeting on a boat" while she and Seamus are supposed to be on a date. Jonathan had said cryptically, Your job is to lead the love bunnies to me. I'll take it from there.

But I don't want anything to do with Jonathan, not anymore, and when I tell Josef this, he thinks I'm talking about developments, the multiplex, blind ambition. Josef tells me he's been fighting that type of gentrification for years. Why do you think I hate going out these days? he asks. Every day is a reminder of what has been and what continues to go away. You get old and things die off. That's nothing new. Your family first, and then your friends. But you don't expect the things around you to change. Get smaller, maybe, but never change. It's like going back to your old elementary school—have you ever done that? It's not that the kids are small—the whole building is. Everything is miniature. That's sort of how getting old is. The things that seemed important aren't anymore. The world shrinks them, not magnifies them.

The TV goes to commercial. A family is flopping around happily in the pool, and when the father (presumably the father) gets out it's revealed through a separate diagram that he is suffering from acid reflux. He turns back and gives his best "I'll smile because I have to" at his family, but it's clear he's hurting. Suddenly, the pool feels threatening. What if he swallows too much water and coughs violently into it? What if we're all swimming with underlying conditions we don't know about? The kid actors feign happiness pretty well. The mother, the least skilled actor among them, springs from the diving board and lands in the puddle of the unknown.

Josef drops a lozenge. This time it doesn't make a hollow sound because the cup is too full but instead sounds like a pen connecting with paper. If it could write a story it would start with, *I am sorry for the mess, you'll simply have to ignore it.*

Chapter Sixteen

Take a trip, Josef had said. Take a trip. That's what I'd do.
So I did. I dreamed I went to Pittsburgh to South Dakota to Wyoming, across the Rockies where my breath kept plummeting, and then to Mexico City, a little area called Condesa, where every person looked vibrant and beaming with youth. And I sat down on a bench named for a saint or made for a saint and rested awhile. Then a boy, maybe seven or eight years old, said 'Amigo, you look tired. Maybe you should get some sleep.' So I stretched out my legs on the bench and used my backpack as a pillow. But the boy protested. 'No, not here, amigo, no sleeping here.' Frustrated, I walked around some more, eventually finding refuge in the outskirts of an old theatre, where at night I pretended the shadows were acting out for me, coming closer and then disbanding right when the scene got good.

I dreamed of Condesa before I learned it was a place, and it was sort of like imagining a woman before seeing her up close. But then, realizing how even the dream of a woman must be prefaced by, well, something tangible, I figured Josef had mentioned Condesa and that I was testing reality through fantasy.
But Josef, he made me promise that if I went somewhere at all it would be a place in my wildest dreams.
Condesa, I told him. Condesa it is.
And he asked, Where's Condesa? What's Condesa? Is that even a place?

Nobody wants to hear about dreams. I know this. It's written into the literature of faces when you tell people about them. You might say, *I had the strangest dream last night*, and a person will feign interest long enough to see if they're involved in it. If not, they will nod their heads as you drone on, but they will not retain the information. If you were to ask people to speak the dream back to you, which you'd be a narcissist to do, they'd say something along the lines of your dream being about the subconscious elements of your life that need addressing. Thing is, even people who study dreams use cliches about dreams. Even they are bored by them.

Choosing not to rely on clichés, I decided to go to Benjamin's house for real. Not to tell him about the dream but, instead, to reveal what had weighed on me ever since waking up in Condesa and feeling, not the hands of a small Mexican boy, but the frayed sheets of my bed and wondering whether I was home or so far from it.

Wherever I was, whatever had happened, I would forgive. It's so easy to forgive your dreams. It's harder to forgive that which has never happened.

Chapter Seventeen

But it seemed that Andre had a plan of his own, which he told me about as I was on the way to execute mine.

Have you decided about the film? Have you decided what you want to do?

What about it? I asked.

Are you going to take Josef's advice and re-film it?

Hell no, I said, which made him laugh. Over the phone I could detect his enthusiasm, like clouds breaking open to sunlight.

I submitted it, I said after a beat. All of it, the way we cut it. The way we liked it.

Goodness, he said. He's going to kill us.

No, I said. He won't know either way. Did you hear?

No?

His daughter is going to take him home to live with her. Says she worries about his safety in a big house like that. I don't blame her either. He's slipping you know. Mentally. A lot of mental falls lately. Physical ones too.

Jesus, he said.

Yeah.

How do you feel about that? I mean, what will you do with yourself?

That's what I've been trying to figure out, I said.

I'm sure Peter can hook you up at the shop, if that's what you want to do. Or, well, maybe I can talk to Janine about running her uncle's restaurant. I think they're opening a new location.

I appreciate it, I said, but I think I'll try out the west coast for a while.

Oh, so that's for real then?

Yeah, I said.

There was a long pause, and I could imagine him puzzling out the logistics of where I would live or where the money would come from. And they were fair considerations, I imagined, but I wasn't ready to think about them yet. I saw instead the Rockies in my dreams flattening out to deserts that pulsed in the afternoon sun and shivered at night, and the desert sage dotting the landscape with color. I saw Josef going out there to retire and living the rest of his life on a ranch where apple cores littered the floor and coyotes came to collect them at night. But Josef was not to die alone, despite how many times he claimed the contrary. He deserved that dignity.

So, I think there's just one thing left to do, Andre said.

And, nearly simultaneously, I told him my plan and he told me his.

We waited until dark and bought two dozen eggs from the IGA, Andre even opting for the more expensive cage-free ones because they were bigger. Then we got in his car and hauled ass to Josef's.

I was convinced that by the time we arrived and turned off the headlights so as not to alert him to our presence that Andre would have changed his mind, that he would have seen the absurdity in egging an old man's house. But Andre was compelled, not by anger or even immaturity as I originally thought but by an insecurity that bordered on helplessness. He detested Josef for stealing his notebook and for telling him what he should and should not put in our film. And when I tried to talk him out of it, to explain that Josef's time was nearing, he used that information against him, saying that a man on the precipice of mental collapse should know better than to fuck with those still living.

And I asked, Does that hold true for war criminals too?

And he said, Let's not be absurd now, okay?

We parked on the street outside the gate and let ourselves in through a gap in the bushes that I had made years ago for convenience. Andre carried both cartons of eggs, and when we got to the part of the driveway that broke off into the walkway to his door, a sensor light went on and we dashed to a portion of the grass where it couldn't reach us.

From where we were standing, I looked for the sign of a TV, a flicker, something that would tell me that he was awake and that we should turn back. But nothing came, and the only sensation of his being there was a curtain dancing in the breeze of the open window, which made me think his fingers were orchestrating a puppet show for us.

A car passed outside the gate, and in the escaping headlights I saw Andre's eyes briefly panic.

I don't think we should, I said.

The car was gone, and with it the sound of the motor, and then Josef's sensor turned off.

Ready, Andre said. One, Two...

Like describing one's dreams, it would be a cliché' to prolong Andre's inevitable decision by focusing on the countdown and on my silent protest. Suffice to say that by the time he counted to three he had launched a half dozen eggs at the side of Josef's house before I was able to draw one from the carton. When his hands were empty, he took the lead and ran to the front of the house—and thus back into the light—where he unloaded the rest of his carton onto the door, the windows, the eaves that caught some of the yolk and dripped it slowly back down. Then he unloaded the carton onto the driveway and took my portion from my hands. He whispered, What's the point in holding them if you're not gonna throw them? But it wasn't a whisper so much as a threat, and when I tried to return his question with an innocence I can only describe as self-protection, he stepped into my shadow just as a downstairs light turned on.

Throw it, he said.

I stared at the six remaining eggs, math I was able to perform because for some reason Andre had grabbed the eggs in even rows.

Throw it, he said.

I heard the front door swing open, and just before catching sight of Josef's slouching figure, I launched one egg and then another and then another until I was sure that whoever was standing there would've been doused in egg. Would've become an egg head.

But when I looked up, I saw that there wasn't a figure but an empty door with only light emanating from it. And then I saw that Andre had run off and that standing in the light of the sensor that had flashed on was only me and a couple of empty cartons and a hand that was squeezing an invisible egg, confident that if Josef had seen me, I had seen him. But I didn't see him, I couldn't find him anywhere.

Chapter Eighteen

I ran.
 Ran like I hadn't since telling Janine I was in love with her and punching my rejection into a stranger's face. I ran and didn't look back, that night or this one. And then I realized: resentment is a both a terrible and wonderful motivator for speed.
 I didn't even bother to run in the direction of Andre's car but booked it the other way: turned a couple times until I felt assured that I had made proper distance from Josef's house and came out onto the main road. I ran east and made a left at Hunter Point Drive, where my old high school stood, and a right onto Dickinson Avenue and followed it down, past the potato farm and the orchard that had since been bought out and was awaiting ordinance to be rebuilt into condos. I ran and let the cars blind me with their oncoming lights, unafraid of being noticed if I was noticed. They passed and so did the fear.
 I ran to the North Road where the BP stood and through the acrid smell of gasoline and into the darkness where the streetlights disappeared and the two-lane road became one. Then I turned left at Ageid Way and followed its trees and their shadows spidering around me until I got the small bridge that leapt over the bay where the water wasn't yellow or brown or even blue but a spotted black with a dollop of moon on its surface. There were no high school kids partying even though it was summer and every day could've been a weekend. I crossed the bridge, didn't bother to look down, and entered the other side where the road curved and led to a small ridge that led to Benjamin's house.
 I saw the yellow door before I took in the entire house, something about that color being augmented by the porch light made me think about how no one had yellow doors, not even in the movies. Maybe in children's

books or in children's illustrations where creativity hasn't been siphoned yet, but rarely in real life and never in Holdam.

The lights inside were on and the dining room flashed an image of my father that I hadn't seen. He was seated at the table with a mess of papers around him, and he was so still. Franny lingered in the kitchen behind him, fiddling with dishes and trying to remove grease from the stove, and she was so busy. They weren't talking, though if they were it was the punctuated talk of familiarity, when talking was just an excuse to be listened to.

I wanted to knock on the door, but Benjamin poured himself a drink and walked slowly to another room, out of sight. Then Franny followed after her part was cleaned, leaving only the papers unaccounted for on the table. They turned off the light.

Worried about being seen, I went to the side of the house, past the garage, where some lawn furniture was scattered. I wasn't sure whether this was furniture he wanted to sell or that he actually used, and I sat down on the one chaise lounge on which a cushion sloppily lay. The usual items that had been scattered on Benjamin's front lawn were gone, either brought in for an impending rain or sold off. Or maybe the papers occupying his table were indication that he was pivoting the business since he and Franny were getting married.

I wished I had more eggs. I would've used them. Maybe I would've used them.

The sky showed no stars. A full moon, yes, but also a lot of clouds that took from it its brightness. Rain was imminent, but we also needed a good rain. The air of late had been chalky and the temperature hotter than previous summers. Josef said it reminded him of Florida, which he hated. Too many old people without identities. Nothing to talk about except the weather.

But now, now the air felt cooler. The sky was about to break open and display the guts it was made of. As I sat there, I realized I had no guts left.

I woke up and it was morning and I was dry. The clouds had gone away except for one that was suspended over the house opposite the street, like an immaculate cartoon cloud. The air felt weighted down again and my legs felt hot from having lain too long.

In the distance, a lawnmower wailed. Its motor did that stop-and-start thing when it changed gears. There was a crunching behind me that sounded like a rabbit scurrying out of brush, but then the crunching stopped and a loud epithet was hurled my way.

What time was it?

I turned around and met Benjamin's eyes.

Henry, oh! Fuck you scared me. What are you doing here?

I fell asleep, I said. I must've fallen asleep. What time is it?

It's well past nine, he said, then checked his watch. 8:48.

I can't believe I fell asleep, I said.

Did you mean to come here? he asked. And it was a strange question. Because I was there: because there was no other way I would've gotten there if I hadn't intended to.

I mean, were you looking for me?

I wanted to find you, I said. And then I stopped, thought about the rain. That if it had rained it would've drawn me home and into my bed and away from the chaise lounge. How a rain would've prevented my being there. How it would've washed away the egg yolk from Josef's house.

Are you in trouble?

No, no.

Okay, good. Let me get you a coffee, he said. No—don't you want to come in for a coffee? I'll get Franny to make us some. Franny! he called. Franny!

No, don't, I said bitterly. Leave it.

The lawnmower cut off for a second, which protracted the silence between us. He softened his voice.

I'm sorry I didn't tell you, he said. About the marriage. Franny said she ran into you and wanted to tell you, but I didn't think it was right if she did. I should've been the one, he said.

And I said, It's not that, though some part of me knew that it was.

Then what is it?

I keep having these dreams, I said. About a place so far off I don't know if it's real. And you're chasing me in them. But you're not you, you're a shadow of you, I can't describe it. It looks like you, has your same features, but I can never see the face. Only the outline. There is always some play going on, which you're part of, that I'm trying to watch, but then the actors disappear and I wake up on the ground with the shadows standing over me. They tap me awake and there I am in my bed again, sweating. Sorry, I know they're just dreams. Nobody wants to hear about dreams.

I stood, finally at level with him.

Jesus, he said.

Sorry, I said. It's not even that, though. It's not the actual dream. It's this sensation of waking up and feeling guilty for something I can't place. Like watching the play had somehow disrupted it, had made the actors resentful and incentivized them to get me. So when I wake up, I feel like there's something still after me.

You get all of that from a dream? He pondered the question for a moment, and then said, Hmmm. I can't imagine how you feel, he said. But I don't blame you for anything. You know that, right? I don't blame you at all.

The lawnmower had started again, and I tried to outperform it.

You don't blame me for anything? I asked. I was waiting for him to take the bait, to both pardon me while also castigating himself. I wanted his vulnerability to shake itself clean like the whites of an eye.

I don't blame you, he said. Do you blame yourself?

I would never, I said.

Good, he said. In my age, what I've learned is that you can never hold onto regret. Never. It'll eat you alive.

So you don't have any? Regrets I mean?

None, he said. None at all. It'll kill you.

He smiled. Is that what you came to ask, Henry? If I regret anything? Is that why you slept outside?

I didn't mean to, I said. I fell—

Then what did you come here for?

I tried to speak, but nothing came. His head shook from side to side.

Henry, hi! It was Franny, who came from the backyard and was now close up. Benjamin relaxed and let out a balloon of air.

I wanted to tell you that I'm leaving, I said. I'm going away.

For how long? he asked with disbelief. Where you gonna go, son, with all of that regret? Where you going?

I'm going away for a while, I said, and I don't want you following me.

Where are you going? he asked.

I don't want anyone following me, I said.

Just tell me where you're going, he said, laughing. Where is my son going?

I ran. Quick as I had run there and maybe even faster. I ran and didn't respond to Franny calling my name. Ran and felt my legs waking up with each step, and it didn't feel like it had the night before but more painful. More like exercise, and the kind that will hurt the next day. I ran to the pulse of throbbing and saw my shadow beside me, and I ran until I didn't see it any longer.

Chapter Nineteen

Jonathan had prepared the boat, hoisted the sails, even hired a crew and dressed them in white pants and polos. Although I didn't want to go through with his plan, my mother had taught me one thing: never break a promise. And Josef, well he had also articulated that advice even though he broke promises all the time. So, what I summarized all that to mean was this: Show up. And if you don't like what you see, break someone's goddamn heart.

According to Jonathan's plan, I was supposed to meet Alma and Seamus by the port where I was treating my mom to a birthday lunch. This would have two effects: the first being that I would join him and my mother for a nice meal, which she would be delighted by given her knowledge of my distaste for her boyfriend, and second, from the restaurant where we we'd be eating, my mother would get a glimpse of Jonathan Bartlett's boat and fall rapturously back in love with him that she would have no choice but to leave Seamus in the dust. This was, remember, all in Jonathan's wildest imagination. He had even named the boat *Alma*, and though she was more resplendent than my mother—younger, richer, taller, more athletic—she was also at the whim of Jonathan Bartlett, or so he believed.

Just after 1:00, my mother showed up at the port's greens. Behind her, sails reflected the light back into the water, so that the entire area looked like a virgin canvas. Mom had dressed up for the afternoon too and wore a dress that went to her ankles and heels that raised her to my height.

Where's Seamus? I asked. He was not with her or trailing her either, the way I expected he would've been.

He's not coming, she said. She didn't seem upset. I wanted to do this with just you.

You didn't have to, Mom, I said, but I was relieved.

I walked her to the restaurant, but it was not the restaurant that I had promised Jonathan I would go to. This one was opposite his boat, close enough for her to see the boat but far enough that she would not have been able to make out the name or the person aboard it.

When we sat, I let her take the seat facing the water, and she remarked how silly it was that there were so many boats docked and that none of them were doing what they were intended to do—to sail.

And I nodded aggressively, said, Yes, you're so right. You're so right.

I mean, if it were me, she said, and stopped. I'm sorry, ever since Seamus I just don't like talking that much about boats. But if it were me...

Yes?

That'll never be me, she said.

You sure about that?

She took a sip of water, but the ice was too cold and water escaped at the sides of her mouth. Sorry, she said.

Her apology was sincere and clipped, like our roles were reserved and I was now forced to mete out acceptance.

Here, I said, take this, and handed her a napkin.

Thanks, she said, and laughed.

It's so beautiful out, she said. I feel bad you're not seeing this. Do you want to switch places?

No, no, I said. I've seen it, the water. I've even seen waves, believe it or not.

You're kidding, she said.

That was Mom—facile and easy to get along with, whenever Seamus wasn't around. I turned to look at the water and saw Jonathan's boat rise across the bay. It was the Starship Enterprise, it was the bleeding heart of romanticism. In faint blue lettering I saw my mother's name—Alma—and thought about how the word meant "soul," thought about how it had been a while since I made that connection. But I didn't have to; Jonathan made it for me. Though he and the boat were a good sight away, I saw him pacing about the boat like he was looking for something. Her soul, maybe. Or his own.

Beautiful, right? she asked. Told you.

Yeah, I mumbled.

Come on, now, trade spots with me. The sun gets in my eyes anyway.

And I acquiesced, if only because Mom had pleaded and because it took only a second to look at Jonathan and realize that I could've observed his confusion for the rest of the afternoon. I took pleasure in it.

Fine, fine, I told Mom. Let's switch.

We did an awkward dance around each other, carrying our forks and napkins instead of simply swapping them on the table, and Mom laughed when my knife hit her fork and they belled-off.

I squinted into the sun—just as she had—and lost Jonathan and his boat somewhere in the sky. The clouds were nonexistent, but the sunspots tricked my eyes into believing there were small islands floating toward me. Then they too faded, and I looked back at Mom who was smiling. I thought that I had all the power in the world.

God, this is so much better, she said.

I'm sure it is, I said. You can see me now, though I can't see you.

You get older and it just hurts to have your eyes open sometimes, you know? Never mind, of course you don't. You're young, she cried. You don't understand—how could you?

I think I get it, I said. Sometimes you just have to look away.

Exactly, she said. That's all.

My phone rang and I peered down to see who it was. I didn't need to check; I knew. I slid it back into my pocket and silenced it.

You can take that, Mom said. Really, it's okay.

And I said, Thanks, but I'd rather not.

I get it, she said.

I looked back out into the harbor to see if I could spot *Alma* this time more clearly, but then the waiter came to drop off our menus and Mom took hers and flipped it dramatically open in front of her. I couldn't see Alma anymore.

Chapter Twenty

When I got to Josef's house to say my final goodbye, I saw a petite woman with blonde curly hair and glasses picking up eggshells left over from two days earlier. She was on her knees sweeping them into a dustbin. Upon hearing the footsteps, she turned around to look at me. It was a face like Josef's, her wide-rimmed glasses obscuring her flimsy nose, and seeing her on the floor picking up little pieces resurfaced the guilt I had felt after throwing them in the first place. Throwing them at Josef was like throwing them at her.

Can I help you? she asked.

I should've been trying to help her, but instead I said: I'm here to see Josef. Is he around?

Ah, you must be Henry, she said. Josef's inside, I'll get him. I'm his daughter, Lucy. She stuck out her hand, but she was too far away for me to grab, so I hastened my step to get there in time and tripped over my own feet.

My gosh, she said, laughing. Are you okay? I'm sorry, but that was funny.

I picked myself up and extended my hand.

It's a pleasure to meet you, Henry. Be careful next time, she said.

What happened here? I asked.

Some childhood prank, she said. Some stupid asses.

She said it like Josef would've.

Hey, at least they had good aim, she said, looking back at the house. Maybe it's revenge.

For what? I asked.

You know the kind of stuff people say about him. I live seven hours away and could tell you all these things. It's all bullshit, you know.

You know that more than anyone. He's told me about you. Says you're one of the smart ones.

I shook my head. Kids are stupid, I told her.

They are, Henry. They are.

Do you need any help?

No, she said before acquiescing: You know what, yes. Go inside and tell my father to make sure he's packed. We leave as soon as I pick up the rest of these shells. We have a prospective buyer coming today and I don't want them to think that this is routine over here. Like it's Halloween every day. Will you do that for me?

Of course, I said. Hey, will everything be okay? With him?

We'll see, she said. He doesn't want to go, but sometimes we have to do what we want least to do. That includes me. I don't want to take him in. I mean of course I do—he's my father and he's sick—but I have two children of my own that I take care of. I'm a stay-at-home mother. I know, I realize it's not okay to say that these days, but it's the truth. And god forbid I put him in a home. I don't think I could do that either, banish him.

I can't imagine, I said.

Your parents, they're healthy? she asked.

Yeah, I said.

I hope you don't have to ever go through with this, she said. But you've been good to him, Henry. You've made all our lives easier in a way. You taking care of him.

I never looked at it like that, I said. If that's what I was doing.

Oh no, no, no. I didn't mean it that way. You weren't his nurse or anything like that. You were his friend.

Who got paid, I added.

Who got paid, she said, Yes. But it helped me out a lot. Not having to drive and see him every weekend. Especially in the last year or so when all of that wandering started taking place.

The first time he wandered he was found in a neighbor's backyard. He had picked up their clippers and gardening tools in an attempt to do some maintenance on what he thought was his yard. I was at his house when they brought him back; his neighbors said, Son, you're gonna have to do a better job with him. He don't pay you for nothing, you know.

It meant a lot to me, too, I told his daughter. She smirked and then used her hand to cover up her crooked teeth.

Hey, you did that film, right? My dad showed it to me. He said he was so proud of the way it turned out.

No way, I said.

Of course, she said. I wouldn't lie. I don't think he would either.

Well, I said, I'll take that as a compliment.

It is one, she said, smiling. Teeth bared.

Are you sure you don't need help? I asked.

No, go along. Go find him, wherever he's hiding. I'll manage this mess. Little assholes, she said under her breath. Little pricks. Entitled pricks.

I walked up the pathway, climbed the stairs, and opened the door for the final time. In another month, in another few days maybe, the house would be sold off. Renovated and restored, its remnants and hiding places kicked up like fairy dust.

There were so many boxes that I couldn't imagine such a future. Not yet. Boxes lined the walls and crowded the landing, and those that hadn't been propped up yet covered the floorboards like a second carpet. Josef's memories—the ones that were left—clung to the walls while others were stuffed in boxes left unsealed. I saw his younger face peek out of one and side-eye me, as if to say *There's still time. You can still help.*

In the kitchen, a recently brewed pot of coffee steamed toward the ceiling. That's where Josef was—standing in the kitchen and watching the coffee filter its final drops before he could lift the pot and pour himself a cup of black.

How are you feeling? I asked.

Hello? Is that you, Hank? Hank? He flashed me a smile and then said, Don't worry. I'm not quite there yet. There you are, my boy.

He took down a second mug and poured two cups. How you doing? he asked.

So now you stop calling me son, I said.

No time like the present, he said. What are you going to do? For work I mean?

I'm going to take a trip, I said.

That's what I'd do, he said.

You're the one who told me that, I said.

And it felt like a game we had rehearsed, a play in which we wrote and performed all the parts. Now I was watching us play it over and over.

That's right, son. Where you gonna go?

It was the same question Benjamin had asked, but this time I wanted to answer. I don't know, I said. And I didn't. I hadn't even managed to look up whether Condesa was a real place, though I supposed it had to be.

You'll come back though and see me? he asked.

Course, I said. I didn't know where that would be.

Speaking of, your daughter wants you to get ready, I said. Says you have to get out of here before the realtor comes.

She's been telling me that for hours, he said. Come into the library, I want to show you something.

I followed as he sidestepped boxes and garbage bags and led me into the room, where several piles of books awaited their turns at being packed away. I figured these were either rejects or ones that had been saved for something special, and then I saw a book from the library placed on top. It was his own.

You stole that, didn't you? I asked. Jesus Christ.

Well, it's my book. No one is going to miss it, he laughed. It's yours, though, all of these books. They're yours.

I looked at the dozens of boxes and, mystified, said, Josef, I have no room for them. There's no way I can take them.

Well then, fine. But they're staying here. If you want them, take them. If you don't, then don't. He looked out the window where Lucy had started the car's engine.

I could sense his mood changing, as if set to a timer that would buzz at the same time he was about to scream. He didn't scream though, didn't even scowl. Just stared vacantly out the window and gave his daughter the sign for one minute. Then he turned to me.

Well, that's it then. I have nothing else to show you, he said.

You're too generous, I said.

Take what you want, he said. There are only three books a person needs in his lifetime. Who said that? Do you know?

You did?

He smiled.

Thank you, I said. I have to ask: did you really like the film?

You're so young, he said. You need so much validation. I used to be like you.

Is that a yes or no? I asked. For once, I'd just like a yes or a no.

Josef laughed, said he had to get going. He turned away from the window and walked past me until he was halfway into the other room.

Can you do me a favor? he asked. The movers are supposed to come in an hour or so. Lucy wants to take me to say goodbye to some people first. More her friends than mine, if you can believe it. Can you stay here until we get back? I don't want any movers messing with my shit.

Still can't trust anyone, I said.

Fact, he said.

Then Josef shuffled out of the room and down the hallway with haste I hadn't seen in years. I heard only the rapping of his cane and then the door shutting, before I went to stand by the window. I positioned myself behind the curtain, far enough away not to see him get into the car or the car pull away out of the gate and into the street where they'd join all the other cars going somewhere.

Daylight lingered, and for hours I waited, expecting the movers to show or for Lucy and Josef to come back, but they never did. Then daylight bowled into sunset, and then night came faster than it did on other nights. It was well after nine o'clock when I decided that nobody was coming back. Maybe they weren't coming tomorrow or the next day either. As night fell deeper and deeper into its perpetual hole, I left the lights off and the boxes as they were and sat and stared into the giant void that Josef had left and realized that nothing was going to get me to go anywhere. Not darkness or the coming light. Not even resentment. My life was just beginning, and I couldn't rise to meet it.

Acknowledgments

It bears noting that a novel is the sum of its parts, as is the work that goes into it. Thanks to the unrelenting work of publisher Jill McCabe Johnson, editor Gail Folkins, and agent Carrie Howland, who never flinched when I presented a multi-voiced and what some called a "quiet" novel. Thanks to John Trotta, Chad Luibl, Jonis Agee, Emily Hunt Kivel, and Caroline Hagood for reading early drafts and better directing their theatrics. Praise be to Simon Van Booy, Bethany Ball, and Helen Phillips who've kindly endorsed its weirdness.

This novel was written over a five-year period in countless coffee shops, bars, restaurants, libraries, and drab offices. I am especially grateful to the owners and staff at North Fork Roasting Company (Southold), Konditori (Brooklyn), the White Horse Tavern (Manhattan's Financial District), and the Greenport Harbor Brewing Company (Peconic). I don't know whether I spent more on coffee or Pilsner while writing this novel, but it was worth it. All of it.

Mom, Dad, Kaitlin, Julia, Michael, and Olivia, thank you. And to you, Kyle, who became an integral part of the family since my writing *TLOG*. To the future: Kylie, Coast, and... [endless, nameless]. To Arline, who says everything I write is good, which I need to hear more than you probably know.

To friends who listened either intently or passively and whose presence was a form of workshop-therapy: Levy Messinetti, Ian Andrews, Rob Europe, W.T. Grayson, and Chris Lupo.

Thanks to the generous grants, fellowships, and educational support provided by Craigardan, NES Artist Residency, and the Kimmel Harding Nelson Center for the Arts. And to the other intrepid writers and artists I met along the way. To Carrie Thornton and Phil Budnick, who are solid mentors and veritable friends (even if, Carrie, we disagree about a certain musician named Conor. You're wrong).

Speaking of influences, this work wouldn't exist without certain jump-cuts assembled through history by the French New Wave, Roberto Bolaño, and Shostakovich. I am especially indebted to Caravaggio, whose ghastly images provided the 'momentum' for this work.

About the Author

Matthew Daddona is the author of the poetry collection *House of Sound*, which *Publishers Weekly* called "ruminative...a glimpse into a mind on the search for answers." A multi-hyphenate writer, his work has appeared in dozens of publications, including *The New York Times*, *Newsday*, *Electric Literature*, *Whalebone*, *Tin House*, and *McSweeney's Internet Tendency*. He lives on the North Fork of Long Island, where, in addition to writing, he shucks oysters, installs irrigation systems, and volunteers as a firefighter. *The Longitude of Grief* is his first novel.